POLAR MIDNIGHT

A Cassie Ingram Novel

ARIC SHAW

UNDERMOUNTAIN**BOOKS**

To Jennifer

Chapter One

December 12, 1:03 am

Silence reigned in the safe-house. Only a hard winter wind eased the oppressive stillness with occasional rustles past Cassie Ingram's bedroom window. Gauging by the grogginess in her head, it was just past one a.m.

There was no cell service here in Michigan's Upper Peninsula. Not that it mattered; she was banned from social media. For her safety, supposedly.

The electricity had flickered and failed earlier the previous night. Captain Kalov allowed her a candle, but the dry, old gun-identification books he'd given her did not make for good reading. Not that her mind could so easily be pulled from her problems.

Her father, Bryce Ingram, was the CEO of Ingram ECO Power, the second-largest energy company in the world. He had many enemies, and they knew about Cassie. They had targeted her once already, trying to get to her father. She still had nightmares about the incident in the

Houston coffee shop. Immediately after, she had been swept to this safe-house, under the assumption that more masked gunmen were hunting her.

Captain Kalov hadn't let that time go to waste. Her father had hired him to train her to how to behave—and possibly escape—if she were kidnapped. Those skills had showed their worth in Houston. And now Kalov pushed her to learn more.

Cassie pulled her hair from her eyes and sat up in the lumpy bed. The cabin had been furnished before the new millennium. She sorely missed her memory foam mattress and Netflix shows. And her private ensuite bathroom. And the maid. The cook, too.

Pressing her back to the headboard, her eyes came level with the drafty window to her right.

Honed to alertness by Kalov's paranoia, she instantly noticed the light sliding over the tree trunks of the pine forest surrounding the cabin. This wasn't the hazy glow of headlights bleeding into the trees from the road. The road was four miles down a dirt drive. Kalov loved isolation. That meant the approaching vehicle was either a drunk local who had made a wrong turn, or it was someone coming to the cabin.

It couldn't be her father's enemies. If they'd known where she was, they would already have come for her. That left Kalov's one trusted man. Val. At this hour, his arrival meant something was afoot.

Cassie climbed out of bed and stuffed her feet into her wool-lined UGG slippers. Kalov was already up—or still up—when she padded into the small living room. A rag rug, whitened by Husky hair, covered the old plank floor. The dog, Grom, stood motionless, staring at the front door.

A sofa and easy chair hemmed in a coffee table made from some dark wood with palm tree carvings on the legs.

The decor was a mishmash of items Kalov had found in junk shops—or on the side of the road. He was dressed in his usual black fatigue pants with a wide-collared button-down shirt. Cassie had lived with the man for nearly three months, but she had never seen him wear anything else.

"Is it Val?" she asked.

Kalov grunted, his usual way of saying "yes." He did not look any more alarmed than usual, which wasn't saying much. He held his 9mm Serdyukov pistol at his side, finger off the trigger. Cassie knew he was more likely to be holding the weapon than wearing it in his shoulder holster. If he did own pajamas, he'd probably wear the damn holster over them in bed.

"Well?" she said, holding her hands out to the sides.

"I got a call. You are moving tonight."

"When were you going to tell me? And why now?"

"When the car arrives, you will go. Your father said so."

Swearing under her breath, Cassie raced to her room to change and pack. She'd been living out of her bug-out bag, a backpack kept supplied with clothes and necessities —and not much of either. She didn't have much to pack.

But she didn't want Val seeing her in her flannel penguin-patterned PJs. Nor did she want to go out into the cold in them. And when Kalov said she would leave as soon as the car arrived, he meant exactly that. Kalov would carry her out if she wasn't ready to go.

"Damned Russian lunatic," she mumbled. "Not every-thing has to be an emergency drill, you know," she called.

Kalov didn't answer. The growl of a heavy-duty pickup truck rose above the winter wind. Its wheels crunched over frozen gravel in the drive. It pulled right up to the back door of the cabin. Grom barked.

Cassie cast one last look at her room before blowing

out her candle and leaving. Kalov met her at the door. "Your pistol?"

"In my backpack. Should I get it out? Are their bears waiting out there?"

Kalov shook his head and frowned. "Bears hibernate. Men do not. Be wary."

He didn't have his parka on. Cassie realized he wasn't going with her and Val. "Why are you staying?"

"I have other clients. Val will go with you."

"Where?"

Kalov let a rare smile spread his lips. "Alaska." He placed his thick hands on her shoulders and kissed each of her cheeks. His whiskers scraped her skin. "Bye-bye, Cassie. Remember: Live."

He gently guided her out the door and escorted her around the rear of the still-running truck. (One never walked in front of an idling car, he had taught her.) He opened the door, helped her up, and shut the door.

The inside of the truck was warm and slightly tainted with exhaust and Val's cologne. Tired, confused, and suddenly a little misty-eyed, she waved goodbye. But Kalov was already walking away, Serdyukov pistol still in hand.

"Do you want to listen to Taylor Swift?" Val asked. He had on that grin of his. Cassie always got flustered when he teased her. There was nothing wrong with Taylor Swift. But she knew better than to react. Val was relentless once he got you off balance.

When she didn't answer, he laughed softly and gunned the motor. The 445-horsepower GMC Denali lunged forward, headlights blazing across the snowy forest floor. "I turned on the seat warmer so your butt won't freeze."

Cassie turned her face toward the passenger window. The interior of the truck was too dark for Val to see her blushing, but she also knew her expression would give her flustered state away.

"Thank you," she said. Val liked to tease, but he was a good guy. When she'd first come to Michigan, still shaken by the coffee shop incident and still mourning the death of her first bodyguard, Val had provided a sympathetic shoulder. He'd never overstepped their professional relationship—except to break down her emotional walls through the occasional inappropriate joke. And it didn't hurt that he had the face and body he did. Like a swimmer or a dancer. And he knew it.

"Kalov wouldn't tell me much," Cassie said. "Just that my dad wants me to go to Alaska."

"Yes. Do you have a question?"

Damn this Russian man. One moment teasing, the next training. One of the many, many things Kalov had been trying to bully out of her was her propensity for indirect communication. Cassie thought her implied question obvious. Yes, she wanted to know where in Alaska she was being taken. And yes, she wanted to know why.

Val was smiling in that easy way he had. No sour-puss glowers like his boss. But that didn't mean Val wasn't a stickler.

Cassie relented, knowing she wouldn't get anything from him if she tried the usual passive- aggressive stuff that worked on her father. "Where in Alaska? And why?"

"The north. Because your father said so."

Before she could punch his shoulder, he waved one hand in apology. "Truly. I don't know any more than that." His hand returned to the wheel and he guided the truck around a hairpin turn. The roads were twisty here as they wound to follow the gentle hilly contours of a land carved by glaciers. Lakes pocked the entire U.P. and forced the road to wind in sometimes circuitous loops.

"I don't believe you," Cassie said. "If we're to outfit ourselves properly, we have to know our destination. What's the weather? What's the political situation? Are there paparazzi? Do I need a disguise? Is there cell coverage? How many Starbuckses are there within a one-minute walk of where we'll be staying?"

Val tilted his head appreciatively. "Good questions. Most of them, anyway. Advanced work has been done by a third party. I know for a fact that cell coverage is non-existent."

Cassie rolled her eyes. She didn't know much about Alaska, but she guessed most of the population lived along the coast. Juneau and Anchorage and Homer. Did her father have a more secure house set up for her there? Maybe he was bugging out, too. She had begged him to lie low after the Houston incident. But as the CEO of a multinational corporation, he said he couldn't just up and disappear.

Cassie knew the truth. Dad simply couldn't give it up. He loved his work too much. She used to think he loved it more than her. She still did sometimes. Like right now. How dare he disrupt her life like this? What if she had been able to sleep tonight? Did he expect her to just leap out of bed and fly off to Alaska?

The answer was obviously yes. And it irritated her. The whole situation did. Even if she'd been able to stay at the cabin, she wasn't truly living her life. She wanted to finish up high school and have a summer with her friends before everyone left for college.

Kalov hadn't been very enthusiastic about her plans to attend Stanford. He'd suggested the Sorbonne in Paris, and had even mentioned Lomonosov Moscow State University as a possible alternative. "No one would dare hurt you there once I put the word out."

That Kalov held that much sway in Russia, a country where one apparently needed a "word put out," had again made Cassie wonder about who he had once been. All he'd ever admitted was that he had been born in Leningrad, now called St. Petersburg.

She wasn't going to Lomonosov, and that was that. Besides, she barely spoke Russian and had no desire to learn. What she did know, she'd picked up from Kalov and Val.

Paris on the other hand—that idea had some merit.

"You should get some sleep," Val said. "We have a two-hour drive to Wausau."

Sleep was the furthest thing from her mind. She dug out her phone and unlocked it. The glow of the screen hurt her eyes, but she was determined to go straight to the source and find out what the hell was going on: Dad.

No signal.

Blowing out a sigh of irritation, she tucked her feet up and hugged her knees. "I didn't ask for any of this."

"You are a billionaire's daughter. Believe it or not, some people have worse things to worry about than catching a private jet in the middle of the night."

Val was always calling her on what he called her "rich-girl whining." Cassie knew she enjoyed zillions of privileges that most people only dreamed of. But that didn't change the fact that there were men and women out there willing to hurt her to get to her father. Rich or not, she didn't feel safe. And her whole life was on pause. "I just want all of the scary stuff behind me."

Val pursed his lips and grunted. "That's called death, Cassie."

They drove in silence after that, Cassie lost in her miserable thoughts and Val scanning the road for threats as he drove them across the Wisconsin border toward the waiting jet in Wausau.

Chapter Two

4:31 am

"I'm gonna make it up to you, sweetheart. I promise."
Bryce Ingram was a short, slightly fat man with an easy
smile and a hard stare. He enjoyed the same full head of
ice-white hair that Grandpa had, though he was just fifty
years old. But the elder-statesmen vibe he projected served
him well in business. At the moment he had his full charm
aimed at Cassie.

She was dead-tired, having failed to sleep at all during
the truck drive. Something felt off about this sudden trip.
The fact that Val didn't even know what was going on
didn't help matters.

She sat in a rear-facing beige leather seat on Dad's
corporate Gulfstream G650 as it glided 45,000 feet above
North Dakota. Her glass of ice water had just been
refreshed by Dad's private stewardess, a twenty-something
girl with exotic eyes. She took a sip and regarded her father
over the brim of the crystal tumbler.

Dad continued to shine his twinkly-eyed charm at her.

Despite his stature, he had a way with women. His three exes thought he had too much way with women. Despite his philandering tendencies, Cassie's mother, his first ex, still held a part of his heart. That was because she didn't succumb to his masculine wiles as easily as most of his targets. Cassie had learned from her mother that Bryce Ingram was not to be trusted.

So despite his earnest promises to make things up to her, Cassie didn't fall for it. She nodded amiably, agreeing that he believed what he was saying, but also indicating that she didn't. He knew that look well, which was why he kept insisting that it would be different this time. "This Alaska thing is just a side trip. After that I have an exciting little thing planned for us. Just the two of us."

"A trip to where? North Dakota?" She couldn't think of anything bleaker than that.

"Well, no. But we might just pop in there on the way. Our shale oil fields there are producing fantastically. I do have a couple associates there I really do need to—"

"I was joking, Dad."

His smile faltered. Cassie couldn't blame him for his enthusiasm. Oil and natural gas—and more recently wind and solar—were his passions. Cassie honestly didn't understand it.

"Forget North Dakota," he said. "I'm taking you to the Big Apple. Shopping, shows, restaurants, the Ritz. The whole goddamned shooting match. The mayor'll have to send out the whole F.D.N.Y. to hose the streets down, because we're gonna paint 'em red."

One thing about Dad: he could sell. He would sell and sell and sell until you gave in. Cassie liked the sales pitch even though she didn't for one second think he was going to deliver the goods. A trip to New York City was just what her spoiled-princess patootie needed.

"Aren't you forgetting all the dudes who want to kill you?" And me, she didn't add.

Dad leaned back in the rich leather seat and sighed. "I think that's come to a close."

Cassie leaned forward, setting aside her glass of water. "Really?" The last she'd heard, the men who had held her hostage were traced to Mexico. An oil spill from one of Dad's Gulf of Mexico rigs had ruined over three hundred miles of beach, clogging small ports and destroying tourism for an entire season.

No amount of PR had been able to smooth over the disaster, both economic and ecological. And Dad hadn't shirked his responsibility. The company devoted billions to the cleanup. But other companies had soiled the waters in the years before the disaster. Several rigs had gone up in flames, pumping millions of barrels of oil into the Gulf. They hadn't stepped up the way Dad had. In the end, Dad's efforts didn't help his reputation. People saw a rich guy who hadn't put in the proper safety measures, in order to maximize profits. And maybe that was true.

Cassie knew she couldn't be objective about it. Despite his shortcomings as a father, she loved him. And she'd watched him diminish during that catastrophe, never sleeping, living on coffee and Tums, and personally coordinating the cleanup efforts.

The media had raked him over the coals. The Ingram ECO Power stock price fell 30%, wiping billions from his net worth. But he hadn't cared about his wealth. He knew that many people owned his stock in their retirement accounts, and that had kept him up at night.

But then he'd come back from it. Day by day, month by month. The company became a turn-around miracle on Wall Street. Profits climbed to record levels.

But the men whose lives had been ruined did not

forget. And when Dad began to get his picture on the cover of business magazines and guest spots on cable news, the people of that forgotten coast were understandably infuriated.

Cassie understood it. She couldn't blame them for their rage. But she wouldn't just volunteer to be kidnapped or murdered, either.

"Did you pay them off?" she asked.

Dad didn't answer right away, but he looked into her eyes for a long time. He seemed sad, a spiritual echo of those terrible months following the disaster. "You can't buy off everyone. Not even if I cashed in all my shares, sold everything we owned, and handed it over in bales of hundred dollar bills. That's not the justice they wanted."

Cassie was glad to hear him say that. She didn't want to think her father was so shallow that he'd expect to buy forgiveness. "So why do you think it'll be safe for us to go to New York?"

He eyed Val, who sat two rows up, head back as he dozed. "I got word yesterday that the leader of the organization that attacked us in Houston is dead." He looked away from her, eyes suddenly icy.

Cassie shivered and adjusted the air vent over her seat to cut off the flow. There was much more in her father's words than the obvious meaning. She could tell he hadn't wanted to say as much as he had. But three months with Kalov had trained her to notice that Dad had made the same type of vague statement that she often did.

He pretended to sleep. He knew Cassie was smart. He knew he had said too much. He always did with her—and her mom. If the leader was dead, it meant he'd been killed. It wasn't a car accident. And it wasn't a heart attack.

If she had to guess, it was a 9mm to the brain. Kalov's organization offered many services, most of which were not featured on his stodgy, old-fashioned website. Survival training was one thing. But assassination was another. Cassie felt no relief.

Kalov's words rose to her mind, his Russian accent made even more menacing by his gravelly voice. "The bear has no morals. You threaten her cubs, she kills you. This is good. This is nature."

Bears had no conscience. But Cassie did. She pushed her seat back and tried to settle in. The flight to their refueling stop near Anchorage had barely started. And wherever they were going it sounded like a real yawner, with no cell service or Starbucks. Maybe she would sleep the whole time they were there.

But for now, all she could do was think.

Chapter Three

8:31 am

"I thought you said we were refueling," Cassie said. She stood in a shabby office attached to a long metal-sided hangar, looking out a smeared window at the Farewell Airport runway. Dad's Gulfstream had taxied onto a disused pad and they'd been told to deplane.

"Well, they do have to fuel up before we can leave." Dad's chagrined look set a warning bell clanging.

She dropped her bug-out bag onto the blue tiled floor. This wasn't an airport terminal, but more of a grimy office. The seating area consisted of seven mismatched arm chairs probably bought from a dentist office auction. A chipped Formica counter held a Bunn coffee maker and a box of sugar cubes. A TV mounted high in one corner played a cheesy local newscast.

As soon as they'd come inside, Dad had rushed to shake hands with a bunch of men in jeans and L.L. Bean pullovers. Cassie recognized a few faces, all employees of Ingram ECO. One of them was Dev Salah, a regally handsome older man who was like an uncle to her. She had always called him Uncle Dev.

His face was the only bright spot in this whole endeavor. Aside from Val's, of course.

Uncle Dev swept her into a bear hug and kissed the top of her head. "How is my sweet little pumpkin?" he said. "You're quite the young lady, aren't you? Let me send Sila a picture." He pulled out his phone and looked around for someone to take it.

Val volunteered. He stepped back and held up the phone. "Smile, Sweet Little Pumpkin."

Cassie felt her face go hot, and she knew her throat and cheeks had turned bright red. Val got the picture, immortalizing her mortification for the ages. It didn't seem possible, but her face went hotter; she couldn't help but turn away and cover her cheeks with her hands. The last thing she needed was Val using a new nickname for her. He'd just finished wearing out "Sassy." Which she'd hated because her cousin had called her Sassy Cassie at school, and the name had stuck through the end of her sophomore year.

Uncle Dev seemed to enjoy her embarrassment, but he put an arm around her shoulders and guided her away from the Russian bodyguard. "How are you? Truly."

"Confused. I thought we were refueling, but now that puddle-jumper has taxied onto the pad and our pilot has done his preflight on it. I don't like the looks of this."

Uncle Dev gave a dismissive shrug. "Deadhorse is too cold for the Gulfstream at this time of the year. That is a Viking Air Twin Otter. Not luxurious, but it'll get us where we're going."

"Did you say 'Otter'? Why are we flying on a plane named after a cutesy water animal?"

Val had snuck up beside her. "Because those turbo props are good down to -60° Celsius."

Cassie didn't know Celsius, but she didn't like the sound of minus sixty anything—unless it was a percentage off Prada. "Just how far north are we flying?"

Uncle Dev laughed. "There's a reason it's called Dead-horse." He handed her a tattered paper map. "See for yourself."

Chapter Four

8:37 am

Darnell Watson steered his fuel truck around the idling Sno-Cat plow truck. His brakes screeched in the thirty-below-zero air, which metal didn't have much to say about, but which human flesh did. This was not what a Southern California boy was used to. But the pay was good.

He set the brake, then left his big diesel tanker running as he wrapped his scarf around his neck and tucked the tails into the throat of his parka. He drew his hood up, adjusted fleece balaclava over his nose and mouth.

Gloves on, deep breath, open door.

"Eight-thirty in the frickin' a.m. and dark as midnight," he said. "Alaska." The sun wouldn't rise above the horizon until January or something. Crazy.

And cold.

The frigid air didn't penetrate the fabric of the parka or his insulated snow pants. But it found every seam, gap, and bit of bare flesh it could. At these temperatures, skin would get frostbit in less than a minute. With the wind now whipping out of the west, it would take even less time.

He hustled to the rear of his fuel truck and uncoupled the hose from its holding collar. The hose was thick rubber with a metal nozzle. He throttled up the fuel pump and dragged the hose to the Sno-Cat. Like all the big vehicles up here, the plow stood on tracks instead of wheels. The driver wasn't even in the boxy cab, having gotten into his own truck and driven back to Deadhorse Camp, his shift over. But nobody turned off a diesel up here in the winter. The diesels ran twenty-four seven. And that suited Darnell just fine. It gave him a damn job.

He had a fiancée and a three-year-old daughter to take care of. He was making four times what he'd get driving delivery for the furniture store back home.

He inserted the fuel nozzle and pulled the flow lever. The smell of diesel made him wrinkle his nose, and he vaguely wondered if the fumes would give him cancer.

Company policy forbade fuelers from clipping the lever into place, but instead to make a man hold it the whole time. It had something to do with safety—or maybe it was the environment. Whatever it was, Darnell thought it was a stupid policy. He had already devised a way to keep the diesel flowing without him standing there and freezing his ass off. With quick motions, he slid the c-clamp into place and tightened it down to keep the lever depressed and fuel flowing. There.

He scurried back to the warmth of his truck cab. Since he was filling a one-hundred-gallon tank, it was going to take a few minutes. He flipped on the cab light and checked his face on his phone's selfie-cam. He didn't think he'd gotten any frostbite. Thing was, the company took safety seriously. Frostbite was a punishable offense up here. They could dock your pay, and if you were stupid enough to get frostbit twice you'd be on a flight home and never invited back. There were worse offenses—like drunkenness and fighting. But those were the usual stupid things. Frostbite, something that literally froze your skin dead, was stupid on another level. Easily avoidable.

Unless you had to stand next to a Sno-Cat plow in sub-thirty-degree cold while you refueled it. That was bureaucracy for you.

Darnell rubbed his cheeks. They looked and felt fine. He put his phone away and leaned back. A flash of light caught his attention in the side mirror. Somebody was pulling in behind him. Maybe the driver for the plow's next shift. A bit of snow had been falling, and the oil companies were serious about keeping the roads clear.

Well, this guy was going to have to wait. No half-fuels for Darnell. He'd have to track this guy down otherwise, because if the Sno-Cat ran out of diesel—it was Darnell's butt on the line.

He noticed it wasn't just one vehicle pulling in. Looked like a convoy of . . . "No friggin' way."

Snowmobiles. Or "snow machines" as they called them up here. What kind of fools would be out on open-air rides like that? Maybe they were Eskimos, the only true locals in this area. Maybe they were lost.

He went through his bundle-up routine, then hopped down from the cab. A couple snowmobiles had stopped behind his truck, hemming him in. The others were circling. He spotted the drivers in the glare of his own headlights. They were dressed in black and gray snow suits, and each had a rifle slung over his back.

The leader cut sharply and came straight at him. Darnell waved, thinking the driver hadn't seen him. Maybe he'd been blinded by the fuel truck's headlights. But the man kept coming and at the last moment skidded sideways, sending flakes of dirt and ice into Darnell's face.

"What the hell?" Darnell shouted. The man muttered something, but it was unintelligible over the buzz of the other snow machines.

The lead driver dismounted and said something in a language Darnell didn't understand. He didn't hear the single gunshot that would kill him. It came from another snow machine driver off to his right.

As he hit the frozen ground Darnell had less than one second of consciousness to see, but not understand, a man remove a black duffle bag from the back of his machine.

Chapter Five

9:12 am

The narrow seats of the Viking Air Twin Otter were upholstered in a bright blue weave that had probably been in fashion in the 1990s. That was forever ago, and it showed. There was no cockpit door, just a curtain—and it wasn't even pulled shut. Cassie watched the pilot and co-pilot flip through a three-ring binder as they went through their whole preflight routine. She'd never minded flying in the G650 or an airline jet. But she'd never been in an old-time prop plane. It didn't look at all airworthy to her.

"Prop planes are safe," Val said, seeing her worry and knowing its cause.

Cassie took some comfort in his words, since his job was to look out for her safety. But she didn't like his look of amusement as she sneered with distaste at the barebones—and tiny—passenger cabin. Seats for nineteen, with an entry hatch near the tail. It was an overgrown Cessna, with high-mounted wings and . . . she couldn't get over it . . . propellers.

Of the men Dad had met at the desolate airport, only Uncle Dev joined their flight to Deadhorse. The others had just flown down from there. With all the empty seats on board, Cassie couldn't help but make a snarky comment. "This is really environmentally-friendly, Dad. Three people in this empty plane. Maybe we should take a commercial flight." One in a proper jet.

"We're on a tight schedule, sweetheart," Dad said. He was stretched out in the very back where four seats sat against the rear bulkhead, forming a sort of bench. It was obvious he planned to take a nap. "I have tickets for us to see a show in three days, so we need to be able to leave at the time we want."

"What show?" she asked. If Dad had bought tickets already, maybe he was serious about the New York thing.

"That's a surprise."

The pilot revved the engines, making the propellers roar and blur. The whole aircraft shuddered, and the vibrations rattled the window shades. Soon they were racing down the bumpy runway for takeoff. The ground dropped from beneath them, the snow-covered landscape falling away below. White, jagged mountains formed an imposing wall ahead.

The plane tilted for a sharp turn, bringing them north. A snake of river cut through the endless white—the Kuskokwim she saw on the map Uncle Dev had handed her. She searched the vast expanse of nothingness for Deadhorse. When she found it, she swore under her breath. It was going to be a long flight.

Val was sitting across the aisle from her. He waggled his eyebrows, enjoying her lack of enthusiasm. "I trained for many months in Siberia. This is like going home." From the sudden hardening of his eyes, Cassie didn't think his memories of Siberia could be all that great.

Val didn't talk much about his past. She knew he was Captain Kalov's nephew. Kalov had emigrated to the U.S. in the early 1990s, after the Cold War had released its fearful grip on the world. But Val had been a soldier in the Russian Army until joining Kalov's organization, providing security and survival training for celebrities and the scions of Wall Street moguls.

Kalov had taught Cassie how to think about risks. How to behave if she were kidnapped. He had put her skills to the test in many ways. But when it came to fighting, Kalov had turned her over to Valentine.

And Cassie had enjoyed those lessons far too much. Val, it turned out, thought the best self-defense skills were found in the discipline of Brazilian Jiu Jitsu. To Cassie's initial shock—and then delight—this was essentially a form of wrestling, involving her rolling around on the floor with Val's body pressed to hers. That he could get her arms and legs pinned and levered into immobility did not concern her in the least. She might not know much about Val *as* a person, but she had become very familiar *with* his person.

Not that she gave in when they rolled. She was a quick study and had fifteen years of ballet conditioning to draw on, which made her flexible and strong. Val considered her an average student. Or so he said. But that was just his Russian quirk. And his job wasn't to make Cassie overconfident. In fact, it seemed that Kalov and Val did everything they could to make her paranoid.

It was hard to feel too scared with Val around. It was also hard to concentrate with him looking at her like that. He was a scoundrel. A professional one, but still a scoundrel.

"Do you want a pop?" he asked.

"Sure."

Val went back a few seats and opened a camping cooler

one of the pilots had brought aboard for them. He pulled out two cans of Diet Coke and fished a package of Doritos from another bag. He handed her one can and returned to his seat with the chips. Cassie watched his movements with the same fascination one might watch a lion as it stalked through the grasses of the Serengeti. He was beautifully dangerous.

And he was off-limits.

Cassie pulled her attention away from him and flipped through a two-month-old copy of Cosmopolitan. She had found it on the Gulfstream, left there—she assumed—by one of Dad's girlfriends. Having been out of contact with the world for three months, and forbidden to go to even the smallest nearby town in Michigan, she had cheered to find the magazine. She dove into the glossy pages, folding the corners of the looks she wanted to pick up on her shopping spree in New York. But before long her eyes grew heavy.

When she woke, it was fully dark out. Not a single light showed on the ground below. Maybe they had flown into a cloud bank, she thought. But if so they were above it, for the sky was filled with stars. The air was so crisp they didn't even twinkle.

She glanced at her phone to check the time. Noon. She knew it got dark early this far north, but it looked like midnight.

"Incredible, isn't it?" Dad dropped his weight into the seat behind hers. "This is your first time above the Arctic Circle."

Startled by this revelation, Cassie dug out her map. Sure enough, a hazy dotted line showed that Deadhorse lay above the Arctic Circle. "This really is the ass end of nowhere, isn't it?"

The plane pitched hard to one side, sending Val's

empty Coke can tumbling. Uncle Dev woke up and gripped his armrests. Dad let out a Texas whoop and pumped his fist. A moment later the co-pilot leaned from his seat and called to them. "A little light chop as we make our approach. Make sure you're buckled in."

Everything was going to be okay, Cassie told herself. She had been in worse turbulence than this. That one time landing in St. Barths in the Caribbean the drink cart had come loose and tumbled down the aisle. Three passengers had thrown up and one guy had had to take his heart pill. Cassie had braved it with nothing worse than sweaty palms.

But that had been on a real airplane. Not this rattletrap tube with wings. The Twin Otter continued to bounce, the tail yawing in a sickening motion until Cassie thought it would fall into a flat spin.

"I have to pee," she said. This always happened when she got nervous. "I'm not joking."

Dad laughed through his nose. "You'll have to hold it. We'll be landing soon anyway."

Twisting in her seat, Cassie looked back at the lavatory door. Dad was right. If she unbuckled, she'd end up with her skull smashed into the ceiling. Even if she did make it into the lav, she wouldn't be able to use it with the crazy gyrations of the plane threatening her to throw her off. Clenching her teeth, she tried to think about what show Dad had bought tickets for. The only one she could think of was *The Wiz*. That wasn't helpful at all. Maybe it was *Les Miserables*. That would be appropriate, considering her current state.

The Twin Otter's turboprops whined as the aircraft battled gusts and descended toward a patch of lights. Thank God they were close. Cassie clasped the armrest and bit her lip. Hold on. Hold on.

The runway lights flashed by, blue glows like fairy lights. The wheels struck hard, the plane bounced, and then it settled onto the runway. Cassie was thrown forward as the pilot braked, her seatbelt pressing onto her bladder. That was enough. She unbuckled, hurdled her armrest, and hustled to the lav, singing over and over: "Youcanmakeit-youcanmakeit-youcanmakeit."

And she did make it. Sighing with relief—both for her poor body and for the end of the flight—she rubbed her eyes and again pouted about the circumstances that had brought her here.

But only for a moment. She wasn't about to wallow in self-pity because she had been forced to fly on private airplanes to the Arctic Circle. She knew lots of people who would have jumped at the chance to come here, just for the adventure of it.

The plane taxied briefly before coming to an abrupt stop. Cassie decided to freshen up. The faucet let out a mere trickle of water, but she washed her hands and face and scraped her pinky nail under one eye to pick off a clump of eyeliner. The little lightbulb above the mirror made her look ghoulish, throwing dark shadows under her eyes. What she needed was a hotel bed, silence, and ten or twelve hours of sleep. And since this was a business trip for Dad, she hoped the accommodations would at least be a class above the Twin Otter's cabin. Maybe they'd even have a few spa services. She hadn't had a massage in months. And her nails. She didn't want to look at them. She had painted them with the only nail polish she had in her bug-out bag. A royal blue that she had liked two years earlier, but which now looked a bit passé.

A voice barked in the cabin outside the lavatory door. At first she thought it was Dad letting out another of his

Texas hollers. But then Val's voice came through the door, low but clear. "Stay in there."

There was no teasing or humor in his voice. She recognized his serious tone. Something was up. She put her hand on the latch, but stopped when she heard a gasp.

"How many are there?" That was Uncle Dev's voice. The side hatch thunked open, admitting a wash of icy air that instantly seeped under the lavatory door. Loud men called out warnings in accented English. "Get down. Get down!"

Dad shouted, "Hey! Don't shoot!"

Captain Kalov's training took over. Without thought, Cassie removed her jacket and pressed it over the light above the lav mirror. The small space went dark except for a thin band of light seeping under the door.

"Mr. Ingram," a man said in hard tones. "You are coming with us. Fight and I am shooting you." Then there came a long string of Russian. Val answered with a simple, *"Nyet."*

A gunshot made Cassie lunge away from the door, letting her light-shielding jacket drop. She managed to stifle her cry of terror. Frantic, she got the jacket back in place. If they didn't see light coming from beneath the door, maybe they wouldn't check in here.

Dad was shouting, "You didn't have to do that! Why did you do that? Let me help him. Please. I'll do whatever you want. Just let me—" A sharp crack cut off his words.

More Russian was exchanged. Cassie listened close. Three different voices. So at least three men. Her training was working even though her heart was in her throat. She wondered who had been shot. Her heart ached. If it was Val or Uncle Dev, she thought she would lose it. And then all the training in the world couldn't help her.

It could be one of the pilots. Yes. That would make

sense. They weren't needed in a hostage situation. The kidnappers would use a pilot's death to prove their seriousness. Cassie had seen the same pattern before in the Houston incident.

She felt instantly guilty for being relieved by the idea of a pilot's murder. She didn't know either of them, but they had a families and people who loved them.

Things outside the lavatory had settled down. The voices had hushed. But Cassie didn't dare open the door just yet. Would the men set up a stand-off on the plane, or would they try to take their hostages somewhere else? She thought it more likely they would move Dad somewhere hidden. If they wanted him dead, he would already be dead.

That was good. For two reasons. First, keeping him alive suggested they were willing to make a deal. And second, they would have incentive to get off the plane as quickly as they could so that they would avoid a confrontation with local authorities. She just hoped they were in enough of a hurry that she could remain undetected. Footsteps thumped just outside the door. She held her breath.

Her mind scanned for what evidence of her presence she might have left behind in her seat. The Cosmo was stuffed in a seat pocket. The top edge might be exposed, but that might not draw too much notice. Her backpack was belted into the seat in the row in front of hers. It was her bug-out bag. A serviceable Victorinox backpack that didn't have a single girly quality to it. Just as Kalov had insisted. Unless the men looked inside, they would assume it belonged to one of the men.

Cassie was torn. She wanted the men to leave, but she didn't want them taking Dad, Uncle Dev, and Val with them. Her mind paused on the image of Val's face. She knew how deadly he was. If these kidnappers gave him even one chance, they were all going to die.

That comforted her somewhat. Dad was tough. He could hang in there. She just wished he had taken his own advice and gotten some training. He was the biggest target, after all. But he'd just laughed and said he knew how to fire a pistol, and if he was kidnapped for a ransom the company had insurance for just that sort of payout. He wanted Cassie trained because she was his little girl. She had thought long and hard about that statement, one he'd made many times. She knew he meant it in a loving way, but she found it condescending. It betrayed, she thought, his true opinion of her. That she was weak.

Well, she wasn't weak. She was her mother's little girl, too. And that made her pretty badass.

Her thoughts went back to her backpack. Her pistol was in there, loaded and ready. If she could get her hands on it she might be able to take a couple of these bastards out.

She shook her head. No. Going after them went counter to her training. Her first step was to lie low. If she were discovered, they'd take her. If she fought three men, she would certainly lose. As Val had shown her on the Jiu Jitsu mat, even a skilled fighter could not overcome superior numbers of mediocre ones. Physics, he always reminded her, was a bitch.

Okay. She needed to think. She needed to call for help. She pulled her phone from her pocket and turned it on, shielding the glow as best she could with one hand. She waited for the signal to connect. Surely any town with a motel and airport would have cell service. But all she got was: NO SERVICE.

"Dammit!" she mouthed. She rebooted her phone. While it flashed its startup screen she listened at the door.

There was no sound at all coming from the cabin. The engines had been left running, which struck her as odd. Maybe they planned to hijack the plane.

But no. They would have taken off by now.

No, she thought, reconsidering. They would have to refuel first. She knuckled her forehead. Trying to solve the unsolvable was a waste of time.

There was no talking outside now. She decided to wait another ten minutes. If there was no sound, she would peep out and see if it was safe to grab her backpack.

The phone rebooted and she entered her PIN. The signal bars came up empty, then switched again to NO SERVICE. She stuffed the phone back into the back pocket of her fifteen-hundred-dollar Earnest Sewn jeans. She was thirsty. She let a dribble of water seep from the faucet and sipped at it. The water tasted stale, but at least it was wet.

Still no sounds outside the door. She quickly checked the time on her phone and was horrified to see that not even a whole minute had elapsed. She needed to get to a phone. Kalov and Dad had set up a specific hotline number for her in event like this. All she needed to do was dial it. A trained operator would answer on the first ring. They would know Cassie's name and be ready to act. The call would be recorded, along with an instant tracing to discover where it originated. Within three minutes—max —Kalov himself would be on the call. He would coach her through her next actions, and an entire team of former intelligence agents and special forces personnel would leap into action, with the sole purpose of seeing Cassie through the incident alive. But all of that was worthless if she couldn't make the call.

To hell with it, she decided. Ten minutes was arbitrary. It might make her safer, or it might give the kidnappers enough time to fuel the plane for takeoff. She wanted her weapon, and she wanted off this stupid Twin Otter.

She pulled her jacket back on and zipped it, wishing she hadn't stuffed her parka in her backpack. She eased the latch back and let the door swing open a millimeter. The cabin of the Twin Otter was dark except for the faint light of an open aircraft hangar off to the right. The Otter's props were still spinning and the side hatch stood open. Fold-out steps had opened when the hatch had pulled down, forming a short stairway to the tarmac. Nobody was visible outside. Cassie crept up the aisle toward the cockpit. Her backpack wasn't where she'd left it. All the other stuff they had brought along—even the cooler of pop and the bag of snacks—was gone.

Cassie went forward and peeked into the cockpit. The co-pilot lay slumped over the yoke in the right seat. He might have been sleeping, except the top of his head was entirely missing. Blood and gray tissue splattered the windshield and much of the controls. He had been executed in his seat.

Cassie gagged and backed from the cockpit, covering her mouth. Her eyes burned, and the start of tears dampened them. Angrily, she wiped the moisture away. This was not the time. She needed to get moving.

She remembered watching the co-pilot throw some luggage into plane's cargo hold. Cassie hoped the kidnappers hadn't bothered to look in there. Not that it held any of her stuff. But Dad and Uncle Dev would not have come without their Tumi roller bags stuffed with clothes and toiletries.

She went to the open hatch and crouched in the shadows at the edge. The iciness of the Alaskan air took her breath away. She was a Texas girl, used to highs in the 60s even in January. Her months in frigid Michigan had done nothing to prepare her for the hateful wind coming through the door. It burned her cheeks and slipped tendrils of cold down the collar of her fleece jacket.

Val had promised that a third party had made arrangements. Hopefully they had spare cold weather gear with them. Surely they had arranged for an Uber to pick them up.

Uber? She smacked her forehead. What was wrong with her? There wasn't Uber service in Deadhorse. Dad might have arranged for a company car to pick them up. She just had to find the driver and then get to a phone.

First, she needed to cross the tarmac to that aircraft hangar over there. The wide doors stood open. There wasn't a plane inside. Maybe it had been opened for the Twin Otter. She moved to the hatch, conscious she'd be in view to anyone who happened to look. But who would that be? It wasn't like this was a bustling airport. There were exactly zero other planes moving. In fact, the place had a weird abandoned sort of feel about it.

From her perch, she could see a few other hangars. They were all closed and dark. She peeped out and looked forward along the side of the Otter. The idling props buffeted her with an extra strong burst of chill wind. Her eyes watered so badly she couldn't see.

She slipped down the steps and eased along the side of the plane, heading to the nose. The main complex of buildings—what she assumed was a sort of terminal and office area—was a couple hundred yards away.

Hugging her arms around her body, trying to keep as much warmth to herself as she could, she backtracked and went to the bulkhead hatch where the luggage had been stowed.

The cargo hold was in the rear of the fuselage. A simple white crank handle latched it shut. She pulled it out of its recess and yanked on it. It twisted. The hatch hissed upward on compressed gas cylinders. Inside were two Tumi bags. She hopped into the cramped cargo space to get out of the wind and pulled the door shut behind her.

It felt good to be out of the wind, but the hold wasn't heated. Using her phone light, she found the zipper of the first and opened it. It was Dad's. She tossed out a few odds and ends of suit coats and trousers. His tighty-whities got a sneer and a quick fling over her shoulder. A toiletry bag contained a toothbrush, shaving kit, and an assortment of trimmers, cotton swabs, a half-used roll of Tums and, to her disgust, a box of condoms. "Jesus, Dad. I don't need to see this."

The heavy coat she'd been hoping for wasn't there. She shrugged on a beige wool sport jacket. She had to roll the cuffs to keep her hands free. No weapon at all. Kalov would have gone on a swearing rampage to learn that Dad was going around unarmed.

Uncle Dev's bag was pretty much the same, though the clothes were nicer. He had a tailor in Hong Kong who did work to rival Savile Row in London. Cassie was always trying to get her dad to dress younger. But he considered Tom Ford "too slick" for the folks he had to deal with on a day-to-day basis.

Uncle Dev had no parka or weapon either. No surprise. He was opposed to weapons. He did have one surprise in his bag. A bottle of bourbon. Cassie didn't know one brand from another, but how fancy could a brand called Pappy Van Winkle's Family Reserve be?

She left it there. Yes, it was flammable, but she wasn't planning to make a Molotov cocktail. The last time she'd tried it—under Kalov's watchful eye—she had nearly set herself on fire. Besides, she'd be better off using Avgas than bourbon.

Nothing of use. She shoved things back into the bags in case the Russians came back to retrieve them. With one of Uncle Dev's very fine cashmere scarves wrapped around her neck, she slipped out of the cargo hold and into the freezing wind.

The left turboprop started to cough and splutter. And then it stopped. Out of fuel. Headlights shone from the side of a hangar over on the darker side of the airfield. Had someone noticed the plane sitting there running, or were the Russian kidnappers coming back? Cassie decided not to wait to find out.

She sprinted across the wind-swept tarmac and into the open hangar.

Chapter Six

12:20 pm

The moment Cassie was out of the wind, she heard voices. She stopped, all her senses alert. Lungs heaving, she slipped along the wall and crouched. Kalov had taught her that motion was death when predators were near. She eased behind a stand of fifty-gallon drums.

The lights overhead weren't very bright. There were several banks of fluorescent fixtures not switched on. And while there wasn't a plane parked inside, there were all sorts of workbenches and cabinets lining the walls. An enclosed area in the far back corner looked like an office. Glass windows showed the room beyond was fully lit. Shadowy figures moved inside. Cassie didn't dare approach. It could be airport workers, airplane mechanics, or FAA officials. But it could also be the kidnappers.

Frustrated by her ignorance, she decided to wait for a moment and get her thinking straight. Captain Kalov said that even highly-trained soldiers sometimes got killed because their adrenaline made them act before they had a moment to think things through. That sort of reaction was useful in hand-to-hand combat, but not so much when trying to evade capture.

She leaned back against the wall and hugged her knees. Eyes closed, she forced her breathing to regulate. Kalov insisted on exercise. He liked short, high-intensity bouts of activity that left her gasping for air. He would allow her only as many breaths as she had done reps with the stupid kettlebell weights he loved so much. A kettlebell looked sort of like a cannonball with a handle on top. He was always teaching her new exercises, each one crueler than the last. "Fifteen swings," he would bark. She would do the reps, then while she rested he would count every inhale and exhale. When he got to fifteen, he'd bark, "Fifteen swings."

And on and on it would go until she was having tunnel vision. But here, in this situation, all that torture was paying off. Not only did she catch her wind swiftly, but she was able to control her breathing and not succumb to the panicky feeling of the adrenaline.

Stop being so proud of yourself, she thought. She hadn't *done* anything yet. She needed to think. What was the situation? What did she know for sure?

She moved her lips as she talked herself through it, but she kept silent. "Okay, Cassie. What's the sitrep? Dad said that we would be safe in New York because the leader of the men who tried to kill us in Houston is dead. But how did he die? Kalov killed him. Or someone who works for Kalov. What's the effect of that? They're frickin' pissed, that's the effect of that. That was a tactical mistake. Or was it a strategic mistake?" She thought strategic. It didn't make sense to cut the head off an organization like the FDT. They had modeled themselves after Al Qaeda, forming a few independent cells with general instructions to do oil tycoons harm. The only answer the FDT would have to an assassination would be to hunker down and commit more fully to their cause.

But there was the sticking point. They didn't exist in Russia. The FDT was a Gulf Coast movement. It was in direct response to the oil companies operating in the Gulf.

There was loads of oil drilling up here in Alaska. But would the FDT bother attacking here? Had they hired Russian mercenaries to do their dirty work? Cassie didn't think so. This was something else. This felt like a ransom play. The Russian connection made a sort of sense. Deadhorse wasn't that far from the northeastern reaches of Russia. She vaguely recalled an old Saturday Night Live skit. Tina Fey had been impersonating a politician. The joke was that the former Governor of Alaska felt qualified to address foreign policy because Alaska bordered Russia. Impersonating the governor, Tina Fey had said the famous line, "I can see Russia from my house." Cassie remembered her dad laughing at that joke. He'd even repeated it occasionally when that same politician showed up on cable news shows.

Russia was close. Val had even mentioned it, in a way, referring to his training in Siberia.

"Okay, it isn't the FDT," Cassie mouthed. "But who else?" If Russians had come here to kidnap Dad, why? For money, yes. But there were other oil executives up here from time to time. And now that she thought about it more, the attack had happened within moments of their landing. The kidnappers had known their plane was landing. Which meant they had known it was coming.

Cassie thought about the men Dad had met at Farewell Airport. Had one of them set this up? Her mind blipped for a moment. She had a thought she didn't want to think. What about Val?

He was armed. He never went anywhere without his 9mm holstered at his side. He hadn't fired a shot. Cassie shook her head, denying that Val had anything to do with the kidnappers.

It was more likely that he'd considered the risk of firing to be higher than cooperating. That was Kalov's policy. Don't fight unless all other recourse is closed to you. And it was wise counsel. Just as an expert in jiu jitsu could be overwhelmed by three average fighters, an expert marksman like Val could die when facing down three—or more—less skilled shooters. And if he shot first, the bad guys would surely return fire. That put everyone at risk.

No. Val wasn't involved in this kidnapping.

A door-slam echoed hollowly in the huge hangar. Cassie leaned sideways to peer around a fifty-gallon drum. A man walked across the bare concrete floor. Cassie sucked in a sharp breath. He had a rifle strapped to his torso. Not on a strap, exactly, but more of a harness. This looked military. It kept the weapon tight to his body, just below his chest.

A machine gun. Kalov had wanted her to study pictures and memorize specifications of all sorts of weaponry, but that stuff put her to sleep. She did recognize the curve of a magazine sticking from the bottom this one, though. It curved forward, in the same direction as the barrel. The stock appeared to be brownish. Wood, she guessed. Not anything she would expect to see on a U.S. Marine. He wore gray fatigues, but no body armor.

He ambled and fidgeted with something in one hand. A flicker of light appeared. A lighter. He was lighting a cigarette. Idiot.

Cassie had seen the occasional military guard at major airports in her travels. She had been to 57 different countries by her last count. But she didn't see them at U.S. airports, and they certainly didn't smoke on the job. And finally, why on earth would this Podunk airport need that kind of security? Even if they did have a mall cop on duty, he'd have a side arm at most. Certainly not what she now recognized was a Kalashnikov AK-47.

This guy hadn't looked her way, which was good. She felt hidden, but if he came by these barrels he would spot her. He didn't have on a parka. The air in the hangar was like a deep freezer. He seemed to think so too, because he went to the far side of the huge folding doors and pressed a button. The motors that controlled the hangar doors began to groan and the door scraped closed.

Cassie cursed under breath. She didn't want to be trapped in here with this guy. But she didn't dare get up and run for it.

She stayed put as the big doors closed. There were man-sized doors out of here. One was just a few feet from the guard. The other was in the back. Cassie guessed it led to a rear parking area. That was good. Cars were good. She could hide behind one. She could even try to break into one. And maybe, just maybe, the company car was waiting there, the driver impatiently air drumming on the steering wheel and wondering where the hell Big Boss Ingram was.

The guard wandered in an aimless figure eight, not giving his surroundings more than a cursory glance. He was much more interested in his smoke. Finally he dropped the butt on the floor and smeared it out with his toe.

He returned to the office and closed the door behind him. Cassie moved. The right wall of the hangar was all work benches and cabinets that wouldn't provide any cover. She eyed the office windows. Nobody was looking out. She streaked along the hangar door and came to the man-sized door. She put her hand on the handle, but at the last moment decided not to go that way. She would have to skirt around the outside of the building to get to the parking lot and the driver she prayed was waiting there.

But where there was one guard, there might be more. Outside she'd be even more in the open. And she knew that nobody was in here. The office was a problem, but she thought she could sneak by unseen.

From here she would have to skirt the left wall. And while the office window gave a clear line of sight toward her, there were four large pallets along the way. Each was loaded with oddly shaped parts wrapped in white plastic. They looked like aircraft engine parts. Maybe the Twin Otters needed new wind-up propellers every once in a while.

She slunk to shelter behind the first one.

It felt good to be moving. It felt even better to have an objective. A quick peek showed her that three men were in the office. One was the lazy guard. Tag him "Smokey." The other two wore similar fatigues, but neither had a machine gun. She couldn't see their waists from this angle. Maybe they had sidearms. She had to assume they did.

Two men—one with thick graying hair swept back from his blunt face and the other younger and wiry—were conferring over a document on the table in front of them. The older one was jabbing his finger at different spots on it. Cassie couldn't see what it was. She didn't care. She just wanted Smokey to turn away.

There. He was digging in a pocket. A phone. He answered it.

Cassie ran to the next pallet while his head was down.

A quick look showed her he had turned to face another doorway exiting the office.

The other two men were still focused on their document. Cassie crouch-ran to the third pallet. She was halfway down the wall now. She paused to breathe and make a quick check of everyone's positions.

Boom, she was off. The fourth pallet didn't offer as much cover. It was piled with cardboard boxes, but they were only three feet high. She had to go onto all fours to stay in cover and peek at the same time. But from this low vantage point, she could only see upward through the office windows. The drop-ceiling was not very informative.

Reasoning that if she couldn't see the men they couldn't see her, she crawled the rest of the way to the office and pressed her back to the wall just beneath the window.

The office door opened and shut. It was just around the corner. The concrete floor was like sitting on ice. Her butt was going to freeze if she stayed there long.

Boot-falls echoed through the hangar.

Cassie pressed herself harder to the wall, wishing she could disappear into it like that Homer Simpson meme she always saw online. He just backed up into a hedge and disappeared.

She held her breath as the footsteps grew louder. And then Smokey walked by. He wasn't more than ten feet away. He was fit, with good posture and nicely groomed neck and sideburns. Military?

Something about that question remained open in her mind. Val was ex-military, but even as a private security man he had a sharper bearing than this guy.

The man walked toward the doors, his back to Cassie. He was lighting his cigarette now.

Cassie crawled around the corner. Nobody there.

Now was the time for speed. Keeping low, she made a break for the rear door. She didn't cast a glance behind. No point. If she were seen, he would either shout or shoot. Either way she'd know.

Hand on the doorknob, she turned it and pushed into the frigid darkness.

Chapter Seven

12:31 pm

The cramped hangar office smelled like burned coffee and Gregor Petrevski's cigarettes. The heaters pumped out stale, dry air that ruffled the map on the table between Colonel Alexei Fedorov and Lieutenant Ivan Blok. Col. Fedorov gripped the "#2 Dad" mug he'd found on the cluttered desk and sipped the super-hot, overly strong coffee that Gregor had made. The man was competent at only one thing. Shooting.

"Squads two and three are almost in position," Lt. Blok was saying in Russian. He was a very trim young man, with a sour face and hair buzzed so close to his scalp that he looked bald, a grooming choice that Col. Fedorov approved of wholeheartedly. What he didn't like was the man's overconfidence. This operation had many moving parts, and they all had to come together just so.

They were on American soil. They had kidnapped two Americans, one Russian national, and a Swedish pilot. They were at the start of a very risky operation in the

Alaskan oil fields. Any one of these things could generate an international incident that would be as close to an act of war as one could get.

The coffee soured his stomach. He studied Blok's pencil marks on the map. "No chatter on police channels?"

"None, sir. They are private security, focused on fist fights and confiscating alcohol."

"And what about local military?"

The man shrugged. They hadn't seen anything of a military sort since arriving here. But it was one thing to come in via the airport, as he and Lt. Blok had done. Quite another to traverse the ice and tundra and frequent stretches of open water as the others had done. The rest of his men had come the hard way, from the isolated village of Vankarem on the northeastern fringes of Chukotka, Russia, across the Chukchi Sea, and then through impossible cold and hardship to the barren North Slope of Alaska. They did it with twenty men, all with supplies and snow machines.

It was as foolhardy as it was daring.

But Fedorov had learned that risk yielded rewards. Maybe not in his former capacity as an Army officer, but as a capitalist it certainly did.

That neither he nor any of his men were still in the army was an important point. They were—as Americans liked to say—freelancing. That is, they were here not at the behest of the Russian government, but as self-hired mercenaries. If things went as planned, they would all wind up rich. And quite possibly, they might help Mother Russia in the bargain.

"Did you get what you need from Ingram?" Fedorov asked.

"Not yet." The shaven-headed officer did not look even slightly concerned. Fedorov noted how the man's hand went to the SRS 9mm holstered on his hip. Always quick to punish, that one was. He was a brutal man, and he got results. But he didn't do it with much finesse.

"Perhaps I shall have better luck," Fedorov said. He left his second-in-command and went through the rear door to where the prisoners were being held. The area wasn't heated, and Fedorov breathed in the chill air. He had grown up in Moscow, and he loved the cold.

This area was a warehouse. Row upon row of shelves, all holding boxes and bins full of service parts for the planes that flew in and out. This hangar was leased by Ingram ECO, so he knew it was all top-notch stuff. A pity he couldn't take it with him when he left. Such parts would fetch good money back home.

He had not allowed Gregor Petrevski to turn on the lights in this section, so his way was lit by only a few dim safety lights. The kind of amber bulbs left on so a security guard could see. There was no security guard anymore, of course. His body was in a rear garbage bin, not decaying at all due to the deep cold. Fedorov planned to be long gone by the time the garbage disposal crew discovered the corpse. Assuming they ever did. He and his men would leave such a disaster in their wake that bodies in bins would be the least of the survivors' concerns. And nobody would know who had done any of it.

The key to that was to leave no witnesses.

He heard the voices before he got there. The prisoners were talking to each other. He stopped to listen. The boss, Bryce Ingram, was whispering urgently. Fedorov couldn't make out the words. He understood English better than he spoke it. He'd been an attaché to the ambassador in D.C. for three years. As a spy, of course. Everyone understood that diplomats were spies. In that time, he'd discovered that his American friends loved his Russian accent and peculiar sentences. The women, especially. So there had been no reason to perfect it.

"I understand," came another voice. The young Russian man. He'd given his name as Valentine. He had not carried any personal things besides his knife and a Glock 17, loaded and accompanied by two additional full magazines. Of particular interest to Fedorov had been the man's knife. A folding blade, five inches long and as sharp as a straight razor. Fedorov didn't recognize the make, but he knew military spec gear when he saw it. This young man was not a run-of-the-mill bodyguard.

Of course he wasn't. He was protecting—quite unsuccessfully—a very rich and important man. There was just one problem with that: Bryce Ingram was notorious about skimping on his protection.

Colonel Fedorov did not like being perplexed. Therefore, he would ask some simple questions. And if he didn't get the answers he needed . . . Well, Lt. Blok and Petrevski could use less subtle ways to extract information.

Fedorov strode around the corner of a shelving unit. The men had been bound ankles to wrists behind their backs. They lay on their sides on the icy concrete. They had warm coats. They would not freeze.

Col. Fedorov approached the pilot. He was Swedish, according to his identification. His English was much better than Fedorov's. "Who this Russian is?" Fedorov asked, tilting his head at Valentine.

Splatters of blood marred the pilot's white uniform shirt. Those blobs had come from his unfortunate co-pilot. That had made for an attention-grabbing start to this endeavor. Making an example of him would pay off in the long run. "You are telling me who Valentine is."

The pilot, Sven Nichols, had cool eyes. He was a man with a capital "M." Fedorov supposed it was a necessary requirement to pilot airplanes in climates like this. The man controlled his fear very well. He merely shrugged.

Fedorov walked among the tied-up men. "Why is Mr. Ingram hiring Russian bodyguard? No Americans are doing such job?"

"I don't know why Mr. Ingram hired Mr. Valentine," Sven said. "I never saw him before today. I assumed he was new."

So much for the easy way. Fedorov had expected the pilot to spill the truth in hopes of preferential treatment. But that wasn't happening. Very well. He drew his sidearm, took careful aim, fired into Sven's skull, returned his weapon to its holster, and turned to the next man. "You, Mr. Salah? Are you having insight why young Russian soldier working for oil CEO?"

The older gentleman with the white hair and the flabby belly looked horrified. He had been close enough to the kill that small flecks of blood and other material had spattered his face.

"Valentine is a decent young man," Dev Salah said, face going dark with horror and rage. "He's making a living doing honest work. That's more than you can say."

Col. Fedorov turned finally to Bryce Ingram, the man who leased most of the acreage in the Prudhoe Bay oil fields. He was an essential part of Fedorov's scheme.

Fedorov did not like the unexpected. He did not like finding the Russian guard on the plane. It didn't fit in with his plans. "Mr. Ingram. It is pleasure to meeting you again." He waved a hand in dismissal. "You don't remember me. I was much younger man—of much less importance—when we are meeting last time."

Ingram was a short man. A bit puffy. He looked like a man who ate too well. Fragile. Even his hands looked soft.

"You are expecting trouble in Deadhorse, Mr. Ingram? That is why you are bringing this guard?"

The man stared back. Probably wise from his point of view. But his silence would not do. Not at all. "I am needing your number. Don't pretend ignorance. You know what number."

It was a telephone number, direct to Ingram's security contractor. It would be dedicated to Mr. Ingram. The person on the other end of the line would know exactly how to proceed. Every major American CEO had a similar number. And the call would go easily. The ransom monies were already in a special account. People such as Bryce Ingram didn't like being hostages, and what was one hundred million dollars to him?

Valentine was trying to get Ingram's eye contact. Fedorov pretended not to notice. Ingram did catch on, and there was a fleeting moment of silent communication between the two men. Finally Ingram relented. "I'll happily give you the number. Just release these other men."

To think Fedorov would free them was idiocy. But of course Ingram would attempt to negotiate. It was in his blood to strike deals. That was very well, but what the man asked was—as Americans liked to say—a no-go. "I make counter-offer. You give me number, perhaps I kill them where you are not seeing blood. Yes?"

"Why kill any of us? That only puts more heat on you when you escape."

Fedorov smiled. He liked the man's subtlety. "When" he escaped, not "if." Nicely done. The psychological trick was meant to put Fedorov at ease, make him relax and feel more confident that his mission would go successfully.

But Fedorov did not need the reassurance of this man. "Give me number, or I'm letting second-in-command get it out of you. I am coming to you as courtesy. Perhaps we are avoiding unnecessary pain." He emphasized the last word.

The man took note. His jaw slackened a moment, and then all resistance faded. "Fine. You have the number already. It's in the phone you stole from me. It's under the name Aunt Mildred."

Without acknowledging this little victory, Fedorov turned and marched back toward the office. By now Squad One would have reached the farthest reaches of the oil fields and begun operations there. Fedorov would have just enough time to place his call and prepare for his own mission to the head of the Trans-Alaskan Pipeline. There was much to do, and things needed to proceed like clockwork.

He barged into the office and yelled at Lt. Blok. "Bring me Ingram's phone."

The wiry man hustled away. Through the office window, Fedorov watched with irritation as Petrevski lit yet another cigarette.

Chapter Eight

12:45 pm

John Goodnight sat behind the wheel of his Ford F-250 and guided it along the dead-straight and flat gravel of the Dalton Highway. Deadhorse was just coming into to view, a sparkle of light in the distance. He had been driving for what seemed like three straight days without stopping. But it had only been ten hours. He'd done another ten the previous day, stopping only for a little sleep at the Yukon River Camp in the middle of nowhere.

When he'd taken the job with Ingram ECO, they'd planned on flying him up. But then someone had gotten the idea to have him drive up in a new pickup so they wouldn't have to assign him one of the ones already up there at Deadhorse Camp.

John hadn't minded at first. He was getting paid, and Alaska was beautiful even in these desolate reaches. But damn if he wasn't sick of sitting.

And the darkness didn't help. What he needed was to

get to his quarters and flop onto a bed and get a solid eight of shut-eye.

The Dalton Highway was a hard-packed slab of ice and snow. The Ford's knobby ice tires did okay on it, but when a shadowy figure darted in front of him and starting waving, he was slow to react. And when he did stomp the brakes, the tires skittered and jounced, the anti-lock system pumping mechanically against his foot.

He saw only enough of the person to gather two bits of information: It was a girl, and she was not dressed for the temperature.

The truck slid sideways, then slowly the lights of Deadhorse spun away. He came to a stop, facing the opposite direction.

"Not sleepy now," he said to himself. He pressed a hand to his chest where his heart was laboring away from a burst of adrenaline. "Damn."

A hard thumping came on the window and the passenger door swung open. The icy air took his breath away. The girl hopped in and slammed the door. Her cheeks were bright red from the cold.

"Take me to the police. Now. Better yet, give me your phone. Mine doesn't have a signal up here."

He stared at her, trying to absorb the weirdness of her presence here. "Huh?"

"My dad has been kidnapped by some Russians. I need to get him help. Now drive!"

John continued to stare. "Who are you?"

The girl—no, she was at least eighteen—the young woman glared at him. She leaned a bit closer and dropped her voice. "Listen. I know it's weird that I stopped you, and I know what I'm saying doesn't make any sense, but I need you to take me to the police station."

He understood that much. And something about her

father being kidnapped. Sounded like one hell of a domestic dispute. He turned the wheel and got the truck going in the right direction.

The airport drifted by to his left. He didn't have the faintest idea where he was going. All the buildings here looked similar. With the exception of some tower-like structures in the distance that he assumed were oil-handling facilities, all the rest looked like a trailer park—if the trailers were made out of railroad shipping containers. The low buildings stood on stilts or skids, keeping them off the ground so the heat inside didn't melt the permafrost in the ground and sink the buildings in bogs of their own making.

"Which way?" he asked, craning his head side to side to look for signs.

"What do you mean, which way? I have no idea where the police station is."

"You don't live here?" he asked.

"No. You don't either?"

"I just got here from Anchorage. Just now. I start work here tomorrow."

The young woman swore under her breath. Something about her voice drew his attention back to her. The truck was dim, but he saw something familiar in her profile. "Do I know you?"

"I doubt it. There must be a restaurant or bar we can stop at and ask directions."

"Um. Before I took the job, I read up on the town. No restaurants."

"Hey, there's a sign," the strange young woman said. "Sag River Motel." She jabbed a finger at the parking area where a bunch of trucks and Subarus were sitting. "Just drop me off."

He pulled in and stopped. She hopped out. "Thanks.

And if I were you I'd get someplace safe and hide. The Russians are armed. They look ex-military to me."

She slammed his door and trotted, head down against the wind, to the front door of the Sag River Hotel.

John watched her for a second. Then—because he knew he would never be able to sleep if he didn't make sure she was okay—he got out and followed. He left the engine running, because it was -30°F and he didn't want to have to tell his boss that he'd let the new truck freeze solid as his first official screw-up on the job.

Chapter Nine

12:59 pm

Cassie Ingram shuddered as the warmth of the Sag River Motel engulfed her. The kelly-green carpet and dark wood paneled walls would have made her shudder otherwise. But even hideous decor was welcoming when you were nearly frozen to death.

A woman at the front desk slouched in an office chair, reading a battered Steven King paperback. She looked up and stared at Cassie. "Can I help you?"

"My father has been kidnapped. I need to call the cops."

"The who? Who was kidnapped?"

Cassie wished she had her bag with her ID in it. But she didn't. "I'm Cassie Ingram. Bryce Ingram is my father. Yes. That Bryce Ingram. We landed just a little while ago and some Russians were waiting for us. They came aboard the plane, shot the co-pilot, and took my dad and three other men hostage."

The desk woman absorbed all of this, mouth continuing to fall farther and farther open. Finally she reached for the phone and punched a button. "Harv? Can you come up? We have an emergency."

"I don't want Harv. I want the police."

"We don't have police, honey. But we do have security. If your dad's in trouble, we'll get him some help."

A man in a black dress shirt and black trousers appeared from behind the counter. He'd come from an interior office.

At the same time, the guy from the pickup truck came in the front. For a moment, everyone got confused as the pickup guy started asking questions at the same time as Harv.

Cassie waved them all to shut up. She looked straight at Harv. "I need to talk to whoever oversees policing this place. Now. My dad and others are in extreme danger."

Harv had a salt and pepper mustache as flat and dull as the hair on his skull. He looked at her with that condescending look men did when they thought you were being hysterical. Cassie could tell the guy was going to slow things down. He wanted to ask every first grade question he could think up.

Cassie turned her back on him. Maybe pickup guy could be of some use. "Nobody in this place can help. Give me your phone."

Pickup truck dude handed her his cell phone. It was the same brand as hers but two years out of date. At least it got a signal. She jammed in the number Kalov had made her memorize and repeat back to him five times a day for three straight months.

"It's not connecting," she said, listening to a hiss and odd buzz. "Why isn't it connecting?"

"My plan doesn't allow roaming, and I'm not on the network up here. I just got here."

She shoved the phone back at him and turned to the desk lady. "You said there's security. Where are they?"

Harv stepped forward. "I'm head of security in Deadhorse."

Cassie closed her eyes and sent up a prayer. "Listen to me very carefully. Russians kidnapped—"

"I heard that part. But you won't let me ask any questions."

"Because we don't have time for your Andy Griffith nonsense. Get on the phone and call someone who has a brain. I need to talk to somebody with an ounce of competence." Cassie regretted the outburst the instant she finished it. But these people were not listening.

"Honey, what you're saying sounds crazy," the desk lady said. "You can't expect us to just believe this story. Your father is Bryce Ingram? That's crazy. Russians? Cray-zee!"

Cassie retreated. She didn't want their faces pointed at her. Truck dude followed and looked like he wanted to help. But he was nearly as useless as Harv was.

"Who do you need to call?" he asked.

"I have a special number for cases like this."

"Long distance calls are free for corporate employees here. It helps keep morale up among the workers who are all away from home."

"Long distance?"

The man looked at her, then comprehension came over him. "I guess you've never looked at your phone bill. Did you even know that long distance phone calls used to be expensive?"

"Get me to a phone. I'll pay whatever. I'm good for it."

"Come over here, sweetie," the desk lady said. Harv was standing next to her, shaking his head, as if to say,

"Silly girls, always coming up with something silly to be silly about."

Cassie decided that once this was all over, she would have a long talk with Dad about the men he'd hired for security. And what sort of town didn't even have real police? The whole place was very odd. She took the old plastic phone with the curly cord attached to the handset. The buttons blurred under her fingers as she dialed her hotline number.

Before the first ring completed, a woman with a calm, crisp voice answered. "Hello, Cassie. Please verify."

This was part of the script. Cassie had numerous phrases she could employ to verify her identity. Each would communicate different things to the woman on the other end. Cassie had to think a moment. If she just launched into her story, the dispatcher would have to wait to get voice recognition confirmation. Cassie said, "Distress. Free. Danger."

Other possible phrases—like "It's just me"—would have told the dispatcher that she was trying to get out of a bad date. But if she had said, "I'm Cassie and I have a message," they would know she had been kidnapped and was trying to call while her abductors were out of the room. She had a whole range of phrases to use if her captors were present and monitoring the call.

As it was, the dispatcher confirmed the phrase in less than one second. "Go, Cassie."

And so she did, telling everything she could in clear and calm phrases. By the time she had finished with her arrival at the Sag River Hotel, Kalov was on the line. "How do you know they are Russian?"

"One guy carried an AK-47. Oh, and they spoke Russian."

There was silence on the other end. "We have a call

coming in from your father's phone. Are you in a secure location?"

Cassie hesitated. She had assumed the Russians were confined to that airport hangar, but she didn't really know that. "I'll get out of sight. I don't have my sidearm."

More silence. She could practically feel Kalov judging her over the line. But since this wasn't a training session, he didn't launch into his usual lecture about being caught without protection. "Secure yourself and call back." The line went dead.

Cassie clenched her fist to crack her knuckles. She was still cold and now her fingers and cheeks were burning from adjusting to the warmth.

Truck guy said, "Um, I'm actually staying down the road at Deadhorse Camp. Do you want to come with me, or . . . ?"

She almost laughed. The guy had been useless so far, but now that she had talked to Kalov some of her paranoia was returning. Harv wasn't at all competent to deal with this situation. And with Kalov and his team getting involved, Harv would be a hindrance.

"Yes, let's go."

Back into the frigid darkness, she trotted to the guy's truck. Part of her mind retained a little suspicion about him. She was eighteen, alone. He was a twenty-something random guy.

She gave him a once-over. Heavy parka, gloves, knit cap with a sports team logo on it that looked like a giant G. "What's your name?" she asked.

He fastened his seatbelt. "John Goodnight. So, uh, you're the boss's daughter, huh? And you're sure he was kidnapped?"

"You work for Ingram ECO?"

"Just started. I'm an Ecological Engineer, part of the

ECO Green department." Cassie heard a definite twist of irony as he said the name of his department. She understood. It sounded hokey, like the company's **PR** department had thought it up. They would probably make an emotional commercial to show how environmentally responsible they were. Stuff they should just do anyway and not talk about. In fact, it sounded like something Dad might have cooked up.

"Who's your direct boss?"

"Janet Remarco. She's up here somewhere." He drove slowly, head jutting forward as he peered out his windshield, studying the unlit signs in front of some of the building. He clicked his tongue when he spotted the turn he wanted. "I studied this place on Google Maps, but it didn't prepare me for how spread out everything is. Deadhorse isn't really a town at all."

Cassie was only half listening. She was wondering what Kalov had found out from Dad. Scratch that. It might not have been Dad on the call coming in from his phone.

She needed to bring in the focus. Nothing she could do about the situation yet. "I need a parka and a gun."

"Uh. I have a nice North Face jacket in my suitcase you can borrow. I don't think I can help you get a gun. And I wouldn't even if I could."

"You have something against a person protecting herself?"

He didn't look at her. "You don't plan to use it for protection. I can tell by the tone in your voice. If you had a gun, you'd steal my truck and go back to the airport. "

"You don't know me at all," she said. He was probably right.

"I know your type."

"My type?" she said, indignant. "You've known me for ten minutes and you've got me all figured out?"

"I didn't say that. I just know that some people aren't good at patience. You think security here is incompetent. Who else is going to save your father?"

"So, just to be perfectly clear, your argument sucked. What you just said *makes* me want to go back to the airport now."

"You'll have to find someone else to take you. I may work for Ingram, but I'm not that loyal. Not yet, anyway."

The wind had picked up and now carried a haze of snow, the flakes tiny and hard. They ticked on the windshield, and Cassie had the impression they were aimed at her. This was Alaska telling her what she already knew. She didn't belong here.

John braked hard, jerking the wheel. "Almost missed it."

The building was a nondescript metal-sided two-story rectangle surrounded by large trucks and row upon row of metal-sided barracks. They looked like train-cars on skis. There was no obvious main entry, so John went in through the nearest door. A man in long johns pointed him down the hall to the landlord's office.

"I don't think they're going to like you bringing your girlfriend up here," the man said, then he continued down the corridor to another room.

The comment created an uncomfortable quiet between them. The manager opened the door. She was middle-aged, thin, and had the rugged face of a woman who spent a lot of time in harsh, dry weather, and had not thought about buying makeup—or moisturizer—in thirty years. Her hair was cropped short, and she wore a turtleneck under a sweatshirt that proclaimed: MY OTHER PUG IS A PUG. "No girlfriends or wives. This is a work camp."

John said, "She's not my girlfriend. I'm just helping her out. In fact, she's Mr. Ingram's daughter."

The woman pursed her lips doubtfully. Finally, she stepped back to let them into the apartment. It was just a large room, like a hotel suite. The space was stuffed with a floral-patterned sofa, a La-Z-Boy, and shelves and shelves of Pug figurines. Of actual dogs, no sign.

She fetched a printout from a stack on her kitchen counter. "John Goodnight. Room 402." She opened a cabinet and fished out a key. "Get her out of here. If Mr. Dell sees her, he won't think twice before firing your ass."

Cassie was impatient to get to John's room. She needed to call her hotline and get back in the loop. She hoped something had already been worked out between Kalov and the kidnappers. Maybe they'd already paid the ransom and Dad was being set free. Maybe the Russians had demanded an airplane and were waiting for it to fly them a few hundred miles west to Russia.

None of these scenarios seemed remotely likely. Cassie didn't think the Russians were only after Dad's ransom account. The machine gun was overkill for that sort of thing.

John pushed into his room. She brushed past him and went to the phone sitting on the bedside table. The room was exactly like a hotel room. A cheap one. It sure wasn't what she was used to.

But it was clean. There was a flat-screen TV mounted above a small desk, and the bathroom looked reasonably modern. The carpet, bedspread, and furniture was all beiges and grays. Neutral colors a lazy, uncreative person would choose.

She punched her hotline number into the phone.

At the answer, she repeated her phrase, this time adding the words "lying low." Kalov was already on by the time she finished.

"Your father is in grave danger."

Chapter Ten

1:10 pm

The phone was very nice. An extraordinarily expensive device made in California. They were readily available in Russia if you had the money.

Col. Fedorov had found the conversation with Miss Ko —Ingram's hotline operator—quite fascinating. Discussing ransom money with her had been like speaking to a banker. She truly seemed keen on satisfying him, as if he were her customer. What a strange thing. But sensible.

Most people calling to demand a ransom payment would be agitated and confrontational. Why not treat such people in a cordial manner? Miss Ko was excellent.

So now that Fedorov had relayed the account numbers and amounts he required deposited into them, he could move on to other issues.

The payments would happen, and there would be all manner of communication between Ingram's people and the FBI and the National Security Agency. Oil execs were, fundamentally, political operatives in America. They contributed to everyone's campaigns so that, no matter who won, they won.

Lt. Blok made marks on his map. If this had been a true military operation, he'd have a tablet with all this information, including real-time GPS data coming in from the squads in the field. But this was freelancing, and that required using older and less expensive tools.

"Load the remaining prisoners into the Sno-Cat," Fedorov said. "They're coming with us to Pump Station One.

"Yes, sir." Blok folded up his map, collected his ruler, his radio, and all his pencils. "Gregor Petrevski, come with me."

The man smashed out his cigarette and followed Blok into the back. Sighing at the sloppiness of his man's littering, Fedorov put the fancy phone in his pocket. Next he collected his High-Vis workman's vest and hardhat. No reason to stand out when blending in would serve better.

It was time for the next phase of this operation. The one that would make the real money.

Chapter Eleven

1:15 pm

"That doesn't make any sense," Cassie said. "Why would he demand that?"

Kalov had played her the recording of the phone call with a man calling himself Ivan Illych Golovin. He said very little except to recite three account numbers and routing information, then demanded $33 million be deposited into each. He sounded like he was reading from a script.

At the end he said, "Evacuate Pump Stations Two, Three, and Four."

Kalov grumbled to someone in the room with him. Cassie didn't catch what he said. Then he spoke up. "Those stations are along the Trans-Alaska Pipeline. It is possible there are more teams of these criminals in Alaska. But why pump stations? I can only guess he means to destroy them."

"Pump stations?" Cassie said. "Why destroy something so boring-sounding?"

"Did you say pump station?" John asked. He had moved to the desk and pretended not to listen, but in a room this cramped it was impossible to do otherwise. "What about destroying a pump station?"

"Who is with you?" Kalov asked.

"His name is John. He picked me up and brought me to his room. He's an employee of the company."

"Get away from him. He could be one of them."

Cassie eyed him. "He would have to be awfully good at acting dumb."

John threw up his hands. "I literally don't know what's going on. That doesn't make me stupid."

Cassie covered the phone with a hand. "Hush. I said you were *acting* dumb."

"The pump stations are part of the Trans-Alaska Pipeline." John pointed out the window. "The whole purpose of this place is to suck oil from the ground and pump it 800 miles south. You do know what your daddy's company does, don't you?"

Kalov must have heard. "I don't trust that man. You should get out of there. Best place to hide is in a cellar with a very heavy door. You should never have told anyone who you were."

"Wait a minute." She turned to John. "The bad guys are demanding we evacuate Pump Stations Two, Three, and Four. What does that suggest to you?"

He ran a hand across his cheek, his eyes looked dead-tired. "Sounds like they plan to take them over. Or maybe blow them up. I don't know. But I don't like it. These stations move tens of thousands of gallons of oil per minute."

"Maybe they're planning to steal the oil," she said to John and Kalov at the same time.

"No," John said, coming to sit on the bed next to her.

"There would be no way to move it, unless they have a convoy of tanker trucks standing by. And if they did, they'd never get away with it. The only way to get oil out of Alaska is on freighters at the port in Valdez. That's 800 miles south. That's why the pipeline was built."

"He's right," Kalov said. "Cassie, you can stay with this man for now. Lock the door. Pull furniture in front of it. I have a team assembling to come to your aid."

"What about my father?"

Kalov didn't hesitate. He always said the direct truth. "He is in grave danger. And there is nothing any of us—including you—can do to help him at the moment. But do not forget, Valentine is with him. There is always hope when a trained soldier is present."

"I'll guess I'll wait here, then," Cassie said. She would do no such thing. "I assume you have this number now?"

"Yes. And we know your exact location down to the meter. Rest assured, we will come."

"So you know where my dad is, too. Where?"

"We believe he has been moved to the pump station."

"How long until your team gets here?"

"Soonest possible is fifteen hours." The phone went quiet as Kalov let the truth sink in.

"I understand," Cassie said. Then she hung up and put her face in her hands. John thought she was crying, and awkwardly patted her back. She lifted her head and blew out a big breath. "So here's the deal. I need to borrow your truck."

"Technically it's your father's truck. As long as you're willing to talk to my boss about whatever happens to it, take it." He paused. "But I'm going with you."

"Trust me, I have more training for this than you. You should stay here and take the call if Kalov needs to get ahold of me."

"Yeah, I'm going." His eyes were firm. Cassie saw a steel in his character she hadn't suspected. She had mistaken his tiredness for weakness, perhaps. Still, he didn't owe her any help.

Come to think of it, she hadn't been very nice to him. "I, uh, I guess I'm sorry for calling you dumb before."

"You said I was *acting* dumb."

"Yeah, but I actually meant you were dumb. I shouldn't have said that. I'm under a little bit of stress."

He smiled and shook his head in wonder. "Ya think? Listen, I don't know your father and I don't know you. But I want to help you. I have other reasons than just because you're a pretty young woman in distress."

John got up and pulled back the window blind. There was nothing to see but hazy lights from the parking lot and a very faint skim of lights on the horizon far away. He pointed toward them. "Somewhere out there is the Trans-Alaska Pipeline, and it starts at Pump Station One. If these Russians—" He paused as he heard himself say the word. He shook his head as if he had to get the craziness of the situation out of his brain. "If the Russians are actually planning to sabotage a pump station, I have to do something about it."

Cassie didn't understand what he was getting at. "You told me you weren't that loyal to the company. I get that. You just started."

"I'm an ecological engineer. I didn't get into this field for the huge salary and the pleasant work environment. I got into it because I care about the environment. If these morons do something that spills oil here, the impact to local wildlife will be devastating."

That steely quality had come to the fore now. His face was set with determination, and he gestured with angry sweeps of his hands when he spoke. For an instant there, he reminded her of Kalov. There was a no-compromise focus and energy in him. She decided he might not be the anchor around her neck she'd thought he was. And Kalov and Valentine had often coached her to seek allies.

"Where's that North Face coat you were telling me about?" she asked.

Nodding grimly, he tore open his suitcase and pulled out a black quilted jacket. Lightweight and full of down, it was like wearing a comforter. It was way too big for her, but it served its function and fit over the wool sport jacket she'd taken from Dad's luggage.

"Let's stop at the cafeteria," John said. "It's supposed to have a twenty-four-seven free-take sandwich bar for employees."

Chapter Twelve

<hr>

1:20 pm

The Consortium Oil Field Monitoring Station, or COFMS, was pronounced "coffems" by administration. Those who worked there had quickly warped that to "coffins." It was a made of four interconnected modular boxcars. They even had the train wheel trucks still mounted on the bottoms. But in place of steel wheels they had short ski-like skids, ideal for dragging over the frozen roads.

These modules had been positioned near the entrance to the Prudhoe oil fields, forming a monitoring center for all of the drilling and pumping in the region.

Jackson Swan was the shift supervisor on duty. His ten reports sat at their terminals, watching the production and flow from exactly 965 wells spread over two-hundred-thousand-square miles of Alaskan tundra.

"Are cams up on the Ingram-Delve sites?" he asked his newest team member, Fox Tils. The young man had the excessive, luxuriously-groomed facial hair common to certain men of his generation. His soft-spoken phrases always ended on a rising pitch, as if he was asking a question with every statement.

Fox tapped some keys on his computer, face lit by the bluish tint of the LED backlighting. "I have most of them. The motion detection algorithms are still, like, a bit sketchy."

Jackson leaned over Fox's shoulder to study the hundreds of thumbnail video feeds coming in from across the oil fields. He had to put on his reading glasses and tilt his head up so he looked down his nose to see the minuscule data readouts overlaying each thumbnail. The numbers showed ambient temperature at each site, along with oil volume per minute, oil temperature, pressure, and a dozen other bits of telemetry.

"Sorry about the small type, Mr. Swan," Fox said, scratching his beard. He treated Jackson like a grandpa, even though Jackson was only ten years older than the young data systems expert. "Is there a particular well you want to see, or something? I can, like, bring any of these up on the big screen."

"Just pick one," Jackson said. The consortium had spent fifty-seven million dollars on this control center. The telemetry feeds and dumb-AI analysis systems were supposed to save the partner oil companies many times their investment over the next few years. But keeping the system operational in this climate had proven more difficult than even the most pessimistic detractor had guessed. Only the arrival of Fox Tils had rescued the operation from failure.

Fox clicked a random video feed, sending it to the big screen at the front wall of their little mission control center. The setup reminded Jackson of movie footage he'd seen of NASA's mission control. Maybe that was a little grandiose, but the room was kept dim and everyone sat at their post, keeping an eye on the production of oil and natural gas, communicating through headsets when needed. Everything was focused on keeping the oil flowing.

"This is oil well Delve-7 over in the Kiki Bend area," Fox said. "The data are good. The cams are running. So, like, yeah. Ingram cams are up." He clicked his tongue. "Yo, look at this. Motion detection alert." He smacked his mouse and a playback of video footage outside the well started. Time code ran at the bottom of the feed in white numerals. "You'll like this. Wait for it . . ."

A polar bear ambled into the frame. It nosed around the door to the well shack. Unlike well pumps in warmer climates, Alaskan ones had cubical shacks set overtop them to protect the machinery from the elements. One benefit of pulling oil from twenty thousand feet beneath the surface was that it came up hot, 120° Fahrenheit. This provided free heating for the shacks.

The bear's shaggy white fur waved in fringes from its flanks and shrouded its legs in snowy wisps. The sloped skull and snout gave the impression of animal stupidity, but Jackson knew the bears were devilishly smart. They focused all their brain power on scrounging for food. The easier to grab, the better.

Company policy on garbage control, combined with an absolute ban on feeding wildlife, had gone a long way to keeping the bears away from the camps. But a field worker sometimes got lazy with a bit of their lunch or candy bar. The bears learned fast. And who didn't love a Snickers bar?

"That's beautiful," Fox said. "I bet he's all, like, 'what the hell?'"

Jackson did not know how to interpret the young man's statement. But that wasn't anything new. The data wiz seemed to speak only in irony and childish narratives of what other people, animals, and inanimate objects were thinking.

"Is the animal tagged?" Jackson asked.

"Yeah. Virtual tag ID number 32. That's based on gait recognition. So maybe the virtual tag isn't so reliable. I'll add a note that its identity is, like, not certain." His fingers skittered over his keyboard as he added a text note to the motion detection event.

In a fervor for good PR, CEO Bryce Ingram had put forward a sizable chunk of funding for wildlife observation and scientific research in Prudhoe Bay. His idea was to use the well sites as tracking points for large animals. An ecological engineer was due the next day to oversee the operation and to work with scientists to provide migration and habit data on polar bears, arctic foxes, caribou, and a number of other creatures of land and air.

Jackson's job was to keep COFMS running. He'd leave the virtual tagging problem to the new guy. "Just tell me the system will be operational when John Goodnight gets here."

"It's operational now, but it isn't, like, providing totally reliable data about the animals yet. The AI isn't good enough to say 'yeah, that's definitely bear 32' based on its face or butt or how it waddles."

"That's for Dr. Goodnight to figure out. We're in charge of the equipment, and that's your only concern."

The young man grumbled something and tousled his own hair. He wore plaid flannel and looked like the scrawniest lumberjack ever seen. "I, like, care about the animals, too, yo."

Jackson let it go. He had other concerns. Namely, he had discovered one of his maintenance staff drinking a beer. Alcohol was simply not tolerated in the fields or even in Deadhorse. Jackson hated having to fire people. Not only did they feel bad, but he was left short-handed until a replacement could be recruited. The pay here was good, but not many people had what it took to work in the endless night of the arctic winter.

Chapter Thirteen

1:30 pm

The commissary was mostly empty. Only two large weary-looking men and one woman sat hunched over plates there. They wore insulated cover-alls and High-Vis orange or yellow vests. All had their hard hats on, with tight-fitting fleece caps underneath. They looked up as Cassie and John came in, like hungry wolves eyeing a passing pack-mate to make sure he didn't steal anything from them.

Cassie scooped up a peanut butter and jelly sandwich and a Diet Coke from the snack bar. The sandwich was wrapped in plastic and looked homemade. She nabbed a package of potato chips and waited for John to stuff his coat pockets with sandwiches and cans of pop.

As they were leaving she heard a man mumble something, and the others all responded with the evil laugh of men enjoying a particularly filthy joke. Cassie liked those, so she wondered what it was. Certainly about her. As long as they didn't say anything to her face they were safe.

John offered a hushed apology for their behavior.

"Women are in short supply up here. Not that that should matter. It's just . . . you know."

"I have more pressing concerns at the moment. But thank you for assuring me of your own personal wokeness."

The new North Face coat was a great improvement. Though the wind still bit at her face, at least it couldn't slip down the gap between her jeans and top anymore. Now all she needed were gloves and a hat . . . and a scarf, and long underwear, and a week in the Caribbean.

The warmth of the truck was welcome. She twisted in her seat to look through the rear window. The payload bed held several lidded bins fastened down with tie straps. "What sort of supplies do you have back there?"

She knew nobody in their right mind would hazard a drive all the way up here without packing some basics for survival.

"First aid kit, two spare tires, some nasty non-perishable protein bars, bear spray, a pop-up tent, tire iron, jack, gas can, flares, hand sanitizer, toilet paper, and . . . uh . . . rubber boots. That's all I can think of right now."

The lights of the worker camp receded behind them as he drove. The snow began to swarm more thickly across the roadway. Far off to their right, a flashing yellow light showed the progress of a snowplow.

Cassie thought the gasoline and flares might come in handy. Now she truly had the makings of a Molotov Cocktail. But that wasn't a subtle weapon. Definitely difficult to come at someone with stealth while holding a flaming bottle in your hand. Also, the flammable fluid dispersed and set everything ablaze. Not at all ideal when there were beloved hostages present. "Sorry, Dad. I didn't mean to immolate you."

"Huh?" John said, alarmed.

"Nothing. Just thinking out loud."

They were quiet for a while. John looked as worried as she felt, if not for the same reasons. Her stomach churned, and she didn't want to eat her sandwich. But she hadn't eaten on the whole flight from Farewell Airport. She was past due for food, especially with a possible confrontation with Russians ahead of her.

John smelled her PB&J sandwich and then futzed with a ham and cheese. He took enormous bites and washed them down huge gulps of Diet Coke. "Tell me more about these Russians. You said they looked like soldiers?"

"Yeah. Kalashnikovs and fatigues."

"Terrorists might wear fatigues. And they certainly use AK-47s."

"These are Russians, not some Al Qaeda cell. Besides, if terror was their goal why not kill everyone as soon as they came on the plane?"

John considered for a few moments before lifting a shoulder. "Maybe they want a bigger audience when they do it."

That didn't make Cassie feel any better. Not at all. "Do you know where you're going?"

"Just following the signs. But I think we have to go through a security checkpoint first. There should be a guard station checking IDs. They don't want tourists out here."

"I don't have any ID."

"Then you'd better hide in the back."

At first she thought he meant the payload bed. That would be one hell of a cold ride. But then he patted the back of her seat. "There's a little back seat. I think you're skinny enough to squeeze behind this. It will only take a moment. They won't inspect the—"

He braked hard. Cassie looked ahead. At first, she

didn't understand what she was seeing. There was a guard post up ahead, the kind of thing you'd see at the entrance to a National Park. A red and white barricade boom should have been barring the way. But the boom lay in a shattered trail leading farther down the road.

As John's headlights shined on the scene, it lit up an arm and gloved hand sticking out from the base of the guard shack door.

"Jesus," John said as he rolled through. He stopped just beyond the shack. "I'd better check this out." He didn't seem eager to do so.

Cassie hopped out, too. She clamped her teeth together, knowing she was going to find another bloody scene. The image of the co-pilot flashed in her memory. She hoped this person hadn't suffered.

He hadn't.

Chapter Fourteen

1:35 pm

The guard had probably experienced a fleeting moment of surprise as a gun barrel poked from a stopped vehicle. Then a high-powered blast had turned his forehead to pulp. The destruction took a fraction of an instant. One second of rising fear, then nothing at all.

"These guys aren't making any sense," Cassie said. Her voice sounded cold to her own ears. But this was the only way she could process the gore in front of her.

John had other ways. Mostly it involved swearing.

Cassie eyed the carnage with dispassion. She had seen worse. She had nearly done this to multiple men in Houston. She had missed her shots, but it hadn't mattered. They had all died anyway when the SWAT team came in.

"Who are you calling?" she asked. John had picked up the guard shack phone.

"Security." He rattled the phone. "Or not. The line is dead."

She could have predicted that. "Let's see if this guy has

a weapon." She stepped over the dead guard. He was dressed for warmth. No obvious sign of a sidearm on him. There was a cabinet and refrigerator in the narrow space at the back. A radio churned out a country song she knew very well. Something about how rain was important for growing corn and that corn was necessary to make whiskey. Not very apropos for this place. The cabinet had a spare coat, a hardhat, and a stash of girlie magazines. No weapon.

"Try the radio transmitter over there," she said. "It's got to be——"

"A bullet right through it. I've got a CB radio in the truck. I can see which channel they use up here. Maybe I can reach that snowplow we passed. He can call this in."

Cassie had been avoiding searching the body, but this was no time for squeamishness. She bent, clamping her lips tight, and unzipped the guard's parka. Just as she hoped, he had a 9mm holstered close to his side. A familiar weapon. A Glock 17.

She removed it, popped the magazine. Empty. She patted his pockets until she found another magazine. This one was loaded.

Safety on, full clip in. She put the gun into the inside pocket of her North Face coat.

When she straightened, she discovered John staring at her. A flicker of fear—no, of reassessment—flitted across his face. He didn't look too pleased, but he didn't try to tell her to leave the gun. Or worse, demand she hand it to him.

"Where did you learn to do that?" he asked.

"Handling a gun isn't exactly difficult. A little training, is all." She bent and removed the security ID card clipped to a retractable badge reel on the dead man's belt. Jason Falson, sec-level four, date of birth: July 13.

Eye color: Blue.

She put the card in her pocket.

John lowered his voice. "I'm talking about how you can do that. Search him so calmly. His head is blown off and you treat him like a CPR dummy."

She pushed past John. "I've seen worse. Let's go."

She headed back to the still-running truck. The tone of John's voice bothered her. She knew she had distanced herself from the gruesome scene. But she was Kalov's creature now. His way of seeing the world, as much as she tried to fight it, was coming to her as naturally as breathing.

When someone tells you every day that you need to X and Y to avoid being kidnapped, raped, killed, or worse, you start to take it in. You don't even realize the hardness is taking root, but then one day a person looks at you like you're an alien. The way John had just looked at her.

He was barking into his truck's CB radio when she got back in. He switched channels again. "Emergency at security gate for Pump Station One. Guard shot. Deceased."

The only response was a hiss and crackle of static. "Either nobody has their ears on or they don't believe me."

But then a man's voice came over the airwaves. "Who is this?"

"John Goodnight. I'm with Cassie Ingram. A guard has been shot at the Pump Station One security gate. Unknown number of highly-trained gunmen operating in the area."

Confused crosstalk came next as truck operators asked questions. CB communication is one person at a time, with no way to interrupt. Eventually a man got through and asked for silence.

This quiet was interrupted by a familiar voice. Harv. "False alarm. The pranksters are known to me. If you're listening, both of you are to return to Deadhorse and come to the security office. If you do not comply, you will be arrested."

Cassie grabbed the handset from John. "Harv, listen to me. There's a murdered guard at the Pump Station gate shack. Check it out if you don't believe us. Russians have threatened the station. At least call the people working there and tell them to prepare to defend themselves against at least three armed men. Call the FBI or whoever you're supposed to call when there's a threat to national security. But for Pete's sake, do something!"

A beat of silence, then two. Finally, Harv said, "Return to security office or you will be arrested. Leave this frequency clear. You are in violation of corporate policy."

Cassie gave up. Tossing the handset aside, she drew in a deep, calming breath. "How much farther?" she asked John.

"Five miles. Ten. I don't know. But it's down this road. I remember that much from studying Google Maps. I took special interest in this stretch due to the arctic fox."

Cassie looked at him to see if he was serious. "The arctic fox?"

"Marvelous animals. Beautiful white coat, fluffy, and you can even domesticate them in a couple generations in captivity. They're weird. Sort of act like dogs and sort of act like cats. Anyway, their habitat is along this stretch of road. I've been thinking about how vehicle traffic might disrupt their patterns. They can listen for small rodents burrowing beneath the snow. But with all these heavy vehicles, I worry that the noise will interfere with their hunting. They'd be fine out in this wind, believe it or not. But nobody really cares about them. Polar bears are more the face of environmental concern."

His eyes gleamed as he spoke. Cassie watched the weariness drain from his face. He sensed her watching him.

"Sorry. I can go on a bit when I get talking about the wildlife up here. It's truly remarkable how life adapts and even thrives in a place as hard and unforgiving as this." He waved a hand at the lights ahead. "All this disturbance does is make it harder." He laughed. "But I do see the other side. Civilization needs gas for its cars. I'm not saying no drilling should happen up here. That's why I'm in this job. I want to make sure that what *is* done up here is done in the least impactful way."

"I can respect that," Cassie said. "I may be Bryce Ingram's daughter, but I care about the environment. I don't want the wildlife hurt. But I bet when you signed up for this, you were thinking you'd have to fight for stricter trash and recycling policies, not get into a fight with a band of Russians."

He let out a half-laugh, half-snort of disgust. "I don't plan to fight the Russians. But I do need to know what they're planning to do with this pump station. There it is up ahead."

A constellation of lights shone through the thickening snowfall. It looked like any large industrial compound: huge, blocky building, smoke stacks, and circular oil tanks as big as the building itself. Several other outlying barns and metal-sided buildings were scattered around the periphery of the place. Trucks and huge service vehicles on snow tracks idled nearby.

Cassie had no idea if anything looked out of the norm or not.

John slowed as they approached the main pump building. Lights on tall poles did little to illuminate the snowy gloom that pressed over the complex. A main entrance was marked only by the concentration of pickup trucks parked in front of it.

"Pull in there." She pointed past the crowd of trucks to

a loading dock farther down the building. A huge quad-tracked plow vehicle was parked near it. In the dim light, Cassie could see it was painted a pumpkin orange. "Sno-Cat" was emblazoned on the rear section. The cockpit was cube-shaped, and the vehicle stood upon triangular tracks. A yellow plow attachment thrust from beneath its blunt nose.

"That looks out of place here," she said. "It's for plowing roads, not a parking lot."

John stopped next to it. Cassie got out, ignoring John's plea for caution. She needed to get inside the building. If the bad guys were willing to shoot a guard, they would shoot everyone here.

Chapter Fifteen

1:40 pm

The door next to the loading dock was locked. It had a keycard reader mounted next to it. Cassie fished the gate guard's security ID from her pocket and pressed it to the reader.

The door clicked. She turned the latch and opened the door a fraction of an inch. There was light inside. No sound other than the distant hum and thump of machinery.

John's boots crunched on the thin layer of new snow behind her. "What's your plan? Go in guns blazing?"

She didn't look at him, but pushed the door open farther. A short entry corridor with a line of hooks and cubbies for workers' personal things. Hard hats hung above empty hooks, while parkas hung beneath hooks where hardhats were missing.

The hats were bright and battered, with names and slogans written across the sides in black Sharpie.

"I'm the one with the gun," Cassie said, "so I guess it'll be *gun* blazing."

"Actually . . ." He coughed and held up a short barrel shotgun. "For bears."

She hadn't had much practice with shotguns, but she was happy to see it. "Do you know how to shoot?"

He nodded. "It's my personal 870. I've got slugs in it."

That made sense for bears, but Cassie would have loved if he had regular shotgun shells, which fire a dispersed hail of shot. Easier to hit a guy. Easier to hit a couple guys. And it would certainly stop them. Still, a bear slug would destroy a guy if it hit.

If.

That was the thing about guns. Sometimes you missed. She stepped through the door. John came in behind her.

She studied the floor. It was grated to catch all the snow and mud tracked in from outside. But it was wet. People had come in this way recently.

"How did the Russians get past the lock?" she said.

She was thinking out loud, but John answered. "Uh, doesn't your dad have clearance to go anywhere he wants?"

"He doesn't own this place," she said.

The pump station and pipeline was operated by an entirely separate company. Each oil company paid hefty fees to put their oil into the system. "They must have grabbed somebody else and taken their security badge."

She opened the next door which led into the loading dock interior. A high ceiling with harsh lights hung over a concrete area with a crane system and a row of fork trucks. Yellow lines marked safe walkways, and every barrel and garbage bin had a spot marked on the floor for where it belonged.

Cassie had expected a messy—even oily—facility. But

this was very clean, like something from one of those NASA photos of the people assembling a Mars rover.

The exception was the trail of dirty puddles leading across the bay to a metal stairway. The stairs climbed to a glassed-in mezzanine overlooking the loading dock. She guessed there was an overseer's office up there.

The windows were dark. "When does the next shift start?"

John didn't know. Cassie checked the time on her phone. "1:42. That's impossible. It's totally dark out."

"Uh, didn't anyone tell you? It's December. The sun won't come up until January 19th."

"What?"

"It's called polar night. We're above the arctic circle. The sun stays beneath the horizon twenty-four-seven. In the summer, it's the opposite."

Something clicked for Cassie. The darkness and the extreme cold were assets to the Russians. They had chosen this time of year for both the cold and the darkness.

She jogged to the stairs and started up. She kept a hand in her jacket pocket, ready to pull the Glock.

Kalov had taught her that an enemy would be more likely to shoot her on sight if they saw she was armed. "Stay behind me," she whispered to John. It wasn't as easy to hide a shotgun from view. "And don't point that thing at anyone unless I tell you to."

Their footsteps rang on the metal stairs, but the sound didn't draw any faces to the window. John mumbled something that sounded like exasperation. And then, "How old are you, anyway?"

The door at the top of the stairs was unlocked. Cassie opened it and peeked in. The office was spartan. Metal desks, aging computers with boxy monitors, and walls covered in a very disgusting dark wood paneling. The air smelled of stale coffee.

She kept low as she padded across the office to a rear door. Muffled voices carried through the wood. She pressed her ear to the door and caught a short burst of Russian, then: "No one will getting hurt. But if you are cowboy, then I'm shooting two of you. Say yes you understand."

A soft chorus of "yes" followed.

"Excellent. Now, I am needing expert in pigs."

Cassie couldn't have heard that right. John hovered behind her, face a pale oval in the dimness of the office. "What's going on?" he mouthed at her.

She shushed him with a sharp cut of her hand. The voice on the other side of the door was the same as the one she'd heard on the recording with Kalov. This man sounded like he was in charge. "No answer? I am shooting this woman? What is name, woman?"

Mumbling. Cassie didn't hear the name through the sobs.

Apparently the threat was sufficient, for another woman spoke up, "I run the pigs. I can answer your questions."

There was no more talking until the leader commanded a man named Petrevski to stand guard over the prisoners. The underlying noise of the pump station was too loud for Cassie to hear anything else.

She pulled back from the door, motioning John to follow as she retreated to the stairs. "They're holding workers in there. I think they were asking for someone who's an expert with pigs. Do they keep livestock here?" The thought chilled her. What purpose would an oil pipeline have for farm animals? And for that matter—

"Not animal pigs," John said. "A pig is a piece of

equipment they put in the pipeline to scrape sludge off the inside walls. They call them pigs, but they're more like augers. Spiral things that get pushed along with the flow of oil." He dropped his head and gripped the stock of his shotgun. The gleam he'd shown when talking about arctic foxes was gone. Now there was worry.

The pig thing was a side mystery. What she really wanted was to find her dad.

She had to see inside that room. She hoped her dad was in there. If only Petrevski remained to guard the prisoners, she and John had a reasonable chance to take him out.

But she wasn't about to barge in with her gun out. And she suddenly realized she had important information that people in Kalov's team would needed know.

She went to a phone sitting atop a tidy desk. A picture of a German Shepherd was featured among an array of stuffed toys. She dialed her hotline number.

The answer came mid-ring. It was Kalov. "Where the hell are you?"

"At Pump Station One. The Russians have taken some workers prisoner. The leader was asking for an expert on pigs. It's a term used for a device that scours the inside—"

"I know the term. You will exfiltrate immediately and return to a safe place. The situation has escalated beyond my organization's purview. The recovery team is still coming, but their ability to move and act in the field will be greatly reduced due to other forces present."

"Other forces? Please tell me the government is sending the Marines."

"I can't be that specific. My contacts have gone quiet in the past half-hour. They won't tell me who we're dealing with, but they hinted he is an ex-Spetznaz officer who earned notoriety in Chechnya and Ukraine."

"That sounds very specific. You know who it is, don't you?"

"I don't. But Spetznaz are special forces. You don't stand a chance against a team with that training and experience. Please confirm that you will immediately exfiltrate and return to a position of safety."

"I will." Just as soon as she found Dad. "Tell the Marines not to shoot the girl with the Glock. Oh, and the guy with the shotgun is okay, too." She hung up.

She could imagine Kalov looking at the dead phone and his knuckles going white with his fury. He knew she was not going to exfiltrate. She knew he knew. If she got out alive, she would happily listen to his diatribe about her foolishness.

But if she left—and her father didn't survive—Cassie knew she would be far more disgusted with herself than Kalov could ever be.

"The Marines are coming," she told John. "But I doubt they'll be here soon.

He tilted his head and gave her a look. "I've been patient and I've tried to give you room to do what you think you need to do. But if the professionals are coming, maybe we should get out of their way. No offense, but you're—what?—twenty years old? You're not a marine."

Cassie made an effort to keep her voice under control. "First off, I'm eighteen. Second, you wanted to make sure they don't sabotage this station. The environment, remember? But if you're too scared to continue, you can go back to Deadhorse and wait for the Marines. But I'm not waiting while that team of Spetsnaz stooges threatens my loved ones."

He looked like he was going to argue, but he must have seen something in her expression that shut him up. She guessed he was thinking he would have to pull her out of this when everything hit the fan. Men always thought the girl needed saving, when it was usually the other way around.

Let him think what he wanted. "I'm not very threatening-looking," she said. "He won't even search me. He'll put me with the other prisoners. Once I'm in there, you make a loud noise. I'll either get the prisoners free, or I'll come help you take him out."

"You're going to surrender? That's your plan? I thought you'd go in there and kung-fu his ass."

She brightened and grinned at him. "Hey, that's an even better idea." Without a second glance, she went back through the office and went through the door.

Chapter Sixteen

1:45 pm

It looked like a storeroom. Prisoners sat along one wall, forlorn and scared, a few with their heads back and eyes closed. The lone guard on duty was Smokey from the airport hangar.

He stood with his back to the opposite wall, a cigarette dangling from his lips. He still wore the AK-47, though it hung carelessly from its harness. His head swiveled toward her, his eyes squinting as he pinched his cigarette and took one last drag.

He tossed it onto the floor and walked toward her, blowing streams of smoke from his nostrils. Remembering that she was supposed to be an innocent girl in the wrong place at the wrong time, she looked around in feigned confusion. "What's going on?"

The other prisoners came alert. They stared at her with a mix of shock and terror. None of them had the slightest idea who she was. All they saw was a lamb who had unwittingly walked into the lion's den.

"*Davai! Shagai k drughim zaklyuchonym.*" He grasped his weapon and waved the barrel toward the other people.

Cassie understood enough to know that he wanted her to join the others. Fine. She would do that. She stood next to a man of about fifty. He made eye-contact with her and mouthed, "It'll be okay."

Hell yes, it would. Still pretending to be flabbergasted, she turned on the Russian. "Who are you? I'm just here to visit my mom."

"You're wasting your breath. He doesn't speak English," said another man, this one with a thin neck and a chin covered by a goatee that looked like a wire brush. "Just keep quiet. They're—"

"Shut up!" the guard shouted. He swept close to Goatee and jabbed the muzzle of his gun into the man's trim belly.

Cassie recoiled, though her instinct was to kick Smokey behind the knee, drive her elbow into his throat, pull him to the floor, and submit him in an arm-bar hold.

But he had a gun, and such an attack would be stupid. Better to let him think she was exactly what he thought she was. A total non-threat.

The man who had made eye-contact with her tried to put a comforting arm around her shoulders. Cassie tolerated it. And she did appreciate the man's sentiment. She recognized that he was obeying his paternal instincts. But it still felt condescending to her.

She put her hand to her mouth and looked all around, like a wide-eyed Disney princess who just realized how much trouble she was in. The soldier had backed away from Goatee. He eyed Cassie and made an obviously rude comment in Russian before returning to his post and digging out another cigarette.

Cassie shrugged free from her self-appointed protector.

She whispered a thank-you to him and put her back to a row of cabinets. The room was twenty by forty and reminded her of an inventory backroom for a shoe store. Except there weren't any lovely Jimmy Choos or Steve Maddens in sight.

It was all boxes and bins. A supply room, probably for maintenance crew. The space had been partially cleared—probably by the prisoners themselves—and a bunch of shelving units were pushed against the rear wall. At the back corner, another door exited the room. The most important detail of all, however, was the absence of Dad, Uncle Dev, Val, and the pilot.

She still had her phone stuffed in her back pocket. It was hidden by the length of John's coat. The Glock was snug in her side pocket. She realized she could draw, aim, and fire before the guard realized what was happening.

She weighed the idea, but discarded it. She didn't know how far away the other Russians were. The machinery noise of the facility was loud, but a gunshot could carry. The sound would be instantly recognized by trained soldiers.

She didn't want the confrontation to be any more violent than necessary. At least two men were dead already. No reason to make more.

Where the hell was John and his diversion? All he needed to do was make a sound. She supposed she had acted a bit precipitously by coming in here like this. That was a weakness of hers. But she was so exasperated by everyone's caution. They didn't act. She did.

A loud crash and curse sounded in the office. The crowd of prisoners stood up and thronged toward the door. Smokey shouted them back and tromped to see what had happened. As soon as he was out the door, Cassie headed for the other one.

She got five feet before Goatee grabbed her by the elbow. "Where do you think you're going?" He was pale and his cheeks splotchy with anger.

Cassie jerked her arm from the man's grip. "I need to go to the bathroom."

"Don't be stupid," the man said, sneering. "The Russian boss said he'll shoot two of us for every broken rule. So, you stay put."

A woman with scarlet hair and matching lipstick nodded in agreement. She had a haggard, lined face that suggested an extreme Vitamin D deficiency. "Keep your head down. Everything will be okay."

The guard was standing in the doorway, his back to the prisoners. Another thunk sounded in the office.

"*Kto tam?*" he shouted. Cassie thought it meant "Who's there?"

The guard wasn't exactly panicked, but he was alert, his posture tense. This wasn't good. The prisoners weren't letting Cassie leave—and for good reason.

She'd had enough of this nonsense. She went directly to Smokey, her strides even and purposeful. But quiet. Come on, John, she thought, just one more sound.

"*Kto tam?*" the guard said again. He took another step into the office. Cassie gripped her Glock, still in her pocket. She didn't dare shoot without knowing where John was. She released the gun and pulled her hand free.

Smokey stood with his back to her just a few paces away. The other prisoners were staring holes into the back of her head. They wanted to stop her, but none of them dared to grab her for fear of drawing Smokey's attention.

Well, they had nothing to fear.

All she needed was one more little pull on the man's attention. She saw in his body language that he was on edge now. There weren't supposed to be any other workers around. The Russian thought he'd gathered all of them into the back room. Now the girl had shown up. And more sounds meant at least one more person was loose. The guard had to be wondering how many he'd missed.

She imagined what he was thinking. Call the boss? No. Smokey had been the one responsible for sweeping the facility for workers in the first place. If he'd missed some then the boss would chew him a new one.

He took one more step, his weapon raised and swinging side to side as he scanned the dim office for threats.

John leapt from behind a desk and threw himself at the man's legs. A stupid, stupid move against an armed opponent.

Cassie didn't hesitate to join the fray. Both men went down under the momentum of John's charge. The guard's elbow struck the floor, jarring the weapon around, making it thunk on the floor. He kicked and yelled.

John reached for the gun, Cassie dropped to one knee, fist gaining power from the move, and drove her knuckles into Smokey's nose. It crunched and Smokey's whole body jerked. The AK-47 fired a short burst.

Someone screamed. Cassie cocked her arm back and mashed Smokey's blood-spurting nose again. His eyes rolled up and he went limp.

The relative quiet that followed the brief scuffle was punctuated by John and Cassie's heavy breaths. In the storeroom someone was shouting something about bandages; it barely penetrated the odd silence that dulled Cassie's hearing.

The smell of gunsmoke brought her around. She realized that the burst of gunfire in this enclosed space had left her ears ringing.

John rolled off the guard. His face was a pale mask of

fear and disbelief. His lips moved, but Cassie couldn't make out what he said.

Cassie tugged at the AK-47. It was secured by a tactical harness. She fidgeted with the buckles, fingers shaking from the sudden flush of adrenaline. Finally she got the weapon free. She was vaguely familiar with the model, having seen a few diagrams of them in Kalov's books.

She released the magazine. It appeared to be a couple rounds short. That meant this moron had killed the guard shack guy—and the radio.

Someone was toeing her in the back. Goatee sneered at her. "You are under arrest." He motioned for her to hand over the gun.

She straightened. "Who appointed you cop?"

"I did. You nearly got Debbie killed. I can't believe the irresponsibility of your actions. And you," he said, pointing at John, "you're under arrest, too."

But John didn't give the man any more attention than Cassie did. He got to his feet and collected his shotgun from behind the desk where he'd been hiding.

"I think he's dead," John said, nodding at the Russian. Cassie felt for a pulse, but didn't find one. She wasn't an EMT or nurse, so she couldn't sure.

"Get some rope or wire and bind his hands," she said to Goatee. She considered giving him her Glock, but decided not to arm a man who wanted to place her under citizen's arrest. "Then all of you should get out of here."

"I certainly do not recognize your authority, little lady," Goatee said. "You've made an unholy mess of things. When those other two come back and see what you've done, they'll kill all the hostages."

"Didn't I just say you should leave?"

Goatee's face reddened and a splutter of fury burst

from his lips, but he was so overtaken with rage that nothing intelligible came out. Then the fatherly guy came in and eased Goatee back. "Relax, Simon. She doesn't know about the others."

Cassie pushed Goatee aside. "What others? Did you see my dad? There were four other men with him. Do you know Dev Salah?"

The man frowned. "I met Salah once," he said, clearly uncertain why she was asking about him. "The other hostages I'm talking about all work here. The Russian boss divided us into two groups just to make sure we behaved."

"So you didn't see Dev Salah? Or Bryce Ingram? Or a man in a pilot's uniform? Or—"

The man was shaking his head, and each name increased the vigor of his denial. Finally Cassie had to accept that he hadn't seen any of the prisoners taken from the Twin Otter. News that there were more workers trapped here did not go down well either.

She squeezed past the guy and spotted the red-haired woman lying on the floor, surrounded by a spreading pool of blood. John swore and dashed to the woman's side. Three other people were crowded around her.

"Where are the other prisoners?" Cassie asked.

"Like I'd tell you anything," Goatee said. "You'll just get them shot."

Cassie stared at the injured woman, but at the same time did not see her. Cassie had caused this. A compressed ball of ache clenched her throat. She hadn't pulled the trigger, but her actions had made Smokey pull it. "I'm sorry."

"That isn't good enough," Goatee said. "You are going to jail if I have anything to say about it. You had no business going all John McClane in here. We told you to sit down, but you just had to play the hero. I hope you die in jail."

The fatherly man had stayed calm to this point, but now he'd had enough. He rounded on Goatee. "Simon, shut up. You're not a cop, or a judge, or anyone of authority. You're getting all riled up because you're scared. Now go get some rope or wire to secure that Russian, or go sit down."

Some of the others gasped and covered their mouths. Cassie sensed that the big man never lost his cool, and that this outburst was not in character. Even Goatee looked momentarily stunned. Finally he walked off, mumbling under his breath about how he would write a comprehensive report on the whole incident and that he would put in the unvarnished truth. And he would certainly file a complaint with the FBI about the teenager who had endangered all their lives with her Die Harding around like a Bruce Willis wannabe.

Cassie had no idea who Bruce Willis was, but she liked the sound of him. Goatee was content to lie low when everyone was in danger. That didn't make sense to her. "Where are the other prisoners?" she asked to all assembled.

It was the injured woman who answered. "I was with them when they separated us. The ones they took went to the main pumping plant. It's the center of this operation."

Cassie knelt next to John, who was holding the woman's hand while another man was trying to stop her bleeding by pressing his own shirt onto her abdomen. "I'm sorry, ma'am. I'll try to make it up to you."

The woman grimaced, but ended it with a smile. "This is just a scratch. We Alaskans aren't china dolls. I'll live. Now, go see if you can help the others."

Fatherly said, "I don't think that's a good idea. I know

you can fight. That's obvious. But two soldiers with machine guns are more than a match for you two."

"My father might be with them. I have to go."

"Your father would want you to go somewhere far from here. He would want you safe."

The man was right, but that had no bearing on her choices. What fathers want for their children was usually at odds with what their children wanted. Dad would rather Cassie live, with no risk, than for her to come to his rescue. But if she followed that course, she would have to live the rest of her days knowing she had run away and left him to whatever fate the Russians had planned for him. Which reminded her . . .

"What do they want with a pig?"

The man blinked, then turned to another man, this one gray-faced and about seventy-five. He had thick neck and fingers, all encrusted with a layer of grease and dirt. "Gergi? Why would they take Becky to mess around with the pigs?"

The man shrugged and spread his hands apart. "Unless they want to get some of them stuck in the pipeline to interrupt oil flow, I haven't the foggiest."

Cassie looked to John.

He raised a shoulder. "I still think they're planning sabotage, but plugging the pipes doesn't seem very dramatic. How long would flow be disrupted?"

"Gergi?" Fatherly said.

"A day or two. The pipeline is constructed in thirty-foot sections. A crew could uncouple a plugged section and get the pig out within a half day. Probably less if it's close to a pump station."

Cassie agreed with John. That didn't sound like a big enough blow to the industry—or the country. It seemed downright lame. "I don't think they're planning on letting anyone go," she said. "They killed the copilot of the plane I came here on. They killed the guard posted at the gate. They haven't kept their faces hidden." It was that last detail that worried her most. Men who showed their faces when they were taking hostages tended to leave no witnesses.

"How far is the pump room?" John asked.

Gergi snorted. "Room. It's more than a room, son." He extended a trembling arm and pointed to the rear door. "There are signs. You can't miss it."

Goatee mumbled something as he passed by with a coil of computer networking cable. Cassie caught the phrase "get us all killed."

As Goatee tied Smokey's wrists behind his back—and very proficiently at that—Cassie rifled through the Russian's pockets. She found two more packs of cigarettes. "Here, he's hopelessly addicted. If he does wake up, you can use these as rewards for good behavior."

She didn't think he was going to wake up anytime soon, but part of her was relieved to see his chest rise and fall in very slow, deep breaths. She had killed once before. It had been a more brutal—almost animal—attack in the coffee shop. And though the man she'd stabbed and scalded had planned to kill her and her father, she hadn't been able to uproot the seedling of guilt that killing him had planted in her mind.

She doubted she would have felt that badly for Smokey, but it was better to not have any deaths—deserved or not —on your conscience.

She discovered a folding knife on Smokey's belt. A four-inch blade. She stuffed it in her back pocket next to her phone. He also carried a protein bar, a small packet of pills, the label in Russian. She thought they were aspirin.

She put the packet in her pocket. He had no sidearm, no identification.

"Let's go," she said to John. "We have one advantage. They don't know we're here. They don't know that I'm even in Alaska."

"I'm sure the mere sound of your name would make them tremble," Goatee said.

She leveled a stare at him. "If they heard my name, they would bring Bryce Ingram out at gunpoint and demand I turn myself over. But they aren't going to learn my name, are they?"

It was funny to think that she wouldn't have dared to stand up to man like Goatee—or any man, for that matter—just a year ago. But a lot had changed in that time. She had no patience for this. "Get everyone into the Sno-Cat plow out there and drive back to Deadhorse." She turned to take in the whole group. "And no, I don't need any of you coming with me. You'll get shot or get in my way."

Fatherly looked like he was going to argue, but then he gave an uneasy nod of surrender. "I have family of my own." He glanced at the AK-47 in her hands. "You look more comfortable holding that than I ever would."

Cassie thought she'd found the safety on the Kalashnikov, but she wouldn't know for sure until she fired it. A hell of a time to find out if she had it wrong. "Then you'd better get comfortable with it quick." She handed the weapon to the man. "In case you run into trouble."

He took it, nodding grimly.

Everyone was watching her. They were solid people, plainly dressed, and serious. None of them were weak. But they hadn't signed on to fight Russians.

"How many other prisoners are there in the main pump facility?" she asked.

"Seven," Fatherly said. "But watch out for Sven. He's like you. He's just looking for a chance to go full Schwarzenegger. You'll recognize him easily. Blond hair, tall, and thick. He lifts weights when he's not working here. But he's a hothead, so if you start something he'll jump in."

"Just what we don't need," she said to herself.

"You're not seriously worried about someone doing exactly what you plan to do, are you?" Goatee said. "You're certifiable."

John laughed. She shot him a glare, but it didn't shut him up. So maybe Goatee had a fair point . . . from a certain perspective. But this was different. Cassie did have some training. And besides, she wasn't a hothead. She planned to proceed with extreme caution. "Why are you people still here?" she said, putting on her own brand of Kalov gruffness. "Go."

She headed the opposite way. The corridor beyond the storeroom was lined with more dark wood paneling. The linoleum floor looked like chimps had thrown a mustard-squeezing party. It was a ghastly color and she wondered who had picked the decor in this place.

Sweat streamed into her eyes. With all the tension and violence of the past few minutes, her North Face coat was too much. She considered taking it off, but she didn't want to leave it behind in case they had to make a quick getaway. It would suck to rescue everyone and then freeze to death during their escape.

She moved ahead, sticking close to the right wall. There were more offices along this corridor, but the doors were open and the lights inside were off.

"Ah, damn," John said.

Her focus snapped back to corridor ahead. A metal door ahead stood open, blocked by a dead body. No gunshot wound on this one. Gauging by the odd angle of his neck, he'd been taken by surprise.

He was obviously a security guard: white shirt, ill-fitting black polyester uniform pants with yellow piping down the legs. A badge was sewn to the breast of his shirt. A utility belt and empty holster told the rest of the story. The Russians had jumped him, broken his neck, and swiped his gun.

"That's three dead," she said in clipped tones. She tried not to look at the young guard's face. He wasn't much older than she was.

She checked his belt for a security card. It was gone.

She and John exchanged a long glance, then she continued. They entered a vast space, like an aircraft hangar but with a much higher ceiling. She stood upon a grated-metal platform with stairs winding down to a concrete floor two stories below. Another set of stairs continued up to a catwalk that led to different portions of the enormous machine that took up the bulk of the space. It was roughly cylindrical, and made of white-painted steel. A mass of tubes, wires, and boxy electronic control boards covered it. The sound of the pumps filled the room with an undulating stamp-and-hiss sound that looped in a perfect rhythm.

She leaned over the railing and peered down to the floor. If the Russians were interested in the pipe-cleaning pig devices, they would likely be near them. So where were the pigs?

As if reading her thoughts, John nudged her. "They have a launch facility in an adjacent chamber. The pigs have to be loaded into a pipe and then nudged into the flow of oil as it starts down the pipeline."

And here she'd been thinking "ecological engineer"

was just a fancy way of saying "biology major." Apparently he did know something useful.

"That way," he said.

She saw the sign. In industrial stencil, it read: PIG BAY. An arrow pointed down the stairs.

At the bottom of the stairs she rushed to take cover behind the bulk of the pump. She saw another sign for the pig bay. She followed the arrow. Ahead, the ceiling lowered to define a section of the facility that didn't need as much headroom. But there was no wall, allowing workers to drive their forklifts and push carts into the lower area without having to go through a door. More tanks were stationed in this area, each twenty feet tall and at least that wide. They stood in ranks of five, with connecting pipes at their tops.

She had no idea what they were for, but they provided good cover. She crept alongside one then slipped the ten feet to the next, working her way toward the back of the space. At the last one, she got onto all fours and crawled around the curve of the tank until she could see just past it.

She spotted a prisoner. The woman was sitting in a metal folding chair, hands in her lap. Her head was bowed. In prayer or sleep or defeat, Cassie couldn't tell. After easing farther around the tank, she spotted the rest of the prisoners. Her dad wasn't among them.

But Val was.

He stood to one side, near the boss and the wiry second-in-command. Cassie's heart dropped, at first thinking Val was working with these jerks after all. But then she saw the wound on the side of his head, a patch of drying blood that mixed in with his black hair.

She realized he was speaking Russian. He was interpreting for the woman sitting in a chair in front of the boss. She must be Becky, the pig expert taken from the storeroom earlier. Val was translating what she said into Russian.

Cassie backed up to get out of everyone's view. The last thing she needed was a prisoner drawing attention to her. Motioning for John to follow, she retreated to the pump chamber. Once hidden behind it she told him what she'd seen. "But there's no way to get close without being spotted." She looked at the gun in her hand. "I don't trust my marksmanship at this distance."

"And just shooting people would be a bad idea," John said, nodding until she nodded in agreement.

"Of course it would. I'm just thinking out loud."

"By all means, don't stop thinking."

She gave him a smirk, but didn't put much fire into it. Where were Dad and Uncle Dev? Had they already outlived their usefulness? She didn't think so. The ransom would require proof of life or the funds would be yanked right back.

She realized the solution to her immediate problem. Since Dad wasn't in the pig bay, she could just leave the Russians be for the time being. The business with the pigs was a separate thing. It might be the main thing to the Russians, but it didn't require Dad's presence. They had him socked away somewhere.

Back upstairs, probably. There had to be more offices here, or maybe another storeroom. "Let's go," she said.

"We're just going to leave those people? We're going to let the Russians mess around with the pigs?"

"Gergi said the worst they could do is plug the flow for a couple days. I say let them. As for the rest of the prisoners, they're still alive. If we go in to free them, we have to be willing to shoot those guys. Are you ready to start a mini war inside this place? Isn't oil flammable?"

"It depends on how much natural gas comes up with it.

But you're not wrong. Shooting around these tanks wouldn't be on my list of bright ideas. But why can't we do like we did upstairs? We could make a ruckus and lure the bad guys out here. Take them out one by one."

"Get all Schwarzenegger on them?"

John took a turn to smirk at her. "I'm just thinking out loud."

"First we get my dad. He may know what they're up to with the pigs. And the other prisoners we rescued are in the Sno-Cat and radioing for help as we speak. We need to get out of here as quickly as we can."

He relented, but Cassie could see he didn't like it. She didn't like leaving those prisoners behind, either. And she especially didn't like leaving Val back there. But her instinct compelled her to get to her dad first. Was that selfish? Maybe. But family was family.

"I don't like this," John said. "Everything here is designed for safety and to prevent contaminating the environment."

Cassie put a hand on his arm. "I get it. I do. We're not letting these bastards kill any more people or any of the wildlife around here. But we have to do it in the right order. Do you understand?"

"I do. Let's go."

They jogged to the stairs and started back up. By the time they reached the door marked REFINERY, Cassie's heart was thumping from the effort. She didn't pause. The door gave into another huge chamber, this one not quite as tall. Enormous gray pumps and tanks lined the floor. John spotted the mezzanine office before Cassie. She had imagined Dad being held on the main floor, but when John pointed she spotted him right away. He was sitting by the window, facing into the office. She would recognize the back of his head and all that thick gray hair anywhere.

She sprinted across a short stretch of catwalk and barged into the office. Dad was tied to an office chair, his hands drawn tightly behind him. Uncle Dev was in another chair, his head lolling to one side.

The office was a control room for the refinery, she guessed, full of monitors and panels of gauges. Dad was unconscious. "Get Uncle Dev," she said to John as she rushed to free her father.

"Dad?" She patted his face. His eyes opened, barely. He seemed groggy, as if drugged. "Did they give you something?"

Dad opened his mouth, but all that came out was a bit of drool.

"Why did they drug you?"

"This man is barely breathing," John said. He gripped Uncle Dev's wrist. "His pulse is weak and slow. Whatever they dosed him with, it's heavy sedation."

Cassie used the knife she'd taken from Smokey to cut Dad free. He slumped forward, but Cassie didn't have the strength to hold him upright. The best she could do was to guide him to the floor. John did the same with Uncle Dev.

She knelt next to her father. "Dad, you need to wake up. Listen to me. I need you to stand up so we can leave."

His eyes remained closed, but he started to mumble. "No. I can't go. You go. Not safe."

She needed to wake him up the hard way. She grabbed a half-full water bottle from the desk.

"Sorry, Dad." She dumped the water on his face.

He spluttered and his eyes popped open. She let some water trickle into the collar of his shirt.

His hand came up, weakly, to fight the flow. "Stop it."

"Then wake the hell up. We have to get going."

Alertness was slow in coming, but he seemed to understand where he was. "Cassie. What are you doing here?"

He tried to sit up, but the best he could do was rise onto an elbow. "They gave me a pill. Where are those bastards?"'"

"They're with Val and a bunch of employee prisoners in the pig bay. What are they doing?"

He rubbed his haggard face and blinked hard. His eyelids seemed weighed down. "Pig bay. They had lots of questions about that. I didn't know much."

"You need to stand. John, how's Uncle Dev doing?"

"Still out cold. I don't think he's going to wake up with a splash of cold water in the face."

"Who's that guy?" Dad asked, eyeing John with suspicion.

"He's a friend. He's been helping me since I got away from the airport." Her father's face bunched and he suddenly pulled her into a tight hug.

"Can you stand?" she asked. "We'll get you out. Kalov says the Marines are coming soon. His own team is still fourteen hours or so away."

Dad moved unsteadily, but worked his way to his feet. He had to lean on Cassie to remain standing. "Marines. We don't need the Marines. We need the frickin' Delta Force. This is a tactical situation that pure brute strength will make worse, not better."

"What makes you say that? There are only two Russians standing, and both are in the pig bay."

"What are you talking about? There are at least three squads in the oil fields right now. They're rigging the wells to blow."

John and Cassie cursed at the same time. John left Uncle Dev's side. "The wells are spread over several hundred thousand square miles. How many men did they bring on this operation?"

Dad shrugged. "It takes at least three to be considered a squad, doesn't it?"

John's eyes gleamed with growing horror. He turned on Cassie. "We've got to call someone. Anyone. The spills they'll create here would be worse than the Exxon Valdez."

"The what?" Cassie said. Her gut was churning from the vibes coming off John and her father. Both saw a potential disaster looming, and by the looks on their faces it was terrible.

"Let's walk and talk," John said. "I think I can get your uncle out by myself." He returned to Uncle Dev and managed to heft him in a fireman's carry over his shoulders. Uncle Dev was not a thin man, but John kept his balance.

Cassie led Dad out. John was slow, holding the railing and taking one step, resting, then taking another. By the time they reached the storage room, John was dripping with sweat. Dad wasn't faring much better. Mostly because he was talking.

"The thing about pulling oil from the ground in these fields is that we don't need oil derricks to pump the fluid to the surface. Geological pressure brings it right up. Like squeezing a zit. All we have to do is collect the oil and pump it over to this station."

They stopped to catch their breath before going down to the loading dock. Uncle Dev started moaning, which was a good sign, but also made Cassie's heart ache. His health hadn't been great to start with.

Dad kept talking. "Hundreds of well-heads out there. Ours and our competitors', all bringing up barrel after barrel. If they blow a well, they'll release that flow onto the surface. Assuming it doesn't ignite."

She got, then, the magnitude of what the Russians were planning.

Dad coughed. His face had turned red, as if he were

embarrassed. But Cassie realized something else was going on when he gripped his left arm.

"Dad? What's wrong?"

He grimaced. "I need my nitroglycerin pills. They're in my luggage."

"What kind of pills?"

John grunted under the weight of Uncle Dev's inert body. "He's having chest pain. Heart attack. Nitroglycerin is an emergency medicine. It dilates the blood vessels for better blood flow."

"I'll be alright," Dad said. "This might just be a bit of"—He gasped—"a bit of angina. Stress'll do that. Sonofabitch, that hurts."

They pushed out of the loading dock and into the frozen air. The wind hit Cassie like a punch in the face. She was happy to see John's truck still there and still running. She'd half expected stupid Goatee had taken it so he could run off to Harv at the Sag River Motel and tell on Cassie.

They loaded Dad and Uncle Dev into the cramped back seat. Cassie buckled Dad in. "I've got some aspirin. I think." She dug into her pocket and gave him the packet she had lifted from Smokey.

He fumbled with it, so she took it back and tore the tablets free. She put them in his mouth. He made a face as he chewed them and swallowed the extremely bitter pill dust.

"You might have just saved my life," he said. "Twice."

Cassie hopped into the front seat. John already had the truck in gear. He gunned the motor and sped away from the pump station, but Cassie caught him looking worriedly in the rearview mirror.

If the Russians had such a devastating plan to sabotage the oilfields, what were they doing back at the plant? And how was she going to get Val and the rest of the prisoners free?

She found her Diet Coke, still unopened, rolling around on the floorboard. She popped the top and took a long pull. It was still cold. As was her whole body.

But her heart was pure fire. Did these assholes really think they could to come to her country, kill her people, blast her dad's wells, and destroy zillions of square miles of the delicate ecology and get away with it?

And if the look on John Goodnight's face was any indication, his feelings were in complete alignment with hers.

"They're not doing this," she said.

John stared straight ahead. "Hell no, they aren't."

Chapter Seventeen

2:03 pm

Colonel Fedorov paced in front of the pig launcher tube. His plan depended on getting the scouring devices underway as soon as possible. He doubted the military had been dispatched yet. He and his men had been careful to leave no witnesses alive to give warning. But they had not cleaned up the dead either.

That had been deliberate. He figured the local police—or whatever passed for the law in this godforsaken land—would be utterly flummoxed to discover murdered people lying about in random places.

Confusion was his greatest ally. That, and the incompetence of the people who dared to stand against him. These workers at the pump station had not put up the slightest resistance. They were weak.

Valentine was furious, Fedorov could tell. The young man did not like being told what to do by a Russian commander, retired or not. Even now he was scheming, watching, waiting for his moment to attack.

He would not find such a moment. Not one he would survive.

Col. Fedorov had led men like Valentine for the past fifteen years. He knew the look a man got when he grew desperate. That was what he'd been trying to pull out of Valentine. He wanted the young man to do something rash, something his own training told him not to do.

Fedorov glanced at his watch. Soon Squad One would return from the field. Then he'd have more men to guard the prisoners and potential escape routes. "Valentine," he said in Russian, "how much longer before this woman completes her task?"

The young man relayed the question to the woman. She was about fifty years old, stout, and dressed in the slovenly way all civilians did up here. Her hair was cut short and she wore pink lipstick that clashed with her purple knit pullover.

She gritted her teeth and said something not very nice. Fedorov understood English much better than he spoke it, but he did not want any of the prisoners to know that.

So far Valentine had behaved as honestly as a Young Pioneer. But that would not last long. The man was eyeing Blok's sidearm like a starving man would look at a loaf of fresh-baked bread.

"Mrs. Grant says the system is not designed to send so many pigs through the pipeline at once," Val said. "The pressure will need to be increased."

"Then tell her to do it."

Valentine relayed the message, to the dismay of the pig lady. The other prisoners wore faces of weary fear and resignation. "Blok, have you found it yet?" Fedorov asked.

Blok was going through Bryce Ingram's luggage. Each item came out, was inspected, pockets checked, then set aside. Fedorov had it on good authority that Ingram kept his personal sidearm in his luggage. He supposedly did not like carrying it.

Blok shook his head. *"Nyet."* He grabbed a backpack and starting rifling through it. Ingram's weapon wasn't necessary, but Fedorov found it poetic to use a man's own weapon against him.

"Sir. I've found it. No, wait, this is . . ." Blok stared at the open backpack. He withdrew a small pistol. Then he pulled out a shirt and spread it open. It unfolded to expose the famous tongue and lips logo of The Rolling Stones. The red was flaked with glittery material, and the cut of the neckline and sleeves showed it to be a woman's garment.

Blok removed several other items, including a set of flannel pajamas with tiny penguins on them.

And then came a box of 9mm ammo. Three magazines. A folding knife. A small first aid kit. A bundle of paracord. A cigarette lighter, and a small black purse.

Col. Fedorov brushed Blok aside. He undid the purse clasp, noting the famous Louis Vuitton logo. The bag had cost no less than two thousand dollars. An assortment of makeup, hair ties, and typical female odds and ends came out next. He found the wallet and flipped it open.

Ten crisp one-hundred-dollar bills and several of smaller denominations were snugged into one side. Two platinum cards and one invite-only black card. The ID was a shock. The photo showed a very lovely teenage girl. The birth year made her eighteen years old, but the photo was of a sixteen-year-old.

"Keep Mrs. Grant working, Valentine. I want those pigs deployed in the next hour." He marched off. Bryce Ingram had some explaining to do. Why had his daughter's backpack been on the Twin Otter? And, more importantly, where was Cassandra Smythe Ingram at this very moment?

He sensed the wrongness ahead before he got there. Something in his make-up had given him a nose for events about to go sideways. He burst into the refinery office and saw his two valuable prisoners gone. He ran, breaking through to the storeroom. All the prisoners he'd left there were gone, too.

That idiot Gregor Petrevski was nowhere to be found. A pool of blood on the floor. Less than one minute later, Fedorov was outside. He swore, long and hard. The Sno-Cat was gone. The prisoners must have overpowered Petrevski and taken him and Ingram and Salah and made a run for it.

That meant the local authorities would soon know was going on. He went back into the warmth of the pump station.

He closed his eyes and tensed every muscle in his body. He drew in a huge breath, held it, and then let it and all the tension in him go at once. Folding forward, he went limp. This technique was good to reduce the heart rate and to calm one's mind.

Rage still boiled in him, but he held it at bay. Clear thinking was needed, not explosions of temper.

This was not yet a catastrophe. But he needed to act quickly. He raced back to the pig bay and grabbed the radio he used to communicate with the field squads. He had previously ordered them to radio silence, but now he would make an exception. He had to go back outside to ensure good transmission.

Ignoring the biting chill that whipped his face, he barked into the radio. "Squad One. You are to stop the Sno-Cat plow heading from Pump Station One toward Deadhorse. Seize control and return to pump station." He repeated the order three times until he got a terse acknowledgement from the squad leader. It was risky to be so explicit, but the radios transmitted encrypted digital signals. If the military was listening in, they would first have to decrypt the message then wake up a Russian translator.

Keeping those prisoners alive wasn't truly necessary, but for his plan to have its greatest impact he wanted them on camera as things came to a head. The more the scarier, as the American saying went.

Now he could turn his attention to the other issue. Cassandra Ingram. Her presence did not make sense. But it did explain Valentine being here. He wasn't Bryce Ingram's bodyguard. He was Ms. Ingram's. But where was she? He and his men had boarded the Twin Otter before anyone could have jumped out.

He cursed Gregor Petrevski. He must have failed to check the lavatory. Fedorov bumped his knuckles against his forehead. That's certainly where she'd been. So close. Damn it. He should have checked the lav himself.

He decided this development was good, actually. If he could get his hands on her he'd have even more leverage over her father. Smiling, he returned to check on Blok and the pig lady. The pigs themselves had been easy to modify, but inserting them into the pipeline had been much more of a project than he'd expected.

He kept having to tell the lady to skip all her stupid checklists. This wasn't a scouring of the pipeline, after all. If something got damaged, all the better.

"Status, Valentine," he said to the young man when he returned to the pig bay.

"The first one is in. The second is about to insert into the main pipeline."

"Good. Keep them going. Mr. Ingram is quite distressed by your delay."

"Is he?" Valentine said. "I thought he would be much more concerned with where his daughter is. Did he threaten you if you harm here? I'm sure he did. But wait . . . I think you don't have her, do you? Pity. She's very charming."

Col. Fedorov did not act in anger when he took Cassandra Ingram's small pistol from Blok. He studied it a moment. A Ruger LC9s. Very compact. An ideal weapon for a young lady to carry with her. He sneered at the small grip and the external safety, but such was to be expected for a civilian's firearm. He checked the magazine. Full.

He pointed the weapon at Valentine's face. "Where is the girl?"

The pig lady cowered, covering her head. The other prisoners made all the usual shocked sounds. A couple said "no" and one huge man with thick blond hair nearly lunged. He restrained himself at the last moment, which was wise. "I think you know where she is. Tell me."

Valentine didn't flinch. He had stared down the barrel of a weapon before, it seemed. Perhaps he had seen action. "She was in the lavatory when we left the plane. She has never been to this part of Alaska before. She knows nothing about it. My guess is that she's still on the plane."

The young man's Russian was perfect, if slightly accented by his lazy American tongue.

"You don't believe that for one second," Fedorov said. "Who does she call in case of emergency?" Fedorov reasoned that if her father had a hotline, his daughter certainly did. "What is the number?"

He saw calculation on Valentine's face. That hesitation would cost him. Fedorov swung his arm, taking aim at a portly man wearing a hardhat. The mustache quivered a moment as the man's amygdala screamed a warning. Fedorov dropped his aim a fraction of an inch and fired.

Everyone screamed except Blok and Valentine. The man crumpled from his chair, hands clamping his shattered knee. He tried not to scream, but moans and high-pitched whines came out of his throat anyway.

Fedorov regarded Cassandra's Ruger. Not bad. The pull was a bit heavy, but it had a nice snap to it. He tucked the weapon behind his belt. "Valentine, do not make me ask you again. I have no need of these people. They live because I am merciful." And he wasn't quite done with them.

That did it. Valentine started reciting numbers. Fedorov pulled a field notebook from his shirt pocket and wrote the numbers down. Not a single similarity to her father's hotline number, he noticed. Different area codes. And of course that was wise. If someone got both numbers they would certainly attempt to track down who owned the numbers. Fedorov suspected a shell corporation held Ms. Ingram's number. It would be forwarded two or three times to the ultimate operator who served her security detail.

"If this number is false, I will shoot that man in the head." He pointed at a man in a mechanic's shirt. His name—Dave—was emblazoned on a patch on the breast. "See to that other man's wound. He is not to bleed out just yet."

Fedorov raised his voice to address them all and switched to English. "Are you needing to die here today? If cooperating—if Valentine cooperating—you walk away. If one is not cooperating, two die. Simple, yes?"

He collected his satellite phone and returned to the loading dock. Now it was time to bring Ms. Ingram in from the cold.

Chapter Eighteen

2:35 pm

Jay Hansen drove the Sno-Cat through the swirling snow, going slowly due to the low visibility, but also because he didn't know what the hell he was doing. He thought he should still be back at Pump Station One helping that girl rescue the other prisoners. It killed him that he was running away.

And, yes, he knew he had a responsibility to the people crowded in the cab behind him. He certainly had a responsibility to his kids and wife. But he had never backed away from a fight in his life.

It didn't help that Simon was crouching next to him, goatee thrust forward in rage, and would not—for the love of all that was holy—shut up.

"Watch out for that turn there," Simon said. "It's sharp. The Sno-Cat has a wide turning radius. I don't know why they didn't do a better job on the design. But if you keep your center line in the middle . . . well it's hard to see. The turn should be up here. Look out for the sign, Jay.

The emergency clinic is behind that building with the drive-through espresso place. They charge so much for a latte you'd think they were serving liquid gold. Watch out!"

Jay had already lost his patience with Simon once. He regretted having to raise his voice like that. But the man was a pain in the ass. Jay didn't need to be told what his own eyes could see.

There was a swarm of snow machines piling onto the road ahead of him. They didn't go single file, but filled the whole road. They slowed so suddenly he was forced to stomp the brakes. The Sno-Cat lurched to a stop, sending people tumbling.

Worrying about poor gun-shot Debbie more than Simon, who had bonked his forehead on the dash, Jay squeezed from behind the wheel and hustled back to see if she was okay. Piper Swonsen was holding compression on Debbie's wound. She glared at Jay. "Why did we stop? She's lost too much blood. We're running out of time."

"Jay!" Simon called from the front.

"Just shut up a second, Simon." Jay squatted next to Debbie. In the dim light of the Sno-Cat's interior it was hard to even make out her face. She wasn't moving. "Hold on, Deb," he said. "There's a bunch of—"

"Jay! Get up here."

Clenching his teeth to hold in the barrage of swearing boiling up from his soul, Jay Hansen rounded on Simon. His building diatribe drained away as he saw what had the goateed fool so riled up.

Four men in black snowsuits were approaching the vehicle. They all carried machine guns. He knew instantly that they were part of the Russian infiltrators. And now they had found their wayward prisoners.

Well, they could go to hell.

Jay jumped back into the driver's seat and gunned the

huge diesel engine. The approaching men stopped, sighting down their rifles. They were taking aim at him, though he doubted they could see him through the glare of his headlights. He put on the high beams, dropped the machine into gear, and floored it.

The beast lumbered at the men, scattering them. The Sno-Cat didn't have much acceleration. Jay turned the wheel hard, sending it into a sharp turn, forcing the men on that side to retreat or be crushed.

"What are you doing?" Simon screamed as the vehicle jounced off the road and onto the tundra.

"I'm making a run for it."

"They have snow machines. They're more than twice as fast as this stupid thing."

Jay knew that. But if they wanted to come onboard the rig, they were going to have to do it the hard way.

Chapter Nineteen

2:46 pm

Cassie Ingram leaned close to the windshield of John's truck, trying not to breathe too hard. The glass fogged up anyway.

They had been on the road to Deadhorse for five minutes, and the weather had definitely worsened in that time. "Do you know where the emergency room is?"

John shook his head. "I don't think they have a regular ER so much as a small trauma room at the clinic. I don't really know for sure."

Dad was awake, but he was still breathing too hard. Cassie twisted in her seat. "Hang in there, Dad. We'll be there soon."

He didn't answer, but he didn't look as bad as before. Maybe the aspirin had worked. She remembered seeing a TV commercial that claimed aspirin was good for heart patients. It had better help.

They had Smokey prisoner now. She wouldn't let him live if Dad died. The thought bubbled to the forefront of her consciousness. Would she really kill the man out of revenge? Her skin grew clammy at the thought.

"Just get to town," she said to John. "Someone there will know where the clinic is."

"I can do you one better," John said. He lifted the CB radio and called on a general channel for advice about the location of the clinic.

A familiar voice answered immediately. It was Goatee. "We're being chased by Russians on snow machines. This is your fault. If you two—"

The lecture cut off and the fatherly man's voice came over the air. "This is Jay Hansen. Go to Deadhorse and find the main camp building. A little beyond that is a blue metal-sided building. It looks like all the rest, but there's a sign that says 'clinic' on the front. Harv, if you're hearing this, please call ahead to let Doctor Sheldon know they're coming."

"And what's your status?" John asked.

"As Simon was saying, we have a bit of a problem. A squad of men on snow machines is following us. They're carrying machine guns. They tried to board the Sno-Cat, but I wouldn't allow it. They haven't fired at us, but they keep following alongside. I think they're under orders not to kill us."

"What about Debbie?" Cassie whispered. John repeated the question.

Hansen's answer took a few long beats. Finally he said. "She didn't make it."

Cassie dropped her head. Another death on her shoulders. She drew into herself, hugging her arms close to her body. This whole mess hadn't been her fault. But she was failing to live up to Kalov's expectations. To her own expectations.

"I'm sorry to hear that, Jay," John said softly. "We're

almost to Deadhorse. I'll find Harv and see if he can get some people out to help you."

"They'd better be military, my friend. Anyone less is going to get their heads handed to them."

Cassie pulled herself from the blackness. She took the radio handset from John. "How long can you keep this up? What's the fuel situation?"

"About a quarter—"

Cassie waited. But when Jay didn't finish, she said, "A quarter tank? I didn't copy that last bit, Jay."

But there was no further transmission.

Chapter Twenty

2:49 pm

The snow machine swerved in front of the Sno-Cat so suddenly, Jay could only react by jerking the wheel. The right side tracks lifted and everyone in the back screamed.

Instinct lifted his foot from the accelerator. With ponderous slowness, the tracks came back down. Jay stepped on the brakes.

The whine of high-revving snow machine engines swarmed all around. A *thunk* in the back told of boots on the outside of the vehicle.

Simon clutched the AK-47 Cassie had pulled from the Russian they'd subdued at the pump station.

The side hatch burst open and a furious-eyed young man leapt in. He aimed his machine gun at Jay.

Simon dropped the weapon and put his hands over his head. "It wasn't my idea! It wasn't my idea!"

Jay had enough time to curse Simon before the Russian's weapon flared. Jay never heard the shot that killed him, and so was spared the screams of all the others on board.

Chapter Twenty-One

2:57 pm

The chairs in Coffins control center were lousy. The coffee was a shocking pre-ground blend that came out of a can. The industrial design of the buildings was utterly utilitarian, and the people were obsessed with a clothing brand called Carhartt.

Fox Tils had recently learned that it was a brand of hunting clothes. Apparently good stuff. He'd grown up in Palo Alto, California. A totally different vibe.

Still, the young data analyst thought the culture here was kind of awesome. Coming out of MIT, he had been looking for an authentic challenge. The data systems job in the Alaskan oil fields had seemed too cool an opportunity to pass up, even though the pay was one tenth of what he could have gotten working for one of the tech companies there in Palo Alto.

But Fox didn't care that much about money. He just wanted to travel the world, following a lifestyle practice of extreme simplicity, and maybe doing some good for the world along the way.

He took another sip of the ridiculous "coffee" they served here. It tasted like someone had run hot water through a can of coal dust. But it had the requisite amount of caffeine, and that's ultimately what mattered. Fox swore that when he got back to San Francisco he would hit up Blue Bottle Coffee for some really exquisite java.

And if he ever did come back here he'd be sure to bring some choice beans, a burr grinder, and a French press. He smacked his lips and put his cup down. The screen in front of him had just started to flash motion alerts.

"Let's see who you are . . ." he said. Probably another polar bear tripping the motion detection algos again. Those roly-poly bastards were just, like, "whatevs."

Fox wished he could pet one of their babies. Those little fuzz-balls were epic.

The video feed came up. It was just some dude poking around. Disappointment sent Fox's finger to close the video window. He stopped himself at the last second because another alert popped up in the corner. It was from a bit of software he'd cooked up the other day. Nothing official, but potentially useful.

He'd tapped into the work scheduler app the foremen used. It contained a maintenance schedule and technician to-do list. Fox's idea was to use the cameras to see when a worker arrived on site and compare that to when they checked into the scheduler. If they were goofing off and not checking in right away, then the program could tell on them.

Fox didn't think it should be used that way. Life was crappy enough as it was up here in the frozen tundra. The last thing a dude needed was Big Brother watching his every move.

Fox had decided that the app could be used instead as a kind of security system. If a dude showed up at a site where no work was scheduled, then it would ping the foreman so he or she could look into it. That was still kinda Big Brotherish, but it might save a life—or a well.

At this well there was no work scheduled for another ten days. That was odd. Fox zoomed in on the dude. Another dude appeared carrying a duffle bag and a frickin' gun. "No way."

Dudes up here often carried guns for protection against bears, but none of them were machine guns. Fox watched the first man pry open the well shack door. The other man pulled a small brick from his bag, stuck it inside the shack, fiddled with something, then closed door. "He just planted a bomb, yo."

Fox leaned back in his chair and combed both hands through his shaggy mane. "I did not just see that."

"What are you mumbling about now, Fox?" Jackson Swan called from his observation desk in back. The dude was like a study hall monitor, always giving everybody a suspicious look.

Fox sent the feed to the big screen. "Check it."

The footage replayed, and the other workers in the room went quiet. All eyes were on the replay which Fox set to infinite loop. Finally Jackson got up and went to stand right in front of the big screen. "Pause it. There."

They stared at the freeze-frame for a long time. The man with duffle bag had a radio to his mouth. "There are more folks in on this," Jackson said. "This is sabotage."

"So, uh, like, what do we do?" Fox asked. Standing around with their mouths hanging open wasn't going to accomplish anything.

Another video flashed a motion alert. And then another. Fox sent the feeds to the big screen where they played in a row.

Jackson turned, mouth opening to answer Fox's question. The outside door slammed open and four men with machine guns swarmed into the monitoring center. They held the weapons forward, like movie Marines rushing into a building somewhere in Afghanistan. They shouted, "Get down! Get down!"

Fox obeyed. He didn't want to get blown away by any of these crazy dudes. He still hadn't been to Japan to test out his Japanese language skills. He hadn't spent months trekking across Europe and staying in hostels and sleeping on strangers' sofas. He hadn't even been to Rio for Carnival. This was not the time to get his head blown off.

So as he got down from his chair, he decided not to close the video apps on his monitor. Instead, he found the power plug beneath his desk and gave it a hard yank. The room brightened as the video feeds vanished from the big screen. Now the big screen glowed bright blue, white letters reading: CHOOSE INPUT SOURCE.

Once the general hubbub died down, the invaders started patrolling the room and making everyone congregate under the big screen. The man in charge was about Jackson's age, red-headed and freckled. He had wide features and large teeth. When he spoke, his words were heavily accented. It sounded like Russian to Fox.

He addressed them like poorly performing soldiers under his command. "What is happening now, you vill not speak. What is happening now, you vill not move. Am I make myself clear?"

"As a bell, yo," Fox said. This earned him a scowl and the barrel of an AK-47 pointed at his face. "It's clear! It's clear!"

Jackson stayed on his feet, legs wobbling. But he found the courage he needed. "I'm the supervisor here. These people are my responsibility."

The leader of the armed men stood toe-to-toe with Jackson Swan. "I relieve you of burden. A little." He swung his weapon and fired a single round into a heavy-set man. Devin Boone, an engineer who monitored the smaller pipelines that fed to the main pump station that carried all the oil south. The man's forehead sprouted blood and his eyes fixed on something nobody on this plane of existence could see.

The report of the shot snapped against Fox's eardrums, making him wince and swear. The stink of gun smoke made him cough. A couple people cried out. Tanisha Gold started sobbing. Jackson Swan gaped at the lifeless form of Devin Bonne, mouth working but unable to express his horror or outrage. Fox admired his supervisor's ability to remain standing in front of the gun-toting Russians at all. He wanted to crawl under a desk and cover his head.

"Perhaps I saved lives," the Russian commander said. "You understand I make serious."

"What do you want?" Jackson asked. His face was bunched into fear-fueled rage. "We'll cooperate. Just tell us what you want."

"I want for you to sit down and not speaking."

Fox wanted to tug his boss to the floor, but he couldn't bring himself to do anything that would draw the slightest attention to himself. It ended up not being necessary. The Russian merely sneered at Jackson and jabbed his finger at the floor. Jackson slowly complied.

The other gunmen were positioned around the room, keeping suspicious eyes on their prisoners. One approached his leader and said something in Russian. The man took his radio and headed for the outer door.

Jackson sat to Fox's left, sending his most furious glares at the Russians in the room. Fox didn't like the open defiance. That was a good way to get beat up or shot.

He leaned into his boss's shoulder. "Relax, yo." He barely got enough breath behind the whisper to make a sound. Jackson heard it, though. He shifted his glare to Fox.

He dropped his eyes, and Fox saw he was patting his front pocket. Fox knew he had a satellite phone since the cell reception out here was one hundred percent non-existent. The landlines worked just fine, too. But neither Fox nor Jackson was going to amble over to a desk and start dialing.

A gunman marched by, making a circuit of the control center. When he continued on, Jackson started to ease his sat-phone from his pocket. Fox put a hand on his arm to stop him. He nodded to the two remaining guards.

They were eagle-eyed now. "Just wait," Fox mouthed. If he knew one thing for sure, it was that a dude's attention faded as monotony increased. Right now the men were at their most alert.

Jackson relaxed slightly, resting his back against the wall. Fox did the same. He closed his eyes and tried to get into his transcendental meditation mantra. Not so easy given the circumstances. His mind kept going to the explosives he'd seen men planting in the oil well shack. Given the other feeds lighting up just as the Russians had barged in, there were at least a dozen other shacks being rigged to blow. Given time, they'd get a ton more wired and ready.

So why hadn't they blown them immediately? Was America now at war? Fox's younger brother was seventeen. It would suck if the whole world went nuts and suddenly Jayme was getting drafted. He had bad asthma.

Fox returned to his mantra, but the sound of Russians' boots kept him on edge.

This situation sucked.

Chapter Twenty-Two

3:00 pm

John swung the truck past a bank of street lights. The snow fell in wispy veils, blurring the world. Small drifts had accumulated around parked cars and trucks, and along the sides of the buildings.

"Here's the clinic," John said. He parked and they both got out to collect their passengers. Dad was able to get Uncle Dev down from the truck with Cassie's help. John still had to carry the unconscious man. Dad walked under his own power as they stumbled into the brightly lit clinic. Nobody was there to greet them. A voice called from an inside an office. "Burn, cut, or broken limb?"

John shook his head and smirked. "So much for Harv calling ahead."

Cassie called out, "Heart attack and drug overdose."

A squawk of surprise preceded a thump and a sharp swear word. Then a woman in scrubs and white coat came out, stethoscope draped around her neck. Her hair was a kitchen sink dye job that made her head look like a floof of strawberry-blond cotton candy. She had spectacles on her face, the thick plastic frames a decade or two out of date. She took one look at the half-frozen interlopers and motioned to a doorway. "In there."

After Cassie and John got the patients situated on gurneys, the doctor began her examination. She checked Dad's pulse.

"He had two aspirin about fifteen minutes ago," Cassie said. "It seems to have helped."

The doctor snapped her fingers and pointed at a nearby cart. "Wheel that EKG machine over here." Cassie did as she was told. With the fast, competent movements of someone with years of practice, the doctor got Dad's shirt unbuttoned and the electrodes of the EKG attached to his chest.

"What drug are we dealing with?"

"I don't know," Cassie said. "I found them like this."

"Pills," Dad said. "Heavy stuff."

"Go get a vial of naloxone out of the medicine cabinet. It's unlocked." She glanced at John until he moved. He fumbled with the small vials and pill bottles in the cabinet.

"They're sorted alphabetically," the doctor said. Her voice was pure calm.

"Will they be okay?" Cassie asked. Dad seemed to be in a lot of pain, and Uncle Dev's face was pasty.

The doctor ignored Cassie and instead peppered Dad with a bunch of questions. Was he short of breath? Nauseated? Did he have a history of heart issues? Was he on any medications?

John appeared, holding a small vial. Without looking, the doctor said, "Shoot that into the other man's arm. There are syringes over there in that drawer. Sterilize the insertion point with an antiseptic wipe first."

John stood there dumbly, his brows sinking into view

from the hem of his knit cap. Finally he shrugged and did as he was told. Cassie watched with alarm as John uncapped the syringe and jabbed it into the vial. "I've only seen this done on TV. Do I really need to flick it to get the bubbles out?"

"If you don't want him to die, you will." The doctor watched the EKG machine print lines and numbers on a narrow strip of paper. She tore off a section and eyed the readout. "I don't think it was a heart attack. Probably a case of angina. Where are your nitroglycerin pills?"

"In my luggage," Dad said. "I couldn't get to them because of those Russian kidnappers."

"They're more useful when you have access to them," Dr. Sheldon said. Dad gave her a blank stare.

Dr. Sheldon fetched a packet from a drawer. Pills. "Put this under your tongue. Don't chew it." She poked the tablet into Dad's mouth.

John injected the naloxone into Uncle Dev's arm. The effect was instant. Uncle Dev's eyes popped open and he lurched upright. On a huge inhalation he groaned, then he fell back, hands clenching his chest. "Oh, geez!"

His eyes were wide with terror. Cassie went to him, and placed a comforting hand on his forehead. "It's just something to wake you up."

Dad was looking better. His shoulders relaxed and he was breathing easier.

"We don't get too many opioid ODs in here," the doctor said. Cassie wasn't sure if the woman was joking or not. She started to object, but the doctor stopped her with a look. By the seriousness set into the lines of her face, she was used to people doing exactly what she wanted.

Cassie clamped her lips together.

"Here's what I'm wondering. I'm wondering if the

Russian story this man told is for real," the woman said. "Or are you all so delusional you didn't think it odd?"

"The Russians are real," Cassie said. "There are at least two still at Pump Station One, and there are squads out in the oil fields sabotaging well sites. Harv doesn't believe us. But John and I just came from the pump station. There are workers being held hostage there right now."

The doctor took this in. "The smart thing to do would be to call the police department. Did you try that?"

"What police department?" Cassie said.

John echoed her, "Yeah, what police department?"

The doctor went to a phone and jabbed in a number. She eyed Uncle Dev and Dad like a watchful mother eagle as she waited for someone to pick up on the other end. Finally she said, "This is Doctor Sheldon at the Deadhorse clinic. I have a report of a group of saboteurs in the oil fields and at Pump Station One. Two victims of an apparent drugging are in my clinic. One is Bryce Ingram. Yeah, the CEO of the company with his name in it. The other is an executive. Along with them are Mr. Ingram's daughter and a young man I've never seen before."

"Wait," Cassie said. "How do you know who we are?"

Dr. Sheldon covered the phone with her hand. "Your face has been all over TMZ recently."

Cassie wanted to laugh at the absurdity of it, but she didn't have any humor to spare. Instead, she looked to John for a moment of shared amazement.

"Yes. Both are still here. If this is true, then we'll need —" She turned toward the window and pinched open the venetian blinds. "I don't see any. Okay. So they're on their way? How long?" A long pause. "That's a long time, sir."

Whatever 'sir' said in response, it had the effect of making Dr. Sheldon blanch. Finally she said, "I'll do that."

She hung up. "Do you have weapons?" she asked. She went to a small file cabinet next to the refrigerator. She pulled out a gray metal lock box. Drawing a key from the throat of her scrubs, she unlocked it and withdrew an enormous revolver. "My bear bagger," she explained. She flipped out the magazine and started loading .45-caliber bullets into the chambers.

She flipped it closed, checked the safety, and set the weapon on the desk. "We are advised by the administrative director in Fairbanks to batten down for the next five hours until the Marines arrive. I bet that was a euphemism. What he really meant was that a SEAL team is coming. They've practiced HALO jumps in the area. I did medical checkout on the whole squad here once when they'd done some practice jumps last summer. Quite stunning young men. I was intrigued."

Dr. Sheldon delivered this incredible narrative without the slightest show of emotion. Not until she mentioned her intrigue with the young men. Cassie saw a small smile quirk the woman's lip. Then that fleeting show of humanity vanished. She retrieved a holster from another cabinet and strapped it over her scrubs and jacket. It wasn't a tactical holster, nor was it a plain nylon job. This was a worked leather piece that would have been right at home on the waist of a movie cowboy ready to defend the town from a band of cattle rustlers.

The huge .45 went into the holster and then Dr. Sheldon returned to her patients. She checked Uncle Dev and announced he would be fine. He mumbled a prayer and eventually his breathing returned to a more normal pace. Dad got another pill from her cabinet and then he, too, relaxed.

"We can't wait five hours," John said to Cassie. He

handed her a Styrofoam cup of black coffee. "If they mean to blow something up, they won't wait that long."

No. And whatever the boss Russian was doing at the pump station, it wouldn't take that long either. But Cassie wasn't sure what to do next. There were prisoners back at the pump station, but she and John alone wouldn't be able to rescue them. And if they'd been told to wait by the local authorities . . .

"Why aren't the cops doing anything?" she asked.

Dr. Sheldon said, "Because they are four hours away by car and nobody's flying tonight. Besides, the NSA told them to stay the hell out of Dodge."

Cassie went to her father. He was sleepy-looking. "Do you remember anything the Russians said?"

Dad just raised his hands, helpless to remember and a bit beyond caring. "They spoke Russian most of the time. I heard one mention the oil field squads."

Uncle Dev spoke up, his voice breathy and weak. "There's a new monitoring facility out by Camp Prudhoe, Cassie. If there are people sabotaging wells, they'd know about it. Telemetry from all the well-heads and substations feeds there."

Dr. Sheldon pursed her lips. "That's a half-hour southeast, past the security gate. The gate isn't a very formidable barrier. I always thought it was a soft-point."

"Why didn't you say something?" John asked.

"I did. But nobody listens to a doctor when it comes to these things. They only want me to mend what's broken, not stop things from breaking."

"The Russians will have blown through that gate without stopping," Cassie said. "And they would go to the monitoring center for sure. But did they kill everyone or did they take hostages?"

"You could call them," Dr. Sheldon said. "The number is on that sticky note. Ask for Supervisor Swan."

Cassie found the sticky and dialed the number. It rang seven times before the line went live and the sound of people talking came through. Someone barked a command in Russian. At the last second, a man gasped and said, "Four Ruskies here."

After a sharp blast, the line went dead.

Four Russians. Probably kept behind to monitor the fields while others continued operations. If that voice had been Supervisor Swan, he had done a foolish, and possibly heroic, thing by answering.

Cassie told John and Dr. Sheldon what she'd heard.

"We need to let the military know that bit of intelligence," Dr. Sheldon said. "That sounds pretty ominous. Would they really blow the well-heads?"

Cassie knew they would. John knew it, too. She saw his growing concern in his stiff and agitated posture.

What could they do about it? Anything they did could get themselves killed. And even worse, it could risk the lives of more innocent workers. The people were here to provide for their families. They were away two weeks at a time, all year 'round, often working in dangerous jobs in miserable conditions. Cassie had no right to add more danger to their jobs.

But she thought of the polar bears, and the arctic foxes, and of the desolate beauty of the land here. How could she stand by and allow these fools to spoil all that?

John had turned to study a map pinned above the coffee maker. It showed the whole region, labeling different portions of the oil fields with names like Jack, Hive, and Delve. "It will be an ecological disaster unlike any seen in our lives."

Cassie could only nod. Dr. Sheldon bowed her head,

showing a hint of emotion for the first time. Uncle Dev was praying under his breath, face still pale as a ghost's.

Dad coughed, then whispered through his groggy haze. "This will end me. That has to be the end-game to all this. They knew I was vulnerable to this. They wanted me to be present when they ruined the land, and ruined the business in this region. The effects will last a decade. Not just the wildlife, but the stoppage of oil from this area will damage the economy, cost millions of jobs as fuel prices spike. But you know who won't be adversely effected?"

"Russia," John said quietly.

"They'll benefit. They have their own oil fields, and with this area offline the world will demand fuel from somewhere else. Russia will be only too happy to provide it. And the oil producers in the Middle East will again flex more power over us with their pricing collusion."

Cassie listened to Dad go on and on about the economic travesty they were about to endure. But she couldn't focus on such abstract ideas. She kept seeing Debbie's face, the woman who had tried to comfort her when she'd turned herself over to Smokey in the store-room. She thought of the gate guard who had lived just long enough to see his murderer's face. She thought about her own co-pilot, whose name she didn't even know. She thought about all the people still held captive.

"None of them will be allowed to live," she said. "Not one."

"No witnesses," John said, agreeing but not wanting to.

"Dad was right. This is going to be pinned on him. And think about it, if I hadn't been on the Twin Otter nobody would even know the Russians were here. None of the prisoners would've escaped. I'm the fly in their ointment."

Dr. Sheldon said patted her .45. "I'll go with this young

man to check in on the monitoring station. You, dearie, will stay here. I will not condone you putting your neck on the line for any of this."

The phone rang, a jangling old-timey phone with a physical bell inside. Dr. Sheldon picked it up, listened, then handed it to Cassie. "Someone called Kalov is very angry with you."

Cassie took the phone, then placed it in the cradle. "He would waste time trying to tell me to lie low. There comes a time when you have to take a risk. You have to take action or else face yourself in the mirror for the rest of your life, knowing you were a coward. My mama didn't raise no coward."

Chapter Twenty-Three

3:30 pm

The phone immediately began ringing again. Cassie stared at it. Finally, her respect for Kalov got the best of her. She answered. "Safe and warm."

"The man leading these criminals is a retired Russian Army officer. His name is Colonel Alexei Fedorov. He is as wily as a fox." That was typical Kalov, not even saying hello before launching into whatever he wanted to say. "You will remain where you are until my extraction team comes for you."

"There are still prisoners at the pump station. Val is one of them."

"Valentine knew the risks of the job. You are not to attempt any rescue or reconnaissance. Stay put!"

This was the argument she'd wanted to avoid. "The military is how far away? You know they won't get here in time to do anything. And this Fedorov idiot won't let any prisoners go free. He'll shoot them. He—"

"I spoke to him," Kalov said. "I spoke to him just a few minutes ago."

"You did? How?"

"He forced Valentine to give up your hotline number. It is easy to game out the scenario. He merely threatened one of the other prisoners. Do not blame Valentine, Cassie. He is soft-hearted. You did that to him. He thinks of you like a little sister and it makes him soft."

First of all, Cassie didn't blame Val for doing the right thing. She could get a new hotline number, but you can't un-shoot someone. Second, she didn't like any of this talk about Val considering her a little sister. She decided it was just Kalov's scheme to get her to drop her ridiculous crush on her lovely Russian bodyguard. Well, she would crush on him all she wanted. She knew nothing could happen between them. But that didn't mean she was willing to let him get killed.

"They're sabotaging the oil fields," she said. "Did your buddy Fedorov tell you that?"

Kalov didn't bother objecting to her use of the word "buddy." He merely growled. "How do you know this? In what way will he sabotage the fields?"

"Probably blow up the wells. Dad says there are multiple squads in the field, according to Fedorov. I don't know what they're doing, but I'm not going to stay here and let them destroy the ecosystem."

"Fedorov demands you come to the pump station." Kalov's voice was uncharacteristically reluctant. He hadn't wanted to say that. Cassie's scalp prickled. John must have sensed her sudden unease. He frowned in a questioning way.

"How does Fedorov know I'm here?"

"He found your bug-out bag. He has your weapon. And your identification."

"He threatened Val, didn't he?"

"No. He threatened your father. He didn't know I knew your father was out of his grasp. That's good. You have no responsibility to do as he asks."

Something wasn't adding up. Why was Kalov telling her this? An odd thought rose to mind. It was so at odds with everything she thought she knew about Kalov, that she dismissed it. But the idea returned. He thought she *should* act, but in his professional capacity as a teacher and protector he couldn't say, "Go, Cassie."

"I understand, Misha," she said quietly. She rarely used the familiar form of his name, Mikhail, but it felt appropriate at this moment. "I will not disappoint you."

"U.S. forces will be there in a few hours or so."

"I understand." Whatever she was going to do, she had better be off the battlefield when the military arrived. Anyone out and about brandishing a gun would be considered an adversary. She hung up.

The door swung open, allowing in a burst of frigid air. A middle-aged man with a gray mustache stomped his feet and shivered as he entered. "I got your call, Dr. Sheldon. I'm confused about why you have to leave during your shift."

Dr. Sheldon grabbed a parka from a coat tree by the door. "I'm sorry, Dr. Limon. We got a disturbing call from Jackson Swan. I'm going to see what trouble he's gotten himself into. I owe him that much."

"Doesn't Harv have guys for that kind of thing?"

"I'll fill him in," Cassie said, pretending to be resigned to staying. She approached John, hugging her elbows. "Thanks for helping me. I'll put in a good word with the boss."

"Fill me in on what?" Dr. Limon said. He hadn't taken his coat off and still stood by the door.

John had locked his intense eyes on Cassie, and she could see him weighing a decision. If he chose wrong, if he decided she couldn't take care of herself and make her own decisions, she would never be able to respect him. Whatever calculations went into his thinking, he came to that realization on his own. He finally said, "Shoot straight, Cassie."

She didn't say anything, didn't even nod to acknowledge that he knew she would be going to the pump station alone.

"I'm not working your shift," Dr. Limon said to Dr. Sheldon. His cold-reddened cheeks had taken on a darker flush and his bushy brows were bunching together like kissing caterpillars.

"You've had three hours sleep," Dr. Sheldon said, zipping her parka. "That should be more than enough. Besides, you're a better trauma doc than I am."

"These men don't look to traumatized. What do they have, acid reflux and gout?"

"Angina and some sort of sedative overdose," Dr. Sheldon said, pointing at each case in turn. She turned to John. "I'll drive."

John looked at Cassie uncertainly. She knew he was desperate to get out to the oil fields and find out what the Russians were up to.

"Take care, John." She turned away from him and went to her father. The door opened and closed. She heard Dr. Limon's coat rustle as he shrugged it off. He mumbled curses under his breath.

Cassie wanted to join in. With Dr. Sheldon and John gone off to the monitoring station, she had to deal with the pump station by herself. She knew how desperate such an undertaking would be. Kalov might understand that she felt a duty to fight, but he would never suggest she run in headlong, guns blazing, against two trained soldiers.

On the other hand, Fedorov didn't know she was armed. He had her Ruger, which irritated her. She had grown fond of the little pistol. The most Fedorov could deduce from it was that she'd had a little training in hand-guns. Like all folks older than twenty-five, he would under-estimate her.

Still, she would prefer to have competent backup with her. Even just one helper. She didn't need to kill Fedorov or his sidekick. She just had to disable or distract him long enough that Val or the other prisoners could help subdue him.

"I'll go," Dad said. He was awake, but very obviously gorked to the gills. He'd be as useless as Tommy Harka, her high school football team's kicker, who managed to miss every field goal attempt of the season.

Besides, Dad had just been brought in for severe chest pain. No way would she take him back into a stressful situation.

As usual, he read her thoughts by looking at her face. That was just one of those inconvenient things a teenager had to deal with. Parents—some of them anyway—cheated. They knew your tells because they had seen them since you were three.

"If you leave, I'll be more worried than I already am," Dad said. His words slurred and his eyes drooped. Rather than contradict him, Cassie kissed his cheek and squeezed his hand.

Cassie heard an engine rev and the snow compact under the wheels of Dr. Sheldon's vehicle as it drove off. John's truck was still out there. For her. That had been implicit in the silence they'd just shared. So here she was,

Dad now asleep, the smell of devil-black coffee competing with the chemical tinge of the clinic's atmosphere.

She gave Dad one last look, then headed for the door.

"Where're you going?" Dr. Limon said. "I thought you were going to fill me in."

"My dad can tell you all you need to know when he wakes up. Do you have a gun on you?"

"It's in my Subaru."

Cassie stuffed her arms into her North Face jacket. "You'd better get it. Just in case. There are a lot of bears out tonight."

Chapter Twenty-Four

3:40 pm

John Goodnight rode in the passenger seat of Dr. Sheldon's Range Rover. The ride was nearly as terrifying as tackling a machine-gun-wielding Russian. The physician drove like the gas pedal had two settings: off and floored.

John Goodnight stared straight ahead as Dr. Sheldon blasted through the swirling snow. Her Land Rover's huge engine roared as if it, too, were offended by Russian invasion.

She didn't slow as they passed the security gate to the oil fields. There was no point. The gate was half torn off and the guard shack had been shoved off its foundations by means of a blunt vehicle. It lay slumped over on the exit lane.

No sign of any guards, but John figured he knew what had happened to the one on duty.

"That disgusts me," Dr. Sheldon said. "If they have no regard for human life, I won't have any regard for theirs." She gripped the steering wheel and found another half-inch on the accelerator, making the Range Rover lurch forward with neck-snapping acceleration.

"How far to the monitoring station?" John asked.

"A minute or so. I'd better slow down. They may have posted a lookout." She didn't slow noticeably, but she switched her lights to just the yellow running lights. The effect was complete and total blindness.

The doctor didn't seem to care. She kept right on. John supposed there was little risk of hitting anyone out here, and the road was dead straight in this area.

He saw the lights up ahead, tiny and flickering through the snow. As they approached, the shape of the facility emerged from the gloom. A pole-mounted parking light hung over a small array of trucks and Subarus. But more important were the seven snow machines, all of them black and the same model of Ski-Doo.

There were no men out and about. Good.

"So what's our plan?" John asked. He'd been asking that a lot lately.

He absently wiped a smear of sweat his palms had left on the stock of his Remington 870 shotgun. He had a pocket full of spare bear slugs. His brain couldn't get around the idea that he was going into a situation where he might actually have to shoot someone.

"What plan? I'm going to go in through the front door, assess the situation, and treat any injured."

"That isn't a plan. That's suicide." John studied the lay of the buildings. There were four of them, all the same size and shape. They had been connected with narrow walkways between the units. And that gave him an idea. "Toilets."

Dr. Sheldon stopped the Range Rover and turned off the lights. She left the engine running. "Brilliant," she said. "Flashlight in the glove box."

He felt an urge to crouch once he'd left the truck, even though there were no windows on this side of the monitoring center. But knowing there were gunmen inside made him cautious.

He crept around the back of the first building and shined the flashlight under it. He was looking for the drain piping for the toilets. These remote buildings didn't tie into a sewer, and the ground wasn't suitable for local waste tanks. Everything had to be pumped out and hauled away. He knew there would be a heated outlet fitting, probably protected inside an insulated box.

He spotted it on the third module, in the gap between units 3 and 4. Good. But he didn't care about the box, just its location. He scanned the area just below it on the underside of the raised building. And there was the hatch.

"I'll fit through there," Dr. Sheldon said, "but I don't know if you will. Too broad-shouldered."

"That's irrelevant if we can't get it open." The hatch was held closed by clamp latches. Simple enough mechanisms to use if you could get a thumb under and pop them loose. But in this cold, the latches were practically armored with ice.

"Move," Dr. Sheldon said. She squeezed under the building and smacked the first latch with the butt of her .45. The ice shattered, and the building thunked. "They might have heard that, so stand ready with that shotgun of yours."

Figuring he was pretty well committed, John braced himself. Another loud clunk sounded behind him. He couldn't imagine the noise going unnoticed by anyone inside the facility. "Hurry up."

"These last two aren't so bad. They just need a little— encouragement. There!" The hatch dropped open, letting a square of light beam down onto the white earth directly beneath the building. The lavatory hatch was supposed to be for sanitization of the whole lavatory. Nobody wanted the pressure washer and chem-tanks rolling through the hallways. This let the sanitization crew access it from outside. The angle of the sloping floors let all the rinse water drain away.

Dr. Sheldon poked her head through. Suddenly she climbed up and disappeared inside. John ducked under and peered up. The edge of the toilet filled part of the view. Dr. Sheldon stood on the remaining lip of lavatory floor. It was very much like the bathroom on an airplane.

The smell of a heavy chemical deodorizer wafted down to him. The air inside was mercifully warm. He stood up and managed to squeeze his shoulders through. He'd have to wait for Dr. Sheldon to exit the lav before he could climb up.

She was already peeking out the door. Her .45 was in her grip, the tendons of her forearms standing out like cables. She might have been middle-aged, but she was no weakling. And she had no fear.

Without any explanation or signal to John, she pushed through the door. John squeezed the rest of the way up. There was no way to close and latch the hatch since the buckles were on the outside. Besides, he might want an easy exit in the next few minutes.

Habit made him check his shotgun. One round chambered and six in the tube. Safety on. Mimicking Dr. Sheldon, he peeked through the door. She was gone. John wondered what her relationship with Jackson Swan was that she would risk her neck so carelessly.

The small corridor was quiet and dark. He slipped out, trying to keep his steps quiet. His boots were heavy and his frozen limbs were none too steady. But who was he kidding? It wasn't the cold making his legs move like logs.

The corridor ended at a junction. He looked left and right. Empty. Of course it was. The Russians liked to collect all their prisoners in secure locations where they could keep an eye on them. And threaten them with death, should one start behaving badly.

He didn't know the exact layout of this place, but the buildings were all simple rectangles. He reasoned the monitoring center would be in one of the middle two modules. Since he was in the third one, that meant it was in unit two. That was to his right.

"Dr. Sheldon?" he whispered as loudly as he dared. Not loud. No response except a sudden boom from ahead. A gunshot? No. More like a door slam.

He moved. At the end of this hall was a steel door. The sign on it read: CONSORTIUM OIL FIELD MONITORING CENTER. A narrow glass window in the door gave him a glimpse of a dark room beyond, seemingly lit blue from the far side. With a quick look, he scanned inside. Not much to see because of the young Russian gunman standing in the way. Fortunately the man was facing the other direction.

John chanced another look.

"Well, damn," he said to himself. Dr. Sheldon was standing in the front of the room, staring down a sharply uniformed man who carried an AK-47. The man's blunt face and corded muscles spoke of many hours of weight training.

Dr. Sheldon laughed and tossed her head in a flirty way. The motion seemed so out of place given the situation, that John had a momentary flush of uneasiness. The idea that Dr. Sheldon was in cahoots with the Russians vanished as quickly as it had come. The Russian swung his open palm and knocked Dr. Sheldon to the floor.

John didn't hesitate. He knocked on the door then retreated to the short, narrow hallway leading to the toilet.

His gun safety training was so ingrained that he mouthed the words, "Safety off." The phrase served as a little meditative prayer. He kept mouthing the words "safety off, safety off, safety off" as the door to the control center clicked open and thumped shut.

He mouthed the words again as the heavy fall of a gunman's boots filled the quiet of the hall.

He mouthed the words one more time when the footsteps stopped just short of the junction with this hall. *Safety off.*

Chapter Twenty-Five

3:40 pm

John's truck was too hot. He'd left the heater blasting the whole time they'd been in the clinic. Cassie turned the vent down, then adjusted the seat and the mirrors, just as she learned in her Driver's Ed class. She knew how to drive, but hadn't much chance to do it recently. Her own car, a cute little BMW M3, was at her mom's house in Texas.

Dad kept an old Ford pickup at the ranch in West Texas, and he sometimes made her drive it when he was doing one of his "work days," clearing brush that absolutely had no need of clearing.

She backed John's truck away from the clinic and headed toward Pump Station One. Hopefully she'd come up with an actual plan while she drove.

Her headlights illuminated a white sign with block letters that pointed the way toward Camp Deadhorse. There would be a lot of work workers there, sleeping during their 12-hour off-shift. She could try to recruit a team of them, but that would be inviting another session of "Is this girl cray-cray or just dumb-dumb?" Cassie had no time to explain the whole situation again.

A blue back-lit sign caught her attention. It was for the Sag River Motel. She remembered that head of security, Harv, had been there. She decided to try once last time to convince him that he had a responsibility to act. She pulled into the parking lot and in less than a minute was face to face with the reception lady. The woman looked her up and down and sniffed. "Still hunting Russians?"

"Yes. Where's Harv?"

"In his office down the street. He left in here in a frenzy. He was cursing about some little rich girl and her fantasies. Any idea who he might've been talking about?"

"That would be me. So where is the office?"

A country song about living like you were dying started when she got back in the truck. It hadn't gotten to the second verse by the time she got to Harv's office. The security HQ was nothing to write home about. Just another pre-fab metal building on skids. A tiny stenciled sign right next to the entry read: CONSORTIUM SECURITY.

Since the oil fields had several companies working them, they pooled funds for things they all needed but which would be problematic if they did it independently. One was road maintenance, and another was the security detail. That meant Harv worked for the oil companies.

Cassie found him sitting behind his desk, mashing a cruller into a coffee cup and then slobbering up the half-soggy pastry in one giant mouthful. He pegged Cassie with a displeased glare as he chewed. "I been looking for you," he said around a mouthful of mush. He swallowed, Adam's apple bobbing. "There've been at least two murders since you arrived. And the federal government tells me that armed men on snow machines are zooming all over the tundra."

"I told you my dad had been kidnapped. The Russians still have a bunch of prisoners at Pump Station One. I'm going over there now to get them free. Oh, and they're sabotaging the oil fields and probably the pipeline."

Harv's eyes widened with every sentence she completed. He was clearly not prepared to handle this sort of crisis. He swallowed and wiped his mustache on his flannel sleeve. "I got a call from the NSA. Do you know who they are?" His tone was so condescending Cassie thought first-graders would riot if they heard it.

"National Security Agency. What did they say?"

"They said a rogue Russian Army officer was doing all this. They also said to stay the hell out of it. I've called all my men out of the field. I don't want anyone caught in the crossfire when our boys and girls in uniform show up and start kicking ass. So if you think I'm going to let you go out there and get in the middle of this, you've got another thing coming."

He scooted back on his office chair so that his belly could clear the edge of the desk. "Now, if you give me your word you'll stay put in Deadhorse, I'll let you go." He held up some handcuffs. "Otherwise, I'm going to detain you."

Cassie watched him sidestep to come around the desk. If the situation hadn't been so screwed up, she would have laughed. Instead, she held her arms out. She'd always wanted to use the little trick that Kalov and Val had taught her.

"Cuff me, then," she said. "I want to see the look on my father's face when he learns that you arrested me."

"I report to more than just him. Besides, he'll thank me for keeping his little girl safe. If you are who you say you are."

Cassie giggled, which was not the best thing to do when an older man who thinks he's an authority figure is about to "do what's best for you." But she couldn't help it. "Cuff me, or I'm leaving."

He shrugged. "Have it your way, missy." He moved to put the cuffs on. To Cassie it seemed like slow motion. In her training scenarios, Val usually played the bad guy bringing cuffs to restrain her. He was quick and a bit rough. But she'd escaped him once.

The trick was simple: Wait until the cuff was open and approaching one's wrist, and then . . .

Cassie gripped Harv's forearm, twisted, yanked the cuffs from his hand, swung the open one under and around his wrist. With the ease of a sidewalk card magician, she flipped the other cuff open and snapped it onto his other wrist.

She didn't look back as she left. So much for recruiting security to do anything. But the encounter gave her a boost of confidence.

An explosion of swearing followed her outside. She chuckled as she got into the truck. The song was now at its crescendo, heading into the final chorus. Singing along with it, she motored down the road.

Chapter Twenty-Six

3:44 pm

The pump station was just ahead. Cassie took three very intentional deep breaths as she slowed and began to turn the wheel.

In times of stress, the body had an odd instinct to breathe shallowly. She didn't understand why. Kalov had pointed it out to her one day when he had made her traverse his "Hillbilly Ropes Course" in the forest near the safe-house cabin in Michigan. He'd never answered why he'd given the ropes course that name, but Cassie guessed it had something to do with its crude construction out of materials found at a salvage yard.

For instance, in one section where the runner—Cassie —was to ascend thirty feet to the top of an A-frame made of pine poles, the only thing to hold on to were railroad spikes driven into the wood. But Kalov, being Kalov, had sledged them so far in the heads barely protruded.

"Improvise," Kalov had advised. "Quickly. This paintball gun is fun to shoot and your yelps make my heart all warm and fuzzy."

Val had stood by, arms crossed, face amused, while Cassie stared at the base of the A-frame trying to think up a way to make the climb possible, let alone safe.

The answer came to her after the first red paintball stung her butt. She slipped off her white Italian leather belt—Prada—and looped it around one of the slanting pine poles. Holding the ends, she leaned back. In this way she was able to brace her feet on the pole and climb, using the slightly protruding railroad stakes as toe holds. Kalov had shouted encouragement, all the while taking carefully aimed shots at her butt. By the time she'd ascended to the bicycle handlebars that served as a zip-line handhold, her jeans were spotted with red blotches, and she knew she was welted with blue-black bruises beneath.

As soon as her feet touched solid ground, Kalov announced a three mile run.

"I'm out of breath already," she'd said, hands on her knees.

"That's because you forgot to breathe when you were under attack. Always remember to breathe." And then he'd sent her running, giving chase and whooping and shooting with preternatural aim.

"Breathe, Cassie," she told herself now. Her chest felt knotted up, like she was bracing for another of Kalov's paintballs. But this time she was running toward danger . . . and the projectiles were lead.

She kept her eyes ahead as she drove, sparing the occasional glance left and right to look for snowmobiles. None in sight, but that didn't mean none were near. With their headlamps turned off, she'd never see them.

She passed the guard shack. She didn't look to see the dead guard inside.

Now she'd reached the spot at which she'd decided to take her next action. Lifting the CB handset, she clicked it to broadcast and said, "Jay Hansen. Status?" She counted to ten, then repeated her question. She kept driving. The lights of the pump station were drawing closer.

Despite her focus on breathing, her heart wanted to go lickety-split. That cued the respiratory system to speed up, too. With little demand for oxygen, though, the resultant buildup of blood oxygen levels would quickly lead to hyperventilation. Cassie kept her breath on a deliberate in and out cycle, with a pause when she was empty.

"Hansen. Status?"

Static burst over the tinny speaker, then a voice broke through. "Return to Deadhorse security H.Q. immediately. You are under arrest."

It was Harv. She ignored him. "Jay Hansen. Report your status."

Harv went into another diatribe. Since the communication was one way at a time, Cassie couldn't interrupt him. Worse, if Hansen was trying to communicate Harv was monopolizing the frequency with his blabbering.

Cassie turned the CB down and put the handset on the seat next to her. The pump station was right here. All the usual trucks and cars were still there. But there were a dozen snowmobiles and a very familiar Sno-Cat.

"Dammit," Cassie said. The whole escape had been for nothing. Debbie's death, too. Cassie hoped that Smokey never woke up. She'd hated him before; now she wished she'd finished him when she had the chance.

The sign for the pump station passed and disappeared behind her. So here she was. No way was she going in through the loading dock like last time. She continued around the rear of the huge pump building. She knew the layout well enough to know roughly where the pig bay was.

She doubted there was a direct entrance to that area. It had seemed like a central part of the building.

But she was looking for something else, anyway. And there it was. The refinery.

Chapter Twenty-Seven

3:50 pm

This place is hell, Yuri Romanov thought as he crept toward the toilet, his AK-47 at the ready. Not that he was in the least fearful of the pasty-faced Americans who worked here. He simply hated the cold.

His friends had always made fun of him for it. And though he'd complained all through his training in Siberia, he'd gotten through it. How else was one to cope with such conditions?

His mother had taught by example that to complain was to cope. She complained about Yuri's father's drinking —but then, what Russian mother did not have such a complaint? She complained about the demise of the Soviet Union, the rise of Putin, the elections of Obama and then Trump. She complained about the melting ice caps. She complained about the fact that it was Monday, or Tuesday, or Wednesday, or any other day, or week, or month, or holiday. She complained that her cakes were too delicious, for her boys ate them too quickly and left none for her. She complained that her boys were too skinny and that she could never get them to eat enough servings at dinner time. And why? Because there was never enough food. Prices were too high!

Yuri had his safety off, but he was relaxed. There was probably another crazy woman in here. The only thing formidable about the woman claiming to be a doctor was how she'd whipped out her cowboy pistol and clicked it at Denya's face.

A misfire. Almost too lucky to be believed. But such were the fortunes of enemies and allies alike. It would give her something to complain about, so that was good for her —assuming she survived, which she wouldn't. Too bad.

The little bathroom was empty, but there was also no floor in it. Odd. At first Yuri was surprised, for he thought Americans too used to luxury to allow for a simple hole-in-the-floor toilet. But then he saw the barrel of the shotgun emerge.

His reflexes were very fast. His AK came up, his head already doing the slight side tilt for him to aim down the sights. But the 24.8 gram bear slug traveling at 2600 feet per second was much faster. What chance does a Russian soldier-gone-mercenary stand against such a thing?

Yuri didn't have time to complain about the unfairness of it, for his time on Earth was at an end.

Chapter Twenty-Eight

3:52 pm

The only times Fox Tils had heard real-life gunfire had
been on Memorial Days—when the parade stopped at the
Veteran's Cemetery and fired a 21-gun salute—and when
he'd visited his grandfather in Truckee. There, he always
got a stern lecture about his parents' intolerable "hippie
politics," and that no grandson of his would grow up
without a .22 of his own. Those visits had been sort of fun,
filled with long afternoons shooting pop cans off of logs.

But Fox was never going to be a hunter. He was a lousy
shot. So when the chest-shaking boom erupted in the next
building module over, Fox needed a moment to figure out
what the hell it was. An explosion obviously, but he
couldn't think of what might have blown. All the
compressed LP tanks were in module one, where the
kitchen was. The Russians figured it out long before Fox
did. And suddenly they were swarming toward the rear
door, their machine guns at the ready.

The lady who had come in with her revolver drawn

leapt to her feet. The Russian squad leader had socked her pretty hard, but Fox could tell by her facial type that she was a tough one. Fox wasn't an expert in face-typing like his mother was, but this lady was definitely a Type Three —like a middle-aged MMA fighter in doctor's scrubs. She had a shiner rising on her cheek, but Fox suspected this wasn't her first.

The Russians were all distracted. Not this lady. She snapped her fingers and pointed behind him. He looked, but there was only the big screen, still shining blue and demanding that someone choose an input source. There was also a fire extinguisher mounted just to the left of the screen.

He looked back at her. "What?"

"Oh, for Pete's sake," she said. She crawled past him and yanked the extinguisher from its wall mount. She pulled the pin and yanked the nozzle free. The nearest man was the Russian boss. She put the nozzle to the back of his head and blasted him. A plume of white powder engulfed him. He doubled over, coughing and shielding his face.

The doctor moved the nozzle to direct the blast into his face. Choking and gagging, the man shoved at her. She dodged, raised the canister over her head and brought the bottom down onto the man's skull.

Fox winced as a dull crack sounded and the man crumpled to the floor. The other gunmen were going through the rear door to investigate the gun blast. None noticed their leader going down.

The doctor pressed a gun into Fox's hands. She'd pulled it from the fallen Russian. "Go secure the door."

"Huh?" He stared at the gun—sleek black and meant for dealing death—as if she'd handed him a wriggling eel.

"Make sure none of them comes back in. Lock the

door. Shoot anyone who tries to break through." She grabbed his hand and turned the gun to face away from her. "Only aim it at bad guys. Here's the safety."

She had retrieved her enormous revolver. The Russian squad leader was face down, head completely whitened by the fire extinguisher dust except for one nasty red spot at the back of his skull. The doctor swiveled the cylinder from her revolver, checked the rounds, snapped it back into place, then started shouting commands at the others in the room. "Out! This way! Now!" They obeyed, scurrying to the opposite door, faces looking half-melted from fear.

Fox went to the other door. The dangerous door.

This was definitely not what he'd signed up for. Sure, he liked the occasional first-person-shooter video game, but he knew for certain there would be no respawning if he got killed here—no matter what his mom said about reincarnation.

Another horrific blast rattled the door.

Fox locked it and risked a peek through the narrow rectangle of glass. He back-pedaled as a Russian soldier came rushing toward him. The man looked scared. He smashed into the door and rattled the knob.

He turned, sprayed bullets down the corridor, shouting in unintelligible Russian. Then all fell quiet.

Chapter Twenty-Nine

3:54 pm

Nobody ever mentions the smell when they talk about gunfights. In movies, you see the cowboys duck behind feedbags, or water troughs, or behind windows in the bank, and they shoot and shoot, puffs of smoke floating from the tips of their gun barrels. And in the theater, or at home on your sofa in front of the TV, you think about how loud the guns are, or how terrifying the zing of ricocheting bullets must be.

But John Goodnight had gone mostly deaf in the first moments of the fight. His shotgun blast—compressed in the tiny space of the lavatory—had even made his vision go jittery for a few seconds. He imagined the shockwave of the blast shaking the intraocular fluid of his eyeballs.

Now the smoke stung his nose and eyes.

Three dead Russians lay piled in the doorway of the lavatory. Two shots. Three kills.

At this range, the bear slugs could not have missed. John had barely aimed. The first man had lost his entire face in a spray of red. The second two had piled in, rushing to see why their comrade was lying on the floor. John saw their weapons and pulled the trigger. No more than a tenth of a second between seeing and decision.

The second bear slug had hit one man in the neck and passed right through to smash the third man's forehead. The carnage was total.

The thick, acrid gun smoke in the lavatory didn't sweep down through the hatch. It swirled about him, a brimstone tendril of the devil's breath. His feet were still on the tundra, frozen.

Warm air rises, he thought absently. His soul felt as cold as death. He wondered if it would ever rise again.

A shout from the hallway brought him back to the moment. How many more could there be? He pumped the action on his Remington 870. He could barely hear the *chick-chunk* as the spent shell popped out and the fresh one seated into the chamber. But whoever was in the hall heard it. They went quiet.

John's legs were freezing. Literally. The arctic air loved idle muscles. Like a spirit of death it sought out warmth, sapped it, turning flesh to ice. If John didn't climb out of the cold, he would lose mobility when he needed it most. Yet all of his instincts were screaming for him to retreat, escape the smoke, the violence, the impossible choice of dealing out death or having death dealt to him. But the chill of polar midnight was like a granite wall keeping him from going that way.

"I don't want to shoot you," he called.

He could barely hear his own shout. The smoke made him cough, but he didn't dare take his eyes off the door. Eyes watering, he elbowed a dead man's booted feet aside, clearing a step for himself. He hefted himself fully into the lav, catching himself on the sink as he wavered.

The Russian struck, sweeping into the doorway, already firing. Holes appeared in the wall next to John's head, bits of insulation foam fluttering like snowflakes. The mirror shattered, the lights to the left and right smashing into an infinitude of shards.

The attacker's eyes were wild, face contorted with rage-fear. He swung the weapon side to side as he fired, like Arnold Schwarzenegger in one of his old movies. And that undisciplined panic saved John's life.

John's shotgun bucked. The bear slug went wide, tearing a chunk from the man's left arm and spinning him to the floor.

John thunked the shotgun for one more round. The Russian crab-walked backward, screaming and bleeding. John didn't pursue him. His heart was slamming and his breath seemed to bring no air to his lungs. The crush of adrenaline made his arms and hands shake.

A spray of gunfire sounded around the corner. The man was panicking. John heaved himself forward, fueled by determination to finish the job but not relishing it. Like a farmer who had to slaughter a pig. Filthy work. Grit your teeth work.

Sometimes the only way out is forward.

He stopped at the corner where the lavatory hall turned toward the monitoring center. He heard heavy breathing, moaning. But no talking. And, most importantly, no gunfire.

"I don't want to shoot you," he called.

"Yes. Yes. No shooting. No shooting." The man's voice sounded awfully young. And frantic.

John wondered if the guy had been given a choice about this mission. He'd probably been told that there wouldn't be any shooting. Poor kid. Maybe there was a way to end this without killing him.

"I'm coming around. Don't shoot me, I won't shoot you."

"Yes. No shooting. I will no shooting." This was followed by a gasp of pain and a groan. That wound on his arm had to be like having a chunk bitten off by a polar bear.

John pushed the tip of the shotgun around the corner, extending it until he was sure the injured Russian could see it. The man didn't fire at the sight of it. That was a start.

John risked a quick look. Just a fraction of a second. No shot. He'd seen enough. The man was leaning against the monitoring room door. His weapon was in his hand, but drooping to the floor. His wounded arm hung limp as an airport windsock on a still day.

John stepped out, keeping the shotgun aimed to the side.

"Drop your weapon," he said, trying to keep his voice firm but calm. The shudder in his syllables betrayed his fear.

The man didn't comply. He looked up at John, though it seemed a struggle for him to do so. Blood poured freely from his hand to splatter on the floor.

John repeated his demand, motioning at the kid's weapon with the tip of his. The Russian reacted with lightning quickness, raising and firing in one motion. He straightened as he fired, the dire effects of his injury now revealed as a ruse. He got off a short burst. John felt a tug at his parka sleeve.

And then the Russian's face came apart. Wet splatters pelted into John, warm and thick. The soldier fell onto his face. In the doorway behind him stood a bearded man in red flannel, pistol aimed down the hall. His eyes were wide with shock. He stood there in a frozen moment, then bent over and puked.

A flurry of snow drifted around John, confusing him. Had the bullets blown holes in the roof? No, the white fluffs weren't snow. It was bits of down stuffing from his parka. The tufts drifted on soft currents before settling onto the floor.

The silence was total. It suited John. He felt wrapped in a numb cocoon now, the downy quiet of not-dying. It occupied the space between the fact of survival and the realization of it. The profound beauty of it—of the total absence of thought—captured John as he stood in the blood-and-brain-spattered hallway. Only the feel of hands on his shoulders brought him back to the place where he stood.

The bearded man was shaking him. "Dude, you got shot."

Stupidly, John looked at his arms and legs. There were holes in his parka sleeves. But no pain. He shrugged the coat off and shook it. More white fluff spilled out like dandelion seeds. He checked his arms and body. "I'm not even scratched."

"No way!" the bearded man said. His pallor was somewhere between snow white and the yellow green of unripe limes. The smell of sickness wafted from his mouth.

And there he went, bending to retch. John stepped back, but realized there was no point in avoiding a little vomit. He was already filthy with gore. He had no instinct to be sick, though. Hundreds of animal dissections had cured him of his gross-out reflex. What he felt instead was the revulsion of violence. And, oddly, gratitude. This puking guy had saved his life just now. John appreciated the toll that act had taken on the young man.

"Thank you," he said. "We'd better get somewhere safe before more of these bastards come in here."

The man finished gagging, and wiped his mouth on his

sleeve. "No more. That was it. The doctor took out their boss."

Relief slammed home. "Dr. Sheldon is alive?"

"And kickin', yo," the man said. "I'm Fox, by the way. Are you a cop?"

"No. I'm John Goodnight. I'm an ecological engineer."

That got Fox's attention. "No way! I work on the telemetry stuff in the field. I was expecting you tomorrow."

"Where is everyone?"

"The doc with the revolver took them all outside. I guess we should, like, go tell them it's safe. . . . Unless they put explosives on this place, too." He scratched his beard and looked around as if he might spot a bomb he hadn't noticed before.

"What do you mean, put explosives here, too? Are there bombs somewhere else?"

"Dude. They're, like, everywhere. The Russians put them in a bunch of the well shacks. They must have a transmitter somewhere. All they have to do is, like . . . you know?" He made a button-pressing motion with his thumb and then spread his hands, fingers waggling to outline a mushroom cloud explosion. "The oil fields will go up like geysers of fire. It's gonna be all Mordor out there, yo."

The oil would spew out, igniting and turning into liquid flame. Black smoke would whip away in the wind. And the fires wouldn't go out until someone put them out, or the well lost enough internal pressure to stop pushing oil to the surface. That was the best case outcome.

If the oil didn't ignite, then hot crude would flow onto the tundra, covering everything with sticky, black gunk. The wildlife would die, unable to escape the oil that coated their fur, robbing them of insulation. The bottom of the food chain would be wiped out. In an environment Nature had built upon the delicate edge of a blade, having hundreds of wells spewing contamination all over the tundra would make for a disaster the wildlife might never recover from.

"And we killed all the guys who knew where the explosives were," John said.

Fox's eyebrows fluttered as if were just coming awake. He got really excited all of a sudden. "Dude! Like, I know how to find all the bombs. I just need to tweak my algos and it'll spit out a spreadsheet of all the wells they plan to nuke."

"Tweak your algos?"

"Algorithms. It's the software for identifying animal motion at the well sites. It's supposed to identify individual bears, but it isn't working. Sorry, dude. But that doesn't matter right now. Yo, as long as the cameras are working, I should be able to see which well had Russians screwing around with them. And like . . . then we'll know!"

It was a start.

Fox went back to the monitoring center, his stride unsteady, but his shoulders squared with purpose. "Somebody should tell those people to come in," Fox called over his shoulder. Since John was the only one left here, it fell to him to go fetch Dr. Sheldon and the others.

He found them packed into her Range Rover. Many of the others had gotten into their cars and trucks and headed to Deadhorse. He filled Dr. Sheldon in on the situation in the oil fields. She looked grim, and the bruise on her cheek was making her eye puff up. But she walked with the swagger of an Old West sheriff, and she bossed the remaining few workers back into the control center. "We have work to do. Get on the phones and get some folks out here to start removing bombs. We need snow machines. And I know someone else to call. I'd better do that one myself. What're you all looking at me for? Go! Chop chop!"

Fox greeted John and Dr. Sheldon by holding out five pages of printouts. His excitement from before was dampened by the sheer magnitude of the task ahead of them. "The system recorded 235 wells that had non-animal motion. The animal identification algos actually worked, like, pretty awesome on the humans. We sort of borrowed the code from the NSA which uses it for IDing terrorists in crowds and stuff. Anyway, the system thinks there were a total of twenty different guys out there. And, yo, check out this map." He hit a key on his keyboard and a map of the region appeared on the big screen. Shadows blocked part of it as Dr. Sheldon ordered two men to move the Russian leader's body outside.

The map had four circles on it, each showing a concentration of red dots. "These are the sabotaged wells," Fox said. "It looks like they hit them in teams. Like, we need to send some dudes out in teams to get these bombs the hell out of there. But we have a problem."

John Goodnight studied the map. There was a scale printed on it. And gauging by that, the most remote wells were over a hundred miles away. On a snow machine going fast, it would take an hour and a half to get there in this weather.

"You said there was a problem? What more could be wrong?" He tried not to think about what Cassie might be facing at that very moment.

Another image popped onto the screen. A wider view of Alaska and the vast empty regions of sea and polar ice around it. A satellite view, John realized. A band of dense white was curving in from the southwest. "A storm?"

Dr. Sheldon confirmed it. "Phase 3 visibility. High winds, blowing snow, and extreme wind chills. It'll make a

SEAL team HALO jump nearly impossible, though I won't stake my reputation betting they won't try it. Those bastards are tough. But anyone *we* send out there will be in extreme danger, and we can't let them split up because visibility will be basically nil."

John pointed at the most remote sights. "That area is so far away. I don't know how much time we have. I doubt it's more than a few hours. If even that long. Once the Russians finish up at the pump station, they'll blow everything and head out while we focus on the disaster they leave behind."

Dr. Sheldon let a long sigh escape her nose. "Leave that to me. I know some people in that area."

"You do?"

She didn't say anything more, but went to the far corner of the room and picked up a phone. Her body language was less eager than a kid on the first day of school after a long summer holiday. "Who's she calling?"

Fox eyed the map. "Yo, I gotta say it's Inuits or whatever. But she's putting her career on the line calling them. If the Marines or SEALS or A-Team get here and shoots one of them by accident . . ." He whistled. "This place is going to draw some serious political heat."

John suspected the political heat was coming anyway. And he would welcome it. The oil fields were obviously too vulnerable. "Explosives," he mused. He knew that none of the people present were qualified to deal with this. "Do people use them here for mining?"

"Sometimes, but this is called oil drilling, not mining. Why?"

"We need somebody to look at these bombs before we have people yanking them out. What if the Russians booby-trapped them to blow if they're tampered with?"

"Excellent question," Dr. Sheldon said as she returned

from her call. She looked relieved, but she was so stony-faced that it only showed in the slight relaxation of the muscles at the corners of her eyes. "My friends are putting together some teams to deal with Sector Four. But we'd better get Denny on the line."

"Explosives expert?" John asked.

"Something like that."

Chapter Thirty

____

4:05 pm

The refinery was mostly outdoors, where a maze of thick pipes and tanks shunted crude oil through a process Cassie didn't understand or care about. The end products here were various types of fuel. Diesel for the trucks and generators. Maybe they made Avgas for the airport, too. She didn't really know the difference. Gas was gas to her, but it all had one thing in common: It smelled hella flammable.

A snow-covered picnic table was standing on end and leaning against the main facility's wall, next to the door. A sign bolted to the wall warned ABSOLUTELY NO SMOKING! That seemed sensible. Cassie swiped the dead guard's badge across the door lock panel. The door clicked and opened.

She didn't think the Russians would have a guard posted this far from the pig bay, but she slipped in as quietly as she could.

She was in an industrial processing facility with more huge tanks, pipes running everywhere, and a constant cacophony of churning pumps and clacking valves. She had no idea what anything was, though she'd visited refineries before with her dad. He'd been taking her to see different Ingram ECO properties since she was old enough to walk. And while she found the enormous complexes interesting in an abstract way, she had not fallen in love with oil the way Dad had hoped. She realized that this Alaskan "side trip" was another of Dad's attempts to draw her into the business. Not happening.

She planned to go to school, maybe study ballet or theater, and then move to New York and make a life in the arts.

But she had learned a few things on those father/daughter field trips. Places like this—ones that could explode—had several layers of safety built in. If there were a spill, or a fire, the control center could shut off the flow, sound alarms, call emergency responders, and usually isolate the problem in order to limit the damage.

Yellow painted stripes on the floors designated the walkways and approved locations for waste bins and hand trucks. Those with diagonal stripes and guard rails were danger zones. She followed the yellow lines to a support column that towered to the ceiling.

Most of the main lights were off, so the whole area was filled with bluish light from the overhead tungsten fixtures. She could barely make out a steel-grated catwalk thirty feet up. It was just like the catwalks in the main pump facility. Perfect.

It took her a minute to find the stairs leading to the mezzanine office. Facility designers tended to put these above the main floor to give a good vantage over the operation.

She and John had been here earlier, to rescue Dad and Uncle Salah.

She stepped into the eerily empty control room. Now she saw all she hadn't had the presence of mind to notice before. One wall was covered with banks of gauges, computer monitors, and buttons. A toolbox sat on a cart next to the door, lid open. A few coats hung from hooks on the back wall. A half-eaten Twinkie sat on the edge of a control panel, next to a coffee cup. It didn't take a detective to see that workers had been interrupted in the middle of their routine.

She scanned the panels for a big red emergency stop button. It turned out to be rather small, and it was protected from accidental presses by a clear plastic shield. She flipped it up. "Here we go." She mashed the button.

Nothing happened.

She looked around for a red button she might have missed. Having to press two of them would be pretty stupid, she thought. But then a beep sounded from the panel. A red-lettered LED display in front of the button read: "PRESS AGAIN TO OVERRIDE SHUTDOWN."

She didn't press it again.

A klaxon started honking in the facility, a two-tone horn that cut through all the other noise. And then there *was* no other noise. The system shut down, one sub-system at a time, in a pre-set order to minimize damage to expensive pumps and piping systems.

In less than a minute, the only remaining sound was the annoying alarm. Cassie accepted that. What she did not like was that the lights stayed on. She had hoped the power would go out and leave the whole complex in darkness.

Her gaze settled on a holding tank just outside the window. She palmed her forehead. The power generators had tanks and tanks of fuel to burn through before they cut out. There were likely dozens of generators around the compound.

She could live with that. The darkness had been a secondary objective, anyway. The main thing was to draw some of Fedorov's men to the refinery. Hopefully Fedorov himself would come to see what was going on.

She didn't plan to wait for him to come into this office.

She scrounged through the toolbox and selected two smallish wrenches and put them in her coat pocket. Just outside the office was a wall-mounted metal ladder climbing to the catwalks. Up she went.

Creeping along the narrow walkway, she did her best to remain quiet in case a Russian gunman was already snooping around. She had her eye on a vantage point that would let her watch the entrances from outside and from the pump station. She kept the Glock in its holster. This wasn't a sniper scenario, and her accuracy against moving targets would be crap from up here.

She didn't have to wait long. The door from the pump station swung open, letting in a sweep of light that fluttered on the floor as men passed in front of it.

There were three of them. She didn't think one was Fedorov or his wiry second-in-command.

So what? she thought. They all had to be dealt with eventually. She had counted fourteen snowmobiles in the parking lot. Jay Hansen had reported each as having one man aboard. That meant fourteen Russians had arrived since she and John had left. Sixteen total with Fedorov and his sidekick. She assumed Smokey was still out of commission.

Kalov's voice seemed to shout inside her head: "You do not take on fourteen men alone. Period."

Cassie smirked. You don't take on three alone.

She pulled one her wrenches out and slung it as hard as

she could toward the far corner of the facility. She lost sight of it immediately, but then a metallic clank and skitter of metal on concrete resounded in the huge open space.

The three gunmen froze. One called out, *"Kto tam!"*

The men conferred in low voices. Two split off to investigate the noise. The other headed for the control office.

She moved like a ghost along the catwalk. She didn't dare climb down the ladder that had gotten her here. It was too much in view of the other men. They seemed pretty intent on where they were headed, taking slow steps and scanning with their weapons. But one glance back would be all they needed.

Cassie looked for another way down. The holding tank near the office looked like a good bet. There were rungs built into the side facing the office, a way for service techs to get to the couplings at the top.

The catwalk passed right over top of the tank. In quick, quiet steps she positioned herself above it. She grabbed the rail, swung over, and hung at the full extension of her arms.

The top of the tank looked a lot farther away from this perspective. She let go anyway.

Her feet slammed into the tank. She absorbed some momentum by bending her knees, but the tank rang out like the world's largest gong.

She couldn't have chosen a worse place to jump to. She scrambled to the rungs and swung down to the office side of the tank. She came to rest on the platform next to the tank and just a few feet from the office door.

The tank was between her and the two men looking for the wrench, but she had to assume her gong had turned them around. She crept to the office door and stopped, holding as still as the ice sculpture at her dad's third wedding.

The alarm klaxon cut off at that exact moment. The resulting quiet revealed her racing breath and the slam of her own pulse in her ears.

Breathe, she reminded herself, bringing Kalov's stern voice back to mind. If the man in the office had heard the gong—and she had no doubt he had—he had left it to his compatriots to deal with. He'd found the controls to silence the alarm. Maybe he was trying to get the refinery running again.

No. Cassie sniffed the air. The idiot was taking a cigarette break.

Cassie peered in. She stayed crouched, keeping her face at his waist level. It didn't matter. He was facing away from her, his attention on the control panel. His cigarette sent up curls of smoke. Was he trying to get them all killed? What a moron.

She could shoot, but that would draw the others here right away. She wanted to incapacitate him with as little fuss as possible. She had Smokey's folding knife. It was likely she could draw the edge across his throat before he had a chance to fight. But if he did fight it was going to go poorly for her, she thought. He was at least as big as Val, and even more thickly muscled.

But now that it came to it, the idea of cutting his throat repulsed her. Even shooting would have been a hard choice to make.

Kalov's voice was shouting warnings to her. When you attack, you use maximum force and aim to kill. If you're not prepared to kill, you shouldn't be in a fight.

Admonishments like that made a lot of sense when you were safe and thinking you wouldn't be getting into any fights. Here in the moment, when Cassie had to act, the advice carried no weight at all.

Cassie was not judge and jury. Striking from behind, she would be a murderer. And even though he was armed with the AK-47 dangling at his side, he wasn't pointing it at her.

Thinking about it more wasn't going to increase her choices or her chances. She decided and acted.

Staying in a crouch, she hustled toward him, looping so she could come from straight behind and avoid any chance of him catching her in his peripheral vision.

The obvious first blow was to the back of his knees to make him fall. Then a transition into an armbar, wrapping her legs just so . . .

Movements flowed, one into the next. The only sounds escaping either of them, grunts. A gasp of surprise rasped from his throat. Cassie's own noises were guttural and explosive. Animal.

She had never gone full-out against Val, fearing she would hurt him by accident. But here she had no such qualms. Adrenaline helped her, finally serving some benefit as it added energy to her grip.

Immobilize. Incapacitate.

The only way to immobilize a foe was to get leverage. Grip his wrist just so, twist his arm to the extreme range of motion. In this position, even a man of his size was at his weakest. She locked his legs, intertwining hers with his so he couldn't use them to kick or lever himself into a roll that would pull her out of her strong position.

Speed is everything when getting your opponent into the most vulnerable state. And so she finally transitioned to wrap her most powerful muscles—her legs—just so. Her left arm jammed under his chin, pressing against his throat. Another animal grunt helped her tense every muscle fiber in her body—like a boa constrictor—pulling that arm against his throat until his blood flow cut off. This is where he would tap out if they were merely rolling at the dojo.

This man didn't get that option. He went limp. Cassie held on a second longer before releasing him. He was out.

But he wouldn't be for long.

Now what?

She was in the same situation as before. She either killed him, or . . . she didn't have anything to tie him up with. She didn't have any rope. She cursed herself for losing her backpack. She had a bracelet of paracord in there. Easily enough to hogtie this man. But just like her gun, it was useless when it wasn't with her.

The toolbox. She remembered seeing some zip-ties in there. She scrambled to it, breath laboring in her chest. The takedown had used a lot of energy.

Screwdrivers, pipe clamps, compass, old-fashioned folding ruler. There, a bundle of white zip-ties.

Bootsteps rang on the metal stairs climbing to the office. No time to think. She left the man where he lay and scurried to the door.

The gunmen were coming up. She back-pedaled into the office. Cornered.

The only thing she had going for her was that they didn't know she was there. She stepped over the unconscious Russian, planning to slip under the control console and hide deep in the shadows. The Russian snatched out and grabbed her ankle, twisted hard, and brought her to the floor.

His weight pressed onto her, his own hand-to-hand combat training giving him the advantage now that the element of surprise was reversed. And he was so strong. Like iron in shirt and pants.

Instinct pulled her hand to the Glock in her pocket. She yanked it free. Trigger safety compressed. The trigger pulled. A muffled snap as the gun lurched.

She pulled again. The Russian convulsed and fell aside. Blood bubbled from a wound in his chest.

Shouts from outside.

She could barely hear the ring of their boots on the metal walkway over the ringing in her ears. What now? What now? Whatnow-whatnow-whatnow? Her thoughts lost cohesion. She felt herself freezing in indecision.

Someone was yelling just outside the office. Cassie went limp, flinging her gun hand out to the side.

Her victim's hot blood soaked through her open North Face coat and into her shirt. Like liquid fingers, it seeped through fabric to graze along her ribs and caress the skin of her abdomen.

With the gun still in her grip, she slipped her hand under an office chair to hide it from view. She let her eyes lose focus and stared at the ceiling. She drew in one last breath and held it. If there was ever a time to ignore Kalov's instructions about breathing, this was it.

If her chest rose, she would die. Playing dead was the worst strategy of all, according to Kalov. But sometimes it was the only one remaining. The trick was to put aside every natural instinct the brain sent to the body. It wanted to curl into a ball, but you had to lie stretched out and vulnerable. The body wanted to gasp for precious oxygen, but you had to keep your chest immobile. The body wanted to look, to see approaching threats, but you must not even blink.

The men stopped in the doorway. They called to their dead friend. *"Fyodor? Ty v poryadke?"* Cassie knew that much Russian. And no, Fyodor was not okay.

They crept into the room. She couldn't see them, but

she could imagine them. Young, afraid, their machine guns held forward, ready to fire. Both barrels were pointed at her. She thought she could feel the pressure of their aim on her head.

Surely they had that much training. They saw the blood on the floor, the girl, torso bloody, her body still. Fyodor had taken her with him. Ah, poor Fyodor, his vodka would be theirs, but they would weep for him as they drank the last swallow.

But now Ivan—she assumed one of them must be an Ivan—was suspicious. Fyodor's pistol was still holstered and his AK-47 was across the room. How did he shoot her and leave such a situation? And what had killed him? Did the girl have a weapon, too? But look at her. So scrawny and just a young thing. What threat could she have been?

Cassie wanted to breathe. Her mind screamed for breath.

Boots stopped near her head. The man knelt, pressed his fingers to her neck, searching for her pulse. It wouldn't be difficult to detect, as hard as her heart was ramming.

Well, the ruse had been good while it lasted. Cassie jerked up with a huge inhalation, eyes wide as if coming out of a dream. The movement had the intended effect, for Ivan fell backward. He fumbled with his AK. He didn't get a chance to bring it to bear.

Cassie swung her Glock, pressing her lips in sad determination as she sighted and fired. That ended him. He fell back as if all the bones in his body had turned to rubber.

Cassie was already slewing the weapon toward the other man. She put the front sight on his forehead.

"*Nyet! Nyet!* Don't shoot!" He held one hand up, palm out. A universal sign of wait. But his gray eyes, just pinpricks of sparkle in the dim light, betrayed him. He had such lovely red curls—and the freckles of fresh-faced youth. He reminded Cassie of a boy she'd known in high school. Chet Spence had been a track star. She and her friends had gone to all the meets to watch his lithe body carry him over hurdles. She would never forget the easy smile and casual way he curled up one side of his mouth to smile. He knew the effect it had on girls.

Cassie didn't have time to wonder if this boy had any girlfriends. He was raising his machine gun one-handed. The gray sparkle of his eyes dimmed as he squinted in concentration, seeking to put a bullet into Cassie's brain.

Bad boy. Why couldn't he just cooperate? Was it because she was a girl? Would it be too embarrassing to be disarmed by her? Was it better to die and have all your friends remember you over their Smirnoff or whatever brand of vodka Russians would drink when they talked about how poor Dmitri had his brains blown out by a teenage American girl? All because Dmitri was too proud.

Cassie's 9mm round penetrated his skull at the exact spot where his mother probably used to kiss him when she put him to bed at night.

Cassie lowered her weapon and wept.

Chapter Thirty-One

4:27 pm

The band of snow that had been dropping dusty snowflakes on Deadhorse finally blew past. According to the forecast, they had an hour of relatively clear weather. The front that would slam them with Phase 3 visibility and estimated wind chills of sixty below zero approached with the implacable disinterest of a god. John Goodnight didn't think they could get all the explosives removed from the field before the storm struck.

He wouldn't ask anyone to do something he wasn't willing to do. But the truth was more complicated than that. Yes, he could take one of the Russian's Ski-Doos and join the removal teams. But there was the big issue of Cassie and the pump station.

While she had suspected the Russians were planning to blow up the oil wells, she hadn't known for sure. As soon as John saw images of the explosives, he put together two pieces of the puzzle. It was obvious in retrospect. Fedorov was using the pigs to send explosives down the Trans-

Alaskan pipeline. John was certain he planned to blow several of the downstream pump stations. That meant he was going to send Pump Station One to Kingdom Come, too.

And Cassie was there.

"Go, John," Dr. Sheldon said. "We're more than capable of coordinating this operation. Steve will be at Slough-7b in a few minutes."

Fox patted John's back and smiled wanly. "And I sent him with an extra cam to aim at whatever explosives he finds. Then Denny here can tell us what's what."

Denny White Eagle was a Sioux Indian from South Dakota. By John's estimate, the man was nearly one hundred years old. He had a toothless smile and a booming voice. Apparently he'd been in a lady's company when one of Dr. Sheldon's associates had tracked him down. "That's the secret to a long life," he'd said without embarrassment. "You gotta keep the good energy flowing."

He had been an explosives technician for road construction throughout the western United States. Then he'd caught a case of gold fever and moved to Alaska to help in mining operations. When that didn't pan out he did several stints on Alaskan fishing boats. Then, in the strangest career shift yet, he signed up to be cafeteria cook at Camp Deadhorse. "His apple cakes are the best food in heaven or anywhere else you'd care to go," Dr. Sheldon had said without the faintest hungry gleam in her eye.

"Steve is at Slough-7b," Fox said. "Video feed coming online."

A rectangle of black appeared on the big screen. Suddenly it brightened. "Can you see it?" a man off-camera said. The image was very close and blurry.

Fox shouted into a radio transmitter. "Yes. But, dude, you gotta put a little light on it."

A murmur of swearing came through, but then a flashlight beam illuminated a brick of explosives. It was in a paper wrapper, labeled in English. C4 HIGH EXPLOSIVES.

A metal object was jabbed into the center of it, two wires leading away.

"Yep. Yep," Danny White Eagle said. "C4. Dangerous. Very dangerous."

"Are those wires connected to a receiver?" Fox asked into the radio.

Steve swung the camera to follow the wires to a small plastic box. It didn't have any lights on it, no dramatic countdown readout. Not like the movies at all. A black wire led from it to where it simply draped over a nail in a wooden support beam.

"That would be an antenna, yo," Fox said.

That explained why they hadn't blown any of the wells yet. Clearly Fedorov intended to use a remote transmitter to send the detonation signals. The puzzle was why he was waiting.

"You're still here?" Dr. Sheldon said to John. "Go find your girlfriend."

John took one last look at the big screen and the brick of explosives. As he was leaving he heard Denny White Eagle tell Steve to pull the detonator out of the brick. There was a moment of quiet and then the room let out a collective sigh of relief.

"Not booby-trapped," Dr. Sheldon said. "Let's coordinate the removal teams and get this taken care of."

John stepped out into the frigid darkness. Dr. Sheldon's Range Rover stood by, still running, exhaust pluming from the back, ready to go.

Chapter Thirty-Two

4:30 pm

Emotion wasn't necessarily bad, according to Kalov. But one must only indulge it at appropriate times. Cassie allowed herself a minute—maybe three—to get some of the tension of what she'd done out of her body.

Crying was a sign of total weakness, she thought. But sometimes her body just did it. It was like food poisoning. One didn't get to decide whether one was going to puke. The body took over and just did it. Maybe tears were a similar thing, a way to purge poison from the heart.

Whatever their purpose, the tears couldn't be allowed to go on and on. She still had to deal with the rest of the Russians. There had been sixteen. Now there were thirteen. Still a ridiculously large number.

The man who had turned off the klaxon hadn't managed to restart the refinery. But that had certainly not been his primary mission in coming here. He and his comrades had been sent to see what was going on. And Fedorov would expect a report back.

Cassie got to her feet and studied the three dead men. The smell of blood made her wrinkle her nose. It mingled with the stink of smoke and the underlying greasy odor of the refinery air.

The men had their AK-47s, their side-arms, and their uniforms that were like military fatigues but which bore no insignia of their country, their military organization, or their rank. That was because they were rogues, not official soldiers.

Cassie set about the grim task of searching their bodies. Cigarettes galore. What was with these guys, anyway? It was a disgusting habit and would be a detriment to their physical conditioning. She discarded these. Two men had Zippo lighters. Both were polished chrome —one with a wondrously proportioned naked lady painted on the side, the other inscribed with the initials I.G.I.

She pocketed the lighters.

No identification, no money. The red-headed kid who had reminded her of Chet Spence carried a photo in the breast pocket of his shirt. A girl. Pretty with cat-eye makeup and false lashes. She smiled with slightly crooked teeth and purple-black lips. What a sweetheart. She might never know what had happened to her beloved Dmitri of the Red Hair and Freckles. Would she have been surprised to learn he carried a lock of her hair taped to the back of her photo?

Cassie couldn't bring herself to search his other pockets. She didn't need these men's knives, nor their guns. She did replace the three spent rounds from her Glock's magazine with 9mm rounds from one of their pistols. She also popped another twenty loose rounds from their incompatible Serdyukov magazines. It was better to have excess rounds than die wishing she'd taken them.

She picked up the first man's machine gun. She had

fired one before—in that horrific standoff in the Houston coffee shop. She hadn't known then that it was an Uzi. In the end, she had gotten off a few rounds. They'd all missed.

She was totally unfamiliar with the Kalashnikov machine gun. She thought she could figure it out, but she could hardly test it here. For one thing, she had stayed at the scene of gunfire way too long. If another team had been sent to check on these guys, then she was in ridiculous danger of being found standing over their dead bodies with one of their weapons in her hands. For another, the racket of gunfire could carry a long way. The walls separating this refinery area from the pump station weren't insulated.

One thing remained for her to take. A small walkie-talkie was clipped to the first man's belt. She snatched it and retreated from the office.

Up the wall ladder to the catwalk, and then to the shadowed spot from which she had observed the three men enter the refinery. The blood soaking her shirt had started to dry. It became cold and sapped the warmth right from her belly. And it smelled.

She could only imagine what her face looked like. There had to be spatters from the first man she'd shot. She didn't know if she'd been hit with anything from the other men. The idea of strangers' blood on her made her skin crawl. She wanted to strip off her shirt and scrub her body with lye.

For now she'd have to stew in it.

She pulled her phone from her back pocket and swore to discover the screen was cracked, the bottom right corner spider-webbed from an impact she didn't even remember. The screen still worked. It was 4:33 pm. So odd, since it was perfectly dark outside.

"Frickin' Arctic," she mumbled.

The Diet Coke and sandwich she'd taken from the commissary were long gone. She needed food, water, and sleep. And yet . . . she felt okay. The adrenaline of the fight was still with her, but she hadn't suffered any real injuries aside from scrapes and bruises.

Her arms and legs felt electrified. And though her hands trembled, she didn't feel out of control. In fact, her vision seemed keener than it had ever been. Her awareness seemed to encompass the entire space of the refinery.

This was good. This was the result of training. This was the strength her mother had gifted to her. With this mental pep talk done, Cassie decided to move out of her observation position. Nobody was coming to see what had happened here. She slid down the ladder and returned to the main floor. The entrance to this area was across a fifty-foot span of open floor.

She sprinted.

Nobody shouted. Nobody shot her.

She continued.

The giant pump station room looked empty at first glance, the huge pump machinery churning away in its constant drumbeat, the industrial concrete floors vacant. But a single out of place flutter of shadow drew Cassie's attention upward.

She had opened the door a fraction of an inch. Just enough to see the man crouching on the catwalk. He held a long rifle with a big scope mounted on top. That made this guy a sniper. He hadn't been there before. He must have come in with the others once they'd finished sabotaging the wells.

He was covering an area leading to the pig bay. Maybe he'd been given the assignment merely to keep him busy. You can't just have a dozen or so guys hanging around doing nothing. They start goofing off almost immediately. Cassie knew this from her two years on cheer squad. Idle boys were a force of destruction on par with a small tornado. But there was more to it than that. The boss, Fedorov, wanted to keep the prisoners in line. What better way than to show them a dude with a sniper rifle?

Several sections of the catwalk remained hidden from her position. But that was okay, because they were behind the enormous pump machinery. Anyone back there wouldn't see her either.

She stayed low as she came out the door. Gritting her teeth, she eased it closed. From here there was no going forward to the pig bay without being captured or shot.

And that posed the central question of this whole stupid plan. Was she truly going to pick guys off one by one like some sort of crazy superhero vigilante in a mask and cape? Or was she going through with her original plan? The refinery gimmick had sort of worked. There were three fewer Russians to deal with. But even if she got Val free, her odds were abysmal.

The sniper had to go. She studied him. He wasn't moving, just crouching there with his weapon trained down the walkway leading to the pig bay. He hadn't looked back even once. He should have a partner, she thought. Someone whose sole job was to watch his six.

The impact took her in the shoulder, a mass of muscle and dark fabric. A vise-like arm pressed across her face while her attacker's legs clamped to immobilize hers. The AK flew from her hands.

That answered the question about the sniper's backup. She didn't have time to wonder where he'd come from. She went totally limp. Any struggle would make noise. She didn't want sniper dude to look. Her ploy was the same as it had been minutes before in the refinery office. The man growled something in her ear. English, but so heavily accented she couldn't understand it.

She assumed it was something to the effect of "Move and I'll break your arm." And that was well within the man's power, given the leverage he had over her. Not resisting—not kicking and clawing like a honey badger—took an enormous force of will. But Cassie had done this to Val once. It was the only time she'd ever gotten close to submitting him on the jiu jitsu mat.

Her attacker eased his grip, thinking the silly, weak girl had given up. She sucked in air, as if in pain and unable to put up the feeblest fight. He eased more and pointed at the AK-47. "Where get you that?"

She turned her face toward him, Glock already rising to greet him. "From your mama, bitch." She fired.

She didn't wait to see him fall. The report of her shot would draw every man to this spot. She scrambled the opposite way, back through the door to the refinery. The door closed behind her, then was slammed by a 7.62mm round from the sniper's rifle.

The steel door stopped it, but a welt the size of a golf ball protruded from Cassie's side of the door, just an inch from her skull. She gave herself three quick breaths before scurrying back to the refinery.

"Subtle as a longhorn at Sunday School, Cassandra," she said.

But what's done was done. They knew she was here. Maybe. They knew *someone* was here. They wouldn't be sending just three of the lowest-ranking men this time.

She climbed back to her observation spot, wishing the backup power would fail but knowing it wouldn't. Darkness would be quite welcome at the moment. She realized the light switches were probably in the office. That was a missed opportunity, and no getting it back.

Think, Cassie. Think. Lights have bulbs. They break easily.

The AK-47 would've been better for this. She counted five light fixtures. They hung high up, in bell-shaped metal shrouds, probably aluminum. She took aim at the closest. Bang.

One out. The others were farther away. Her hands were trembling. She fired. Missed. Fired. Hit. But the light fixture swung wildly around. She'd missed the bulb.

She let that one go. No sense trying to shoot a moving target when there were three more hanging still. She rested her arm on the catwalk railing and took careful aim. Another one shattered.

The place had dark corners now. She wasn't satisfied. The Russians could hear her firing, she knew. They probably figured she was in a gun battle with the three men she'd already killed. Good.

The walkie-talkie in her pocket hissed and a Russian voice said something very urgently. They were waiting to come in until the gunfire stopped. It would be stupid to do otherwise, since they couldn't know what the situation was. Nobody wanted to rush into crossfire.

But then an alternative idea came to her. They were calling to the man she'd taken this walkie-talkie from.

Fine, she thought as she blasted the fourth light fixture into darkness. Enough of this beating around the bush. The light she'd set into wild motion had settled. She took aim, fired, and sighed as it sent a spray of shattered glass to the floor far below.

The entire space was dark now. The only light seeping in came through the high band of windows along the roofline. She couldn't do anything about that.

She sat down and pulled her magazine. The rounds

she'd spent on the lights were quickly replaced with spares from her pocket.

The quiet in the aftermath of her shooting made her breathing sound very loud. It reminded her to take control of her inhalations. Slow them down. She needed to settle, get her mind back to the present moment, and think.

She got exactly ten seconds of thinking before the door burst open and a stream of men rushed in. They fanned out, taking cover behind storage tanks, cabinets, and other machinery. They broke into two squads of four. One went toward the office, the other began a disciplined patrol of the refinery floor.

Cassie watched as they went deeper into the darkness. The light fanning through the door didn't penetrate very far. She made up her mind. The risk here was setting off a massive explosion that would send the refinery and the pump station to the moon.

Bullets and fuel were as dysfunctional as her parents' marriage. But sometimes they combined to make something special. Something that was powerful and beautiful. Something like an explosion.

Something like Cassie.

The largest fork truck sat at the end of an aisle near a bank of pallet-shelves. Unlike the vehicles outside, the fork truck didn't need to stay running all the time because it was warm in here. Also, it ran on LP fuel, a compressed gas stored in metal canisters like the ones Dad hooked to the barbecue—much to the shame of his Texan mother and to the scorn of his Texan friends.

But Dad was always afraid of those tanks. He called them bombs. "Time to hook a new bomb to the cooker," he would say.

Cassie brought out one of the Zippo lighters she'd taken from the dead Russians. The buxom lady on the side seemed appropriate. A real bombshell. She weighed it in her palm. Heavy, small. But serviceable. She hefted it toward the fork truck. It hit the concrete with a sharp click and skittered beneath the vehicle. A pretty bad-ass throw.

The four men patrolling the floor froze. One by one they came back into the faint light bleeding from the open doorway. A murmur of conversation rose among them.

"Come on. Come on. Get closer," Cassie whispered. For a few seconds she thought her ploy had failed. But then the men swarmed toward the fork truck. They held their guns up, all shouting in English, "Get down. Hands on floor!"

Patience. It was so hard to wait to trip the trap, but patience pays. And when she thought they were about to realize their mistake, one man stepped closer, bent at the waist, and peered under the vehicle. He reached under. The others seemed to relax. The squad in the office came pouring down the steps, all shouting and pointing. One of them had figured out that Cassie was dangerous and they knew she was still running loose.

The guy pulled the lighter from under the fork truck and stood. The office squad joined the group. One was waving for them to disperse.

Cassie fired. The 9mm round pinged from the canister of compressed gas mounted at the rear of the fork truck. The ricochet clipped one man's leg and he fell to the floor, screaming.

"You have got to be kidding me!" Cassie said.

She fired again. The Russians were already dropping in reaction to the first shot. But they weren't running. They didn't know where the shot had come from.

Cassie's next round penetrated the metal canister, sparking the compressed propane inside alight.

A flash of red fire burst out, followed by a concussion

that flattened Cassie to the catwalk. Her head bonked off a railing baluster.

The clank and clatter of metal on metal resounded all around the refinery as pieces of the blown-apart fork truck impacted with the tanks and machinery of the place. A wave of heat washed over Cassie. Not mere warmth, but like the heat of being much too close to a campfire. It flushed her skin, then vanished, leaving her face suddenly cold.

The klaxon started up again, two-tone horn blaring. A valve clunked open above, and a downpour of frigid water began to smack and ping on the catwalk. The fire suppression system had kicked on.

Probably a good thing, considering the billows of smoke that floated past her. The thick, acrid stench of burning rubber and grease made her choke. It was carried by super-heated air toward the ceiling. Unfortunately, Cassie was near the ceiling.

She got to her knees and tried to see through the smoke. It was so dark in the refinery from her target practice on the lights that she was utterly blind to what remained of the men who had been by the fork truck. A shout and cough rose from below. Somebody had survived. How many somebodies remained an open question.

Cassie had crossed a line. It hadn't happened with the close-proximity shootings of men whose faces she could see. Oddly enough it had happened at a distance, when the men had not even been aiming their guns at her. She had stepped across the line of self-defense to a realm of strategic, premeditated killing.

This was, she realized, war.

If she didn't get down there soon, she would cough loud enough to attract the attention of any survivors.

Besides, her eyes felt like she'd dumped some of Dad's habanero salsa in them.

She followed the railing to the ladder. The rungs descended into smoky blackness. She climbed down, stepping as softly as she could. The smoke cleared enough that she could see a lighter area in the haze.

That was where the door was. She stopped, went as still as stone. Though her ears rang from the explosion and the close-quarters gunfire earlier, she could hear the klaxon clearly. That told her she was not totally deaf. But the klaxon was muffled, as if heard through earmuffs.

With her hearing reduced, she would have to be extra cautious. Kalov had warned that the notion of a sixth sense was *"chush."* Or in the Texan vernacular, "hogwash." The truth of such heightened senses, he claimed, was the subconscious mind processing the subtle clues provided in hearing, smell, and even the sense of vibration in the ground and air. But the subconscious could not detect these things when the flow of sensory information to the brain went dull.

That meant she had to be extra careful. She got to the main floor and picked her way through the debris field. The floor was littered with twisted metal here, a smoldering hunk of vinyl and foam there, charred pieces of Russian here and there.

Cassie approached the door in a half-crouch. She kept the Glock in the forward, two-handed grip Kalov had taught her.

"This would be an excellent time to flee, Cassandra," she said to herself.

But there would be no fleeing. She was now soaked to the skin and shivering. The only good thing about the fire suppression rain was that it washed some of the blood from her skin. But the water was nowhere near warm. It felt like a November rain shower in Michigan when the leaves had all fallen from the trees and the skies turned permanent gray. The cold there was damp and slipped down the throat of your jacket and made your body shiver. Not Alaska cold, but cold enough to chill your ribs. If she went outside soaked like this, death would close its hand around her heart and squeeze. And it wouldn't take more than a minute to turn her blue.

Forward she went. The air cleared. The door to the pump station was not only open, it was off its hinges. The blast must have been concentrated in this direction.

She got lower, trying to get to fresher air. The sniper had certainly turned his attention to this door now. If she went back to the refinery, she would be able to hide. But she'd be no closer to her goal. The odds were better now. Still terrible, but better. She had cut the opposition in half at least.

She pulled the walkie-talkie from her belt and spoke the lines she'd rehearsed on the drive there. "This is Cassandra Ingram. I've been informed that you demanded I come here. Well, Fedorov, I'm here."

She had debated the next line. She had decided on bravado. That would feed the man's sense that she was being rash. Which, she had to admit, she kinda was.

Everything she'd done to this point had been calculated. More or less. Sometimes less. She spoke the line. "I haven't decided whether I will kill you, or if I'll merely feed you to the bears."

She released the transmit button and waited. If Fedorov was smart, he wouldn't respond at all. Or maybe he would reply with an ultimatum. That would force her to act. He would probably threaten one of the prisoners.

On the heels of that thought a distant gunshot rang out. Cassie ducked instinctively. But it had been far away, the sound attenuated by walls and machinery between the gun and Cassie's ears.

The walkie-talkie hissed and a voice came through. "I shoot Valentine because you are behaving like child. You will drop weapon and coming into open. Or I am shooting more people. It is up to you. Longer you are waiting, more people are dying. Like you shoot them yourself."

Cassie didn't hesitate. "I'm coming out."

She set her Glock on the floor and kicked it through the door so that the sniper could see it. She still had a pocket full of 9mm rounds, but she wouldn't be able to do much with them without a gun. She popped off her right shoe and laid the folding knife inside. She jammed her foot in. It was lumpy and a protrusion on the handle poked into the ball of her foot. She had endured worse; fifteen years of ballet, ten of them on pointe, inured you to minor pains of the foot.

She moved forward, hands up. The blade in her shoe gave her a slight limp. But given how she probably looked, a limp wouldn't cause much suspicion. Frankly, she didn't care. Val's face rose to mind. His sideways smile, his evil eyes. Dead? Impossible.

She believed Fedorov had fired a weapon. He had wanted Cassie to hear it. But Val had been serving as an interpreter. Shooting him before speaking with her made absolutely no sense. But she couldn't be sure. That made her stomach churn and her chest ache.

"That stupid Russian," she said as she stepped into the view of the sniper. She was talking about Val. Her loving torturer. The incessant, but welcome, teasing that made her face go hot had made her fall in love with him. But the barriers that kept him out of her arms were impenetrable. Age, position, life experience. Hell, his job made it impossible. How could she give her heart to a man who could end up in a situation like this? She would worry herself to an early grave.

But none of that mattered in the face of this moment. She could deny the ability to have a future with him, but she couldn't deny that she would cry forever if he died.

"Stupid Russian," she said again. She clicked the walkie-talkie. "I'm out here. I can see your sniper glassing me with that pea-shooter of his."

There was no response. Cassie didn't expect to be shot, but she braced for it. Kind of impossible not to when a high-powered rifle is aiming at your eye.

"Please placing radio on floor," said a new voice. She turned her head to see the wiry guy from the airport hangar walking up to meet her. This was Fedorov's second-in-command.

"What's your name?" she asked. She wanted as much information as possible. And she wanted to get him talking. She wanted him treating her like a human. The theory was that even small amounts of rapport made it harder for a captor to rape, torture, and kill you. She found that theory rather unconvincing but it was better to try it than curse yourself later for being a know-it-all skeptic.

The man didn't answer, but merely waited for her to comply with his demand. She did.

"Come with me and no one getting shot." He turned his back on her. Cassie could feel the sniper's weapon aimed at her. She followed, limping, and casting a longing look at the Glock she was leaving behind.

She didn't consider making a dive for it. There was no way in hell she'd be able to shoot the man leading her away before the sniper gave her a discount lobotomy.

There was no sneaking from storage tank to storage tank this time. They walked straight into the pig bay. The prisoners' faces she'd seen before were more haggard-looking, and their sprits so sapped of hope most didn't even look up when she limped past them.

But one did. A thick, blond-haired man. His face was red with fury, and his whole body trembled with barely-contained energy. Cassie remembered Goatee telling her about this guy. Sven.

And there was Goatee himself. Not talking. Not lecturing. Certainly not reporting anyone to the authorities. He lay on his back, a hole in his chest, a pool of blood spreading away from him like a giant crimson amoeba.

His was not the only body on the floor. A man in yellow high-vis vest and rugged work-pants was also dead. More blood. His hard hat lay ten feet away, the words "Hard as Nails" emblazoned in vinyl letters across the front. She recognized a few other people from the storage room. But the fatherly guy, Jay Hansen, wasn't there, and neither was scarlet-haired Debbie.

And then there was Val. Shot in the leg, a belt tourniquet cinched around his thigh. He looked like a vampire in this light, his dark hair sweat-slicked and drawn back to show his widow's peak. His face was pale from shock or exhaustion or blood loss or pain. Probably all of them.

He shook his head the slightest fraction for Cassie. He was telling her not to worry about him. But of course she worried about him. She loved him.

Fedorov didn't look at her. He was with Becky, the pig expert, looking at a computer screen. It displayed a local map. A dotted line ran down the center. Even from where she stood, Cassie could make out the green dots flashing in several places on the line. Pigs in the pipeline. So Fedorov had gotten them in, and now he was going to cut off the flow of oil. Bastard.

"I'm not accustomed to people ignoring me," she said. "Do you know who my father is?" She had to play up her rich girl, spoiled brat image. "If you think you can get a ransom for me, you don't know my father at all."

Ridiculous statements. Anyone who knew her father even slightly would know he'd pay anything to save his own skin. His little princess would be at least that valuable to him.

"You are giving to me hotline number," Fedorov said, his accent strong but his enunciation precise. He still didn't turn to face her. His voice was deep, pleasant. He likely had a good singing voice. It was the type of voice that carried command in it, even when the words he spoke didn't make much sense. She had known men like him before. They often rose in corporations like her father's because they were good at taking clients to dinner.

Some men built entire careers upon that one skill. This man, though . . . Cassie had an instinctive respect for military types, and usually gave them the benefit of the doubt. In this case, she decided he was exactly as he appeared. A slightly small man with an enormous ego.

"I don't have any idea what you're—"

He aimed a gun at Val's head. She recognized the weapon as her personal Ruger.

"Oh, *that* number. Let me think." She recited the numbers, slowly, then changed the order, then changed it back. "Yes. I'm pretty sure that's it. If not, then I got the seven and the eight switched around. I'm dyslexic."

"You are liar. But I call number. Maybe Valentine is living, maybe is dying."

He dialed. Listened. Then hung up without saying a word. "You tell truth. This is good start, Cassandra Smythe Ingram."

He finally turned toward her. His face was well-formed, and he had likely enjoyed many girlfriends when younger. But the meanness in his eyes betrayed his fundamental cruelty. Cassie guessed he was about 50 years old, maybe older. Fit military men were hard to gauge. His hair was kept short, more gray than black now. His sleeves were rolled to mid-forearm, revealing hairy, pale skin corded with muscle and prominent veins.

"Please, holding still." He raised a phone and took her picture. "Blok, search her. I am not wanting for her to injure herself." He dismissed her from his attention by turning his back on her. He dialed the phone and held it to his ear.

The wiry soldier appeared at her side. So his name was Blok, was it? At least that was something. She gave him a cool gaze, the kind she'd ice a boy with if he made unwanted advances. She had a lot of practice with this particular look.

Blok wasn't even slightly phased by it, which irritated her to no end.

"Hold your arms out," he said, motioning with his own. She spread her arms apart and sighed through her nose as he frisked her. It was business-like and intrusive. She hated every second of it.

But not as much as big Sven. The huge Swede lurched to his feet and pointed at Blok. "I will kill you, Blok. For what you do to her, you must die."

Fedorov turned slightly, raised Cassie's pistol, and fired. Sven went down, screaming. His face was red, but not with blood. Only fury could darken a man's complexion to that maroon shade. He crawled toward Blok, shouting something in Swedish. Blok didn't even look at the man. He squeezed Cassie's sleeves, pressed her pockets. Very thorough.

Any second now he would order her to take off her shoes. He clamped his hands around her ankles and proceeded up each leg. Sven climbed to his feet.

Fedorov was still on the phone. He watched Sven stumble, barely giving him the attention a mother would give a toddler loose in the kitchen while she talked to a friend on the phone. Blood was dripping from Sven's right hand. The bullet must have taken him in the bicep, for his shirt sleeve was matted to his skin, soaked and blood-darkened.

Fedorov pulled the magazine from Cassie's gun and began loading it with more 9mm rounds, thumbing each one into the spring-loaded mechanism with the patience of a man who had done such a task thousands of times.

"Sven," Cassie said, "don't get yourself killed for me."

Val wasn't in view. He still lay on the floor, on the other side of the computer desk where the pig lady sat. The woman was as pale as Cassie had ever seen a living human. Despite the drama unfolding around her, she kept her eyes on the screen.

Fedorov raised the pistol. "Sit," he said to Sven. "You are like fool dancing." An odd phrase, but it seemed to catch Sven's attention more than the gun did. He spun to face Fedorov, eyed the gun drunkenly, then swayed and fell onto his side. It made no sense given the injury.

"He's hit in the side," a short woman in heels said. She was sitting with the rest of the prisoners, but she had a clear line-of-sight at Sven's hidden injury. She made to get up, but Fedorov shook his head.

The bullet must have ricocheted off his arm and deflected into his flank. Probably not all the way to the heart, but if it nicked an artery he would bleed out.

Blok finished frisking Cassie and stepped back. "She is unarmed."

"You are on best behavior," Fedorov said. "Your father comes. I am telling him you are bad girl or good girl?"

Cassie's world froze. Now she understood why he'd

taken her picture. That had been for her father's benefit. Now Fedorov was using her to get him back. Dammit.

She had a little time yet. How long was it from the clinic to here? She had just done that drive. Twenty minutes? It had seemed quick, but she'd been preoccupied on the way.

"You don't need him at all," she said. "I'm more famous. And if you want to send a message, or get a ransom, or plug up the pipeline, you don't need him at all."

"You are knowing nothing," Fedorov said. There was heat in his voice now. Good. She needed to spark that emotion to pry out of him what he truly wanted.

"Then explain it to me," she said, and she instantly regretted her choice of words. And as if reading lines from a script playing out in her mind, Fedorov said, "I am not explaining to little girls."

He snapped his fingers and pointed at a spot on the floor near his feet. "Sit."

Really? He was going to make her sit at his feet? If the idea hadn't been so preposterous, she would've been sorely offended. Clearly it was meant to demean her. And also keep her close so that when her father arrived he would immediately see the danger she was in. That would make him cooperative for whatever idiotic scheme Fedorov had in mind.

Cassie decided that biding her time and at least pretending to cooperate would keep her hands and legs free for when the time to act arrived. Besides, sitting at Fedorov's feet put her much closer to Val.

She didn't move too swiftly. She didn't want to give the impression of total submission. That would just make Fedorov more suspicious. She folded herself onto the floor.

It felt good to sit down. She had been running amok

for so long she didn't even remember the last time she had slept. The chill from her soaked clothes was making her shiver again. If Fedorov noticed, he either didn't care or didn't think her well-being of much long-term concern.

Val was making a point of not looking at her. She supposed he had other problems at the moment. With his leg in a tourniquet, he wouldn't have long before he suffered permanent tissue damage from having blood flow cut off.

The injury had to hurt like a son of a gun. She wanted to go to him and put his head in her lap, to brush his hair back and tell him it would be all right. And then maybe kiss him, ever so softly.

But that was out of the question. Fedorov was back at the screen, watching the progress of the pigs. Sven was still breathing, but he hadn't moved in a few minutes. Blok stood ready to follow whatever order Fedorov issued. His hands were loose at his sides, but he didn't have his sidearm drawn. And he didn't need it, for three other men were posted around the room, their AK-47s in their grips and their eyes scanning for the slightest wrong twitch.

Chapter Thirty-Three

4:57 pm

The snow machines had picked up John Goodnight's trail just minutes after he'd left the monitoring station. They closed in on the Range Rover's rear bumper and tailgated like a Boston cab driver.

John kept an eye in the mirror, but with the blaze of the snow machines' front headlights glaring from the glass, he couldn't see anything of the drivers—or their guns.

They hadn't fired on him yet. He slowed, hoping one would come alongside. The thought that they might be men come to help clear explosives from the field crossed his mind.

He decided to wait until he passed the crossing of the Sag River Highway and the Dalton. There were light posts there. He could see if they were friend or foe then.

If foe, then he had Old Betsy. He patted the shotgun. She hadn't had a name until that moment. But he remembered his grandfather talking about a machine gun he'd operated in Viet Nam. It was monster, firing .50 caliber rounds. A collapsible tripod mount made it a mobile, terrifying machine of death.

Grandpa had called his trusty M2 Browning Old Betsy. Grandpa had been a killer of men, though he had rarely spoken of the war. Except a few times . . . in very quiet moments when he had wanted to pass to John something about what he'd witnessed and done.

John had cherished those stories, and those moments, all of his life.

"You don't get over it," Grandpa had said. "You just get on with it."

The name Old Betsy was not one of affection, John knew. It was a sort of gallows humor. A way to deal with what should not have to be dealt with. "Old Betsy" sounded cute, intended to minimize the weapon.

Now John had his own Old Betsy. He hated her, but he needed her.

At the intersection, the street lights gleamed from the black paint of the following snow machines. There was no mistaking them for local machines, because the men riding them were in black parkas and balaclavas.

John sped up, forcing the riders to give chase. The engine in the Range Rover roared and the wheels dug into the snow-covered road.

On dry pavement, he might have outrun the snow machines. But on this stretch of treacherous road, he simply couldn't go fast enough. So he waited for the machines to close in.

"Here we go," he said, not really believing he was going to attempt what he was about to attempt.

He slammed both feet onto the brake pedal. The anti-lock system pushed back, making a sickening grinding noise as the brakes pulsed. John pushed harder. The tires skidded, rolled, skidded, rolled, the traction system keeping the vehicle as straight as the physics of a 5,238-pound SUV coming to a sudden stop on slick surface would allow.

The impact was sudden and loud. The center rider had less than three seconds to react. If he slowed at all before crashing into the back of the Range Rover, it made no difference to his flesh.

The debris of his snow machine flipped into the rear window, shattering it and sending shrapnel through the vehicle. Stings of glass and metal pricked John's scalp.

The Range Rover canted sideways, shoved by the impact into a flat spin. The traction control lost its mind and the vehicle spun, forcing John to tighten his grip on the steering wheel. The unexpected gyration caught the second rider trying to skirt the accident on the left. The front bumper of the Rover took off one ski and dislodged the man. The machine flipped and skidded away to the ditch, but the man kept going. The Range Rover's left wheels thumped over him as it continued to spin.

The final rider jerked his steering yoke in time to avoid the out-of-control vehicle, but the sudden change of direction flipped man and machine in a blur of metal, plastic, and flesh.

The Range Rover came to a stop facing the opposite direction of travel. John sat frozen in shock at the cacophony and absolutely insane daring of his stunt.

The smell of gasoline was heavy in the Range Rover. The fumes were already making him light-headed. A flicker of light in his rearview mirror drew his mind back to survival. Flames danced on the rear seats, and several chunks of shattered snow machine were wedged between the roof and floor of the cargo area.

The Range Rover's engine still purred. Grabbing Old Betsy, John climbed from the burning vehicle. He could easily imagine Dr. Sheldon's expression when she learned of her burned-out SUV. It would be like her expression at any other time, but perhaps a hint of fury in the eyes. John did not look forward to the inevitable conversation that began with him saying, "I slammed on the brakes so they would run into me."

The wind had picked up, presaging the impending snowstorm. He was at least three miles from the pump station. A walk of 45 minutes under a California sky, but here, going straight into the wind, it would likely be the last walk he took.

He shouldered Old Betsy and started. The land was flat, so he decided to go straight toward the lights in the distance, ignoring the road. The snow was blown away from the frozen ground here, so the footing was easy.

A whoosh sounded behind him as the Range Rover went up in more intense flames. Assuming it would explode once the gas tank got hot enough, he picked up his pace. The flames lit the way ahead, and he saw reflections off something shiny just a hundred yards away.

A snow machine. It lay on its side, skis facing him. The windscreen was missing, and the body was dented. The seat didn't seem to be on quite straight.

John got it upright and tried the motor. Miraculously, it started. He hopped on, tugged his balaclava more firmly over his nose, and gunned the engine. The machine lurched to one side, and he compensated by yanking on the yoke. Something had gotten twisted out of alignment, but it went straight enough once he got the hang of it. The headlight worked sporadically, giving him strobe-like glimpses of the ground ahead.

He twisted the throttle and blazed toward the pump station.

Chapter Thirty-Four

5:03 pm

The smell of blood had thickened since things had calmed down in the Coffins facility. The operation to remove the bombs from the wells was well underway.

Fox sat at his computer, keeping his eyes on the motion alerts coming in. He had a spreadsheet open with all the known bomb sites. As a volunteer entered a well shack and removed a bomb, Fox checked it off.

But since shooting that Russian, and then seeing the rest of the carnage John Goodnight had left in the lavatory, Fox's stomach had been fighting to squeeze out every hint of food. Not that anything could possibly remain.

"Frennly, there has to be a mop around here," Dr. Sheldon said to a man whose expertise was centered on metering the amount of oil flowing into various transfer stations. Despite his name, he was not a friendly man. And he had not volunteered to go into the field to remove C4. So Dr. Sheldon, whose assertion of authority both perplexed and comforted Fox, assigned him to cleaning up.

Frennly had dragged the dead outside, leaving long smears of blood on the floor. The man didn't seem especially grossed out, which was another strike against him as far as Fox was concerned.

Dr. Sheldon had helped remove Jackson Swan's body. Fox's dead supervisor now lay outside, too, but Dr. Sheldon had taken the extra measure of covering him with a tarp. When she'd returned, she'd drilled Fox on the progress of operations and demanded that he calculate the rate of removal and make estimates of when the entire project would be completed.

Fox welcomed these analytical tasks because it took his mind off the stench. "It's going to be close. The storm hasn't slowed and the track hasn't veered. The closer wells should get done in time, but those remote ones are, like, remote. Are the Inuit really willing to—"

"Eskimos," Dr. Sheldon said. "They aren't Inuit."

Fox flushed, chagrinned to get caught in such a cultural insensitivity. His mother would've made him do an extra hour of meditation and probably a three-day juice fast for such a transgression. "Sorry. But I thought—"

"You need to focus on the bombs."

"Sorry. I'm, like, stressed. But the, uh, Eskimos have the most ground to cover, and the storm will hit there first." He had a separate large-screen monitor hooked up to his computer to display a zoomed-in map of their zone of the project.

"What choice do they have?" Dr. Sheldon said. "There are rivers all through that region leading out to prime fisheries."

Frennly was huffing as he carried in a sloshing bucket, the pole of a mop over his shoulder. He spoke as if he were part of the conversation. "Five thousand gallons an hour on average from each of those wells. Each liter contaminates millions of liters of water."

"Well, at least the rivers are iced over," Fox said. "The oil won't get to the ocean."

"Sure it will. The oil is hot. It'll melt the ice and get right into the water. Come the thaw, more of it will wash downstream. The spill on the surface will bleed into the permafrost, destroying the micro-biome. And that's the beginning of the food chain. You'll have fewer bugs, fewer voles, and that means fewer birds. And on up it goes until the foxes and bears are starving."

Fox frowned at Frennly, though he couldn't blame the man for saying it like it was.

"I guess we'd better not fail," Fox said. "How can we help the Eskimos?"

Dr. Sheldon came to stand next to him. "By staying out of their way."

Chapter Thirty-Five

5:10 pm

John spotted his pickup truck idling behind the refinery. A stroke of fortune, and only possible because he had come straight across the tundra instead of following the road. He was only too happy to get off the damaged Ski-Doo.

Cassie had left his truck running, thank God. He got in, closed the door, and pulled off his gloves. His hands felt and moved like semi-frozen jelly. He would give himself just a minute. The ride had sapped all the warmth from his body and he doubted he could reliably pull a trigger in his current state.

From the outside, Pump Station One looked as dull and industrial as any large, metal-sided structure in the middle of nowhere could look. He feared what not-so-boring things might be happening inside. The fact that the facility was still standing provided a small measure of relief. Very small.

He reluctantly climbed out of his truck, noting that the

fuel gauge was approaching E. There was certain to be a supply of gasoline nearby, but he didn't have the time to go looking. And part of him doubted he would be needing the truck soon. If ever. This didn't feel like a situation one lived through.

The acrid smoke that met him inside the refinery almost sent him back into the cold. He wondered if Fedorov had already set the place on fire in hopes it would blow. But the darkness, and the extreme cold inside, suggested that whatever had burned in here had long gone out. The lights were out, and he had to wait for his eyes to adjust to the vague outdoor lights that filtered through the clerestory windows.

The yellow markings on the floor were his only guide forward. Bits of charred debris littered the place. He recognized one of the forks from a lift truck lying in the middle of an aisle. And near it what looked like a charred leg. The boot showed that it had been one of the Russians.

"Cassie Ingram," he said, "what the hell have you been up to?"

The answer became somewhat clearer when he got to the top of a stairway and found an office full of dead guys. All of them shot. It was a mirror scene to what he'd done in the monitoring center's lavatory.

The young woman intrigued him, but she scared him, too. He'd met many extremely smart and capable people in his college years, but not even the most aggressively-minded business majors had possessed Cassie's almost-crazy willingness to walk into danger.

On the other hand, she was the same age as thousands of soldiers going into the line of danger overseas, so he supposed it wasn't that odd. Maybe the disconnect was because of her fingernails, which she kept short, but painted a light blue. That hinted at what her real life was like, the kind where a woman her age could live in peace without the constant threat of violence hanging over her head. In contrast to that, he remembered the look in her eyes as she handled a Glock, or scanned her eyes over a dead man. There was something robotic in it—as if she could unplug her emotions. Or appear to do so.

An odd moment to be thinking of such things. He left the dead men in the refinery office and continued back to the door to the pump station.

A stray AK-47 magazine caught his eye. The weapon wasn't around. Did Cassie have it? He wouldn't be even slightly surprised. He came out into the pump facility, glad to be breathing fresher air. He stood upon a raised plat-form with steps leading down to the main floor.

Beyond the steel railing in front of him stood the massive pump that started the oil flow through the Trans-Alaskan pipeline. It sounded like it was still pumping, a continuous 4/4 beat at the speed of a typical AC/DC song.

The railing in front of him clanged, accompanied by the report of a rifle. John stumbled backward, his eyes lifting to where a sniper was aiming directly at his face. That had been a warning shot. He lowered Old Betsy to the deck and held his hands up.

The sniper didn't move, but he must have communi-cated through a headset radio because two Russians charged forward, guns at the ready. One grabbed him and shoved him toward the stairs, while the other kept the barrel of his AK-47 aimed at him. A bit of overkill, but in light of the devastation Cassie had apparently left in her wake, not surprising. That any remained to take him pris-oner was not a good sign.

John knew he had to play it cool. They didn't know that he had killed several of their compatriots yet. As far as they knew he was just a lone dude who'd come to see what was going on at the pump station. The shotgun would make sense to them, given the wreckage in the refinery. A guy in these parts would have such a weapon in his truck.

They didn't know he was friends with Cassie, either.

"I don't know what's going on here," he said, "but I don't want any part of it. I just work here."

He got a hard jab in the kidney in response. It hurt like hell but he kept going. This wasn't the time to give them excuses to beat him up or simply remove him from the board.

They took him to the pig bay. One of them had scooped up Old Betsy. They led him past the storage tanks and into a scene of blood and tension. He spotted Cassie right away, sitting on the floor near Fedorov, hugging her knees and looking somewhat chastened. A total act, he knew. He noticed her eyes shifting to another man near her. He was dark-headed and had a belt cinched around one thigh. Val. As soon John saw Cassie's face, he knew she loved the man.

Val was too old for her. But in John's experience, women never cared what he thought was good or bad for them. He let it go. A rail-thin Russian with gray eyes and a narrow face approached. "Why are you coming here?"

One of the men handed over Old Betsy. The young soldier took it, pumped the action, and then delivered it to Fedorov. The man was hard, lean, and obviously irritated by John's presence.

"I work here," John said. "I'm an ecological engineer." He nodded at the shotgun. "That's for bears."

Fedorov found this funny. He snickered, annoyance fading. "You are making joke? But no, bears are attacking people here sometimes. Many bears."

The other Russians joined his laughter, and then John caught on. The bear was the symbol of Russia, like the bald eagle was for the U.S. John allowed himself a weak laugh. He shook his head and said, "No, no. I mean real *Ursa Maritimus*." He made clawing motions. This sent the Russians into more bouts of laughter and exchanges of Russian joviality, much of it at John's expense, judging by the way they looked and pointed at him.

Cassie used their momentary distraction to remove a shoe. She rubbed her foot, pretending she had some sort of injury. But then she surreptitiously fished something out of her shoe and slipped her foot back in. John couldn't see what she'd palmed.

The Russians' mirth was interrupted by a jarring ringtone. The pop music was so out of place that John assumed the phone belonged to one of the captives. But the leader of the Russian terrorists picked up a phone and listened. *"Da. Voidite."*

"Sit, ecological engineer." Fedorov pointed at the floor between Val and Cassie. John moved promptly to avoid an accidental execution. He plopped next to Cassie and said, "Explosives in the pigs."

She swore, closing her eyes and making a very clear effort to stay relaxed. The girl was astonishing. Where did she get her equanimity from? John felt like he was going to have a panic attack at any second. Their situation couldn't be worse.

"So when is my dad getting here?" Cassie said. Fedorov ignored her. But John knew she'd been talking to him, not the Russian. She continued, "It's only twenty minutes from the clinic to here. He must be taking his sweet time."

Clever girl. That phone call Fedorov had just answered had to have been her father. He was probably telling

Fedorov that he had arrived in the parking lot. That meant time was about out. Cassie cast a glance toward the computer monitor on the desk in front of Fedorov. John recognized the map of the pipeline and deduced that the green lights on it were pigs in the pipe. The one farthest along was approaching Pump Station 4. The others were closing in on Stations Two and Three.

For the pigs to have traveled so far so fast, Fedorov must have ordered the lady next to him to increase the oil flow to dangerous levels. The pressure in the pipeline was kept fairly low in normal operation. It didn't need to be that high to deliver the heavy liquid to its destination. As long as a continuous flow arrived 800 miles south in Valdez, everyone was happy.

"Four pump stations," he said under his breath. Cassie nodded.

Footsteps echoed in the large space and Bryce Ingram walked in, a heavy, oversized parka making him look almost child-like. His pale face and haggard eyes made him anything but youthful. He looked defeated. His eyes fell on Cassie and a visible war raged on his face. Frustration, fear, outrage, and finally submission.

"Welcome, Mr. Ingram," Fedorov said. "You are in time." Fedorov motioned to the chair in front of the computer. "Please sit."

Ingram sat. "Please let these people go. Let my daughter go."

"Cooperating keeps her safe." Fedorov snapped his fingers and a man rushed forward with a tripod-mounted camera. It looked ten years out of date, the sort of home-movie camera John's mom had used to record birthday and solstice celebrations.

"I have script," Fedorov said, placing a crisp white sheet in front of Ingram.

Ingram's eyes narrowed as he read the script, and his face grew paler. "No. You can't do this."

"I *can* doing this," Fedorov said. "But world is knowing you let it happen."

Chapter Thirty-Six

5:28 pm

Cassie Ingram didn't hold out much hope for success. But she didn't require hope, merely effort. If her next action failed, then she doubted there would be opportunity for another attempt. People were going to die within the next five minutes. She might be one of them. She wasn't okay with that, but Kalov had taught her to move toward many situations she was not okay with.

Dad was now looking at the old-timey video camera Fedorov had brought. Fedorov stood off to the side, stilling holding Cassie's pistol. She had been puzzling over why he seemed so enamored by her weapon. He had an Serdyukov sidearm of his own, holstered at his side, and surely more comfortable in his grip than her small carry.

The puzzle piece didn't fit any explanation other than that he had a personal grudge against her father and that possessing his daughter's gun was a statement of his possession of her. Pretty creepy.

Dad started to read at Fedorov's motion to begin. "My name is Bryce Ingram. I am the CEO of Ingram ECO Power based in Houston, Texas. My company drills oil and sells it for . . . for massive profit. During my career I have encouraged my company to cut the corners and polluting the earth." Dad paused, obviously confused by the odd grammar and the astounding confession Fedorov had put in his mouth. "Today I am in Alaska. The pipeline here has enriched me. But I am never satisfied with the billions of dollars I am skimming from the pockets of the hard-working people of the world."

Dad stopped and stared defiantly at Fedorov. The Russian merely aimed the gun at Cassie. Dad bent to the script and picked up where he'd left off. "I have been given the choice to die here and set the workers free, or I can safely leave and they will die. I have chosen to live—"

Dad stood up and threw the paper aside. "No! Let them go. I will not be part of this." He looked into the camera and said, "I do not agree to that deal. I will not leave while any of these people remain."

Fedorov put his hand over the lens. The operator shut the camera off. The weapon came up again, and Cassie had the extreme displeasure of staring at the wrong end of her own Ruger. Not only did it send chills of fear through her, it infuriated her.

Dad shut up and moved to stand between Fedorov and Cassie. All eyes were on the two men. Even the Russian guards were watching. Cassie made her move, sliding the knife she'd pulled from her shoe to John. "Cut Val loose."

John pulled the blade into his hand and tucked it tight against his forearm.

Fedorov said, "We are trying one more time. Cassandra lives or dies. Your choose."

Dad's indignation faltered and then collapsed. "I'll read it. I'll read it."

The camera started again and Dad began from the top. His voice shook. The faces of the other prisoners turned ghostly pale as realization of what the script meant sank in. They were all going to die.

Dad got to the part about his choice to live and let other people die. But he added something. "I have been given a choice. I will be allowed to live and go free with my daughter, Cassandra, who is with me. My other choice is to die and let the workers go. I make the only choice a father can: To save my daughter."

He paused, waiting for Fedorov to object. The Russian tilted his head. "You are making yourself fool. Starting again."

Risky and foolish. Cassie didn't know whether to admire Dad's audacity or curse him. But the ploy created a few seconds of tense silence between Fedorov and Dad. And that was all John needed. He pretended to get faint. As he leaned back on his right elbow, his hand slipped toward the bindings holding Val's wrists behind his back. A quick jerk and Val's shoulders came forward. His hands were free.

"The knife," Val whispered. John handed it to him. Cassie *felt* Val's movements more than she saw them. She knew how he thought, and she guessed his tactical assessment would place priority on Blok. The thin, young Russian was the closest to Val, and he seemed the most dangerous next to Fedorov himself.

But the method of Val's attempt was nothing at all like what Cassie imagined. Instead of rolling toward Blok and dragging him to the floor, Val sprang up, belt falling away. It hadn't been cinched tightly at all.

In one motion—like a cobra striking—Val's arm extended as he rose to his feet. The four-inch blade plunged into Blok's neck, exactly at the throb of his carotid artery. Blok went down without making more than a gurgle.

Cassie moved with Val, though staying lower. Dad turned from the camera to see what the ruckus was all about. His eyes widened to see Cassie charging him. They went down together as Fedorov fired at her.

Val now had Blok's sidearm free. Pops and cracks resounded as he dropped a Russian gunman.

Cassie lunged to grab John's shotgun from the desk. She had never fired one, but she knew the principle. She dropped to the floor, rolling to keep herself a moving target. Fragments of concrete spat into her face as bullets impacted in front of her.

She had seen Blok pump the round into the chamber when he'd first taken the gun. She flipped the safety, lined up Fedorov, and fired. The blast rolled her completely onto her back and drove the stock of the weapon into her shoulder. Like getting kicked by a horse.

Cassie sucked air through her teeth and tried to get on top of the pain. Her ears rang from the blast. More pops broke through her muffled hearing. She looked for Fedorov, hoping to see him bleeding out on the floor, but he stood calmly in the face of fire, lining his sights on Val.

Because Cassie's dad had been in the way, Val had chosen to take out the other guards first. But it had left him open to Fedorov. The man wouldn't miss. Not at this range.

Desperately, Cassie worked the pump action, discharging the spent shell and seating a fresh one. She rolled and braced. Fedorov squeezed off shot after shot.

Cassie lined up her aim as best she could. She pulled tension onto the heavy trigger, then withdrew her finger as her sightline was obstructed. Becky, the pig lady, had made a run for it, putting herself right in the line of fire.

Cassie screamed for her to get down, but the woman just turned and looked at her in confusion. It was Dad who cleared Becky from the crossfire, grabbing a handful of her skirt and yanking her to the floor. Cassie heard the rip of machinegun fire off to her right. Fedorov lowered his weapon, a tendril of smoke climbing from the hot barrel.

Cassie fired. Fedorov didn't drop. He didn't even stagger. The bear slug had gone wide. She feverishly pumped the shotgun. John was shouting something at her, but she couldn't concentrate on his words.

Suddenly she was airborne, grabbed by her collar and belt. The Russian who grabbed her, tossed her. She tumbled wildly, coming down on a shoulder already throbbing from the shotgun's kickback. Her breath blew out of her body. The shotgun fell from her hands and slid across the concrete, hitting the body of her beloved Val.

He lay face down, cheek to the concrete. His eyes were open, but sightless. Heat tore open Cassie's throat, more painful than any bullet. She crawled toward Val, vision blurring. She got her hands on his face and pressed her nose to his cheek. Not knowing where the bullets had struck, she couldn't pull him into her arms and hold him the way her instincts cried out for her to do.

Rough, strong hands pulled her away, screaming and kicking. Like a wildcat she turned on the man, clawing and flailing. And then she went limp as a blow caught her across the face. Her already-muffled hearing gained a high-pitched ring and her vision swam.

The world of sound and feeling returned slowly from the momentary haze covering her stunned awareness.

Fedorov was holding her shoulders in his iron grip. "Stop." He backhanded her for emphasis, a measured swipe that stung her cheek but didn't break loose any teeth.

The shock of it sent her to her knees. Her hands went to her face and sobs convulsed her body.

"You are reading one more time," Fedorov said to her dad. "Say what writing says. I am killing someone now."

Cassie thought his odd English meant that last bit as a threat, but the snap of the Ruger brought her head up. Another prisoner went down. The rest of them cried out and cowered. Cassie noticed only one remaining Russian machine-gunner, the man who had thrown her through the air. And the sniper, she reminded herself. She must not forget him.

Dad read the script all the way through, not changing a syllable of the English-as-a-second-language wording. When he was done, Fedorov sent his man off with the camera. The man returned with it, now removed from the tripod. The red light on the front flashed, showing that it was still recording. The man panned across the living prisoners. Then he turned the camera onto Dad and finally to Cassie.

She reflexively straightened her hair, but found it still damp from the fire suppression sprinklers earlier. She became disgusted with her own ingrained vanity and the thoughtlessness of it in the face of the present catastrophe.

She looked away from Val, unwilling to have this image of him sink into her memory.

Fedorov opened a duffle bag and removed a thin tablet computer. Its cover folded out into a keyboard. Attached to the tablet by a curly cord was a small box with a thick black antenna jutting up. Fedorov flipped a switch on the box and a green light came on. It was obviously a radio transmitter.

"It goes as I plan," Fedorov said, smiling. "Valentine dead is your choosing." He turned an eye toward Blok, whose lifeless body lay just beyond Val's. "Blok is pity. I would enjoying killing him myself." He raised a walkie-talkie to his lips and spoke a blur of Russian. There was no response, so he repeated his request.

He looked perturbed. Again he spoke into the device. A long silence hung there and was never relieved by a response. He looked at the device, the first sign of genuine worry crossing his face. The moment of emotion drew Cassie's attention and yanked at the part of her mind that Kalov—and Val—had molded into a puzzle-solving machine.

Mourning Val had to wait. She had a responsibility to herself, her father, to John Goodnight—who was sitting on the floor and looking as exhausted as she felt—and the rest of the prisoners.

She even felt a responsibility to Sven, the huge Swede who now lay dead on the floor, the man she didn't know but whose sense of chivalry had forced him to stand when Blok had frisked her so brazenly.

Fedorov was a liar. Nothing had gone according to his plan. She had known that for some time now. She had been the wrench in his machine, the fly in the ointment, the pig in the garden. And she was not done yet.

Kalov had given her several mnemonic devices to help her assess a situation. The one that had saved her life in the coffee shop was L.I.V.E.

She had to skip over "L," which stood for Lie Low. That was pretty much out the window in the current circumstances. "I" stood for investigate. Fedorov, the camera guy, the one remaining gunman, and a sniper.

All men armed. Cameraman didn't have his AK-47 in hand. It hung on his torso, secured by a tactical harness.

Twelve surviving prisoners, including several she had seen in the storeroom with Goatee. Then there was Dad. He wasn't looking so hot.

Where was Uncle Dev? He must still be back at the clinic. Fedorov had decided not to demand that he come. That was interesting. Maybe it was because Cassie had taken out so many of his men. Maybe Fedorov had a ratio of gunmen to prisoners he wanted to maintain. But maybe it was mere oversight due to his mounting stress.

John's shotgun was now back on the desk, but she'd seen the remaining gunman remove the shells. Val's body had been kicked over and the weapon he'd taken from Blok retrieved. Cassie cursed herself for not grabbing the pistol when she'd been next to him.

Blok had taken her remaining lighter and spare 9mm rounds when he'd frisked her. Her pockets were empty. In sum, the "I" part of the L.I.V.E process didn't reveal much. Which brought her to "V."

"V" stood for Viable Plan. Kalov had emphasized that "viable" meant something she could survive. It didn't mean avoid all risk or even avoid all injury.

In the current situation, she could play along with Fedorov and maybe live. Fedorov likely wanted her and her father to leave Alaska intact, to be subject to the scorn and humiliation of the entire world. Even given the chance to explain that Fedorov hadn't given them a choice, most people would only see the hated executive and his spoiled daughter. The blame would be multiplied by the ecological disaster Fedorov planned to set off.

Going along with things was not a viable plan.

There was no viable plan.

The final letter in the acronym was "E." That stood for "execute" and it meant full-out, total commitment to the plan.

In summation, L.I.V.E. revealed absolutely nothing hopeful in this situation. But the process helped anyway, because it revealed to her the simplicity of her choice.

There was only one. She needed to attack, soon, and with total expectation of death.

Chapter Thirty-Seven

5:30 pm

"Status on that storm front, Fox?" Dr. Sheldon said. She had the phone tucked between her ear and shoulder, a legal pad and blue Bic in her hands.

"Right on schedule," Fox said. The radar installation at Barrow showed a band of blue and violet creeping eastward. The first fringes of snow were already hitting the farthest wells.

Dr. Sheldon scribbled on her notepad, then hung up. Fox glanced at the nearly-illegible scrawl when she bent over his shoulder to study his spreadsheet. He'd exed off a third of the sites so far.

Her pad was a simple list of ten names. He couldn't make them out, but he didn't need to read them to know they were the names of the Eskimos who were out in the field. Three had checkmarks next to their names. He assumed those were the ones who had returned to safety.

"How do you know them so well?" he asked, nodding at her list.

"I sometimes see them as patients. But I made good friends with an Inupiaq family through their son, who I knew in college."

"Is that who you're talking to now?"

"No. Their son died in an oil rig accident out in the bay. I'm talking to *his* son, Peter." She looked at the list. For the first time in Fox's brief acquaintance with her, she looked truly distraught. "He's still out there."

Fox pulled up his array of camera feeds from the remote wells. "Do you know which wells he was going to? Maybe I can spot him on the feed recordings."

Dr. Sheldon flipped up a page and scanned her scribbles. "He checked in at a site called Jack-Five. Owned by Ingram ECO. He was going to Jack-Six but hasn't checked in there."

"Maybe there was radio interference from the storm," Fox said, clicking his keyboard to bring up the feeds for the Jack-Five and Jack-Six wells. The video was grainy and had the green cast of the night-vision mode. Fox triggered some macros to skip ahead to the recordings' motion detection points. Time code played in block numerals at the bottom of the feeds. The figure moving around the well shack at Jack-Five was small and bundled head-to-toe in parka, thermal snow pants, thick boots, gloves, and head coverings that disguised all facial features. It could have been anyone out there. John had to assume it was the guy in question. "What was his name again?"

"Peter," she said.

He tagged the figure on the screen as "Peter" and started the gait analysis algorithm. It came back with a medium score, which meant it might be able to ID him again if he appeared in a different video.

The figure had been at Jack-Five thirty minutes ago. The bomb removal took all of two minutes, including the cutting of the receiver wires. Then Peter was out of view and presumably off to Jack-Six.

"Let me see . . ." Fox studied the map. Gauging by the distance between the two well sites, he figured it would take Peter only ten minutes to get to Jack-Six. He skipped forwarded on that well's feed and searched for motion detection. But there was nothing.

Now he was worried. He rewound the video and set it to play back at 5x speed. Fast enough to scan visually, but not so fast that a guy could come and go and be missed.

Dr. Sheldon didn't require any explanation to understand what Fox was doing. She hovered behind him, projecting tense vibes. When it was clear that Peter hadn't shown up at Jack-Six, she backed away and went to a phone in the far corner of the room.

Fox felt useless, but he didn't know what else to do. He set the Jack-Six feed to ping him if anything moved there, and put the well's feed on the big screen.

A few more bomb removals had been completed in the other zones, so he marked them off on his spreadsheet. As long as the Russians didn't hit the red button—wherever they had it—it looked like the nearer wells would be clear in fifteen minutes or so. Even at that moment seven new motion alerts popped up, showing the arrival of team members at more wells.

Chapter Thirty-Eight

5:35 pm

The Russian man with the video camera had it pointed at Bryce Ingram, who now sat in Becky's seat. The keyboard for the computer that monitored the pipeline and the progress of the pigs had been moved aside to make room on the desk for a leather briefcase.

"Say lines," Fedorov said to Cassie's dad. "I am getting many angles for video."

Dad said the lines. "I choose doing this to save my life." He spoke through clenched teeth, as if fighting to keep the words in.

"Now, opening briefcase," Fedorov urged.

Dad thumbed the brass latch releases. They flipped up with sharp snaps. He looked to Fedorov for his next order. The Russian made an opening motion with his hands. Dad did so.

From where Cassie sat on the floor, she couldn't see much. But the briefcase appeared to be tightly packed with paper bundles. Or maybe some brick-like objects wrapped in paper. John whispered, "That's C4."

Dad must have recognized it, for his face went white. "So much?"

Fedorov kept himself out of the frame of the video. He said, "Remove bag. Detonator and transmitter."

Dad pulled out a zip baggie. Inside was a silver cylinder about the width of a pencil. Wires were attached at one end. He removed another black box and set it on the desk.

"Remove from bag."

Dad removed the detonator and set the baggie aside.

Fedorov motioned for Dad to push the silver cylinder into a brick of explosives. Dad obeyed.

"Connect wire at transmitter box."

Dad fumbled with the thin wires. One white, one green. They terminated in plastic connectors of the same colors. There were obvious connection points on the top of the transmitter box.

Cassie thought she understood. When Dad was forced to press a button on the tablet, the black box would detonate the briefcase. But Fedorov had called the box a transmitter.

Ice cut through her stomach, realizing that it would send a signal to detonate the bombs at the well-heads. Everything would blow all at once.

Fedorov would record the catastrophe, and then he would distribute the video for the world to see. For the rest of Dad's life—for the rest of Cassie's—the crime would stick to their names, to their hearts. To their souls.

"You can refuse, Daddy," she said. "I'm ready." She was not at all ready.

Dad sobbed and shook his head. He would make no decision that killed his daughter, no matter the consequences. He continued to fasten the locking nuts on the black box's connectors. Once he was finished, Fedorov made him face the camera again and read from the script. "I leave these people behind to die. They are hard-working and innocent. But they pay the price for my greed and crimes."

"Pressing button. Now." Fedorov pointed at the tablet.

Dad looked at the device, but he didn't push it. Confusion furrowed his brow. But Cassie understood. The button push wouldn't detonate anything immediately. It would start a countdown. That would give Fedorov and his remaining crew time to evacuate with Dad and her.

Fedorov shot Gergi, the septuagenarian from the storage room group who had guessed that Fedorov's interest in pigs had something to do with sabotaging the pipeline. The man didn't make a sound but simply slumped from his chair, hole in his forehead.

"I'm pressing it! I'm pressing it!" Dad said, voice cracking. He thumbed the screen and leaned away from it, lips trembling.

Cassie's eyes skimmed across the scene, searching for any way out. And now that it came to it, she wondered how the Russians would keep the prisoners from leaving once they fled the ticking bomb. The answer to that question came instantly. At a word from Fedorov, he and the remaining machine-gunner began to fire.

Three people fell before the rest understood what was happening. Now that he had the video of Dad assembling the explosives and pressing the button, he didn't need to keep these people alive for the explosion itself.

Cassie leapt to her feet and charged.

Chapter Thirty-Nine

5:37 pm

The chime from Fox's computer terminal cut through all other noise in the Consortium Oil Fields Monitoring Station. A window popped up. MOTION JACK-SIX. Fox whistled through his teeth to get Dr. Sheldon's attention. "We got movement, yo."

He launched the gait recognition algo and zoomed the camera. A figure moved toward the well shack, grainy and barely distinguishable in the flurry of snow that had now begun falling over the area.

"Is that Peter?" Dr. Sheldon asked.

The computer churned as its processor strained to apply its algorithm to the steps it detected. There were only five full strides of clear motion before the figure opened the door and disappeared inside. Would it be enough to make a match?

Yes. With a confidence of 70%, the computer displayed: SUBJECT UNKNOWN. It wasn't Peter. Fox looked down. "I'm sorry, Dr. Sheldon. But if that's, like, not Peter, who is it?"

"He was teamed with his cousin, but they split up to cover more wells in less time. So . . ."

Fox knew what she was thinking. Most likely this was Peter's cousin. But Peter had been clear in his last transmission that he was heading to Jack-Six. Something had happened to him. It could have been anything. The cold, a snow machine accident, or simply a breakdown. Maybe a run-in with a polar bear. "He might have misspoken," Fox said, searching for hope. "Maybe he, like, meant he was heading to . . . " He searched the remaining sites for an alternative, but the only site that would have made sense was Jack-Six.

"I'm his godmother," Dr. Sheldon said softly. "I haven't been a very good one."

The phone in the back corner started ringing. Dr. Sheldon glanced at it. She gave herself a shake and went to answer it. Fox continued to study the map of the Eskimos' zone of operation. It was such a barren landscape at this time of year. The thought of being lost out in that darkness with a storm closing in made him shiver.

Dr. Sheldon snapped her fingers. "Fox. Come here."

She was smiling. No, she was grinning. "Peter called in," she said, hand pressed over the receiver. "He found the Russians' transport caravan. A big track-truck towing a fuel wagon and several cargo haulers for the snow machines."

The bastards must have driven over the frozen stretches of the Chukchi Sea. It was a nutty stunt, but here they were. Fox sighed in relief. "I hope he didn't, like, stay there long. He'll be lost on Hoth without a Tauntaun."

When Dr. Sheldon raised an eyebrow in recognition of Fox's reference, they both shared a grin. Finally, something had gone their way.

"Fox," Frennly called from across the room. "Look!"

On another video feed, a volunteer was backing away from a well shack. He had his hands out in the universal motion of "Easy, easy. I don't want to fight."

"A Russian?" Fox asked.

"Maybe."

Fox raced back to his terminal and zoomed out the camera. What he saw made him go all loose and hot inside. A polar bear was moving forward, head low, and making short, aggressive lunges at the man.

And then it charged. The man went down under the green-tinged image of the polar bear. Fox was grateful for the grainy night-vision video. The bear was not merciful and it was not quick.

"We need to get someone out there to help him," Dr. Sheldon said. "And to clear that shack's explosive charge."

Fox was already on it. Anything to avoid looking at the carnage on the feed. But what he discovered didn't help. The closest man was thirty miles east. In fact, the monitoring facility was closer.

Dr. Sheldon patted her revolver. "I'll go. I'm the only one qualified to deal with his injuries."

Fox looked up at her. "First, that dude's dead. Second, your leadership is needed here. I'll go. We've got, like, a million AK-47s to spare. I should be able to take the bear out with one of those, right?"

What he didn't say was that he felt useless here. He was pretty much duplicating work the computer and Frennly could handle. He expected Dr. Sheldon to stare him down, but she pressed her lips together and nodded. If she left Coffins now, all the communication flow that coordinated the teams would have to go through him. And he didn't have the authoritative snap in his voice that she did.

He got his parka and balaclava and gloves and made

his way into the cold. The well site was just down the road. He looped the strap of an AK over his neck, revved up the snow machine engine, and sped toward a bomb and a bear.

Chapter Forty

5:37 pm

Cassie jammed her chin into Fedorov's side. Her legs wrapped around his. Her forearm shoved into his Adam's apple. The takedown had been fast, violent, and ruthless.

And she wasn't done yet. He still had her gun. She hadn't been able to count the shots he'd expended in his assassination of prisoners—and Val—but she had no doubt that he had a couple rounds remaining. Already he was straining to bring the weapon around.

The machine gun fire stopped, followed by shouts and sounds of struggle. Another burst fired, someone cried out, then all fell into the relative quiet of individual battles of flesh and bone.

Cassie would have had no chance against a man of Fedorov's strength and training without the secret sauce of surprise. But even that wasn't enough to defeat him outright. She strained to keep the gun pointed away from her, but that forced her to release leverage elsewhere.

The barrel of her Ruger LC9s continued to turn

toward her. Fedorov was gritting his teeth, whole body straining. Only the position and leverage she'd gained on him prevented her swift execution. As it was, she was in a slow motion death, like a stranded motorist watching the landslide descending, helpless to escape.

"Desperation makes for desperate moves," Kalov had often said. Here, all that remained to Cassie was one final gambit. Pulling her arm from Fedorov's throat, she clawed up his chin, across his nose, seeking eye sockets with her fingers.

The shot was so loud Cassie felt like the world had blown apart. Her fingernails scraped over Fedorov's face, nails seeking to pull back eyelids, to dig deep into the soft tissue there and probe until she got a grip on his skull.

She didn't hear her own screams, but felt the fire in her throat.

The next shot came from an entirely different direction than she'd expected. From behind. Fedorov went limp in her grasp, all fight draining away in an instant.

Heat dampened her shirt, her face, her hands. A hot gush of Fedorov's blood. She released him, shocked to still be alive, stunned by the enormous blast of the slug than had nearly severed the Russian man's right arm.

John Goodnight stood a yard away, barrel of his shotgun smoking. His nostrils were flared like a raging bear ready to attack.

Across the space, two prisoners stood over the body of the video camera guy. He was lying on the concrete with his head centered in an expanding pool of blood. Three more prisoners held down the final machine-gunner. He struggled, but one prod of his ribs with the barrel of his confiscated AK-47 was all he needed to get the hint. The people guarding him included Becky, the pig lady.

Cassie pulled her hands from Fedorov's face and

pushed his inert body away from her. Her hands were cramping, her thighs burning from clamping Fedorov into immobility. "Am I hit?"

"I don't think so," John said. His voice was raw. He must have been shouting the whole time. "He fired, but—"

Cassie was so exhausted she accepted John's hand to help her to her feet. Her legs trembled—from the exertion, from relief.

Dad lay slumped on the floor, not moving. Gasping and coughing, Cassie waved at Becky. "Get over here and shut these pigs down." She pointed at the screen.

"It doesn't work that way," John said. "There's nothing she can do from here."

"Just get her!" Cassie went to her father and lifted his chin. His head lolled and his body slid from where it was propped against the desk to flop onto the floor. He wasn't breathing. Cassie searched him for wounds, but found none. She pressed two fingers to his throat but found no pulse. "Dad!" she screamed, voice breaking. She rubbed his cheeks. "Daddy!"

"Sweetie, over there." A lady was pointing at a lump of black in the shadows. It was her father's luggage. Cassie sprinted for it, tore it open, hands trembling in her haste to find his toiletry bag. She dumped it out and snatched up the bottle of nitroglycerin pills.

She tumbled a few into her hand and ran back to her father. She shoved a pill under his tongue. "Won't do any good if he's not breathing," the woman said. She was bleeding but she pushed Cassie aside and started CPR on Bryce Ingram.

John returned with Becky. She shook and cried. John got her seated, and in unbelievably calm tones had her explain everything on her computer monitor. Even the things that anyone would intuitively understand. Slowly she calmed and was able to focus on the problem. Cassie took this in through her peripheral awareness. Nothing much mattered if Dad didn't make it.

But then he began to sputter, his chest convulsing. He drew in ragged gulps of air. The woman who had saved his life leaned back on her heels. She wavered, then fainted.

"I can't!" Becky yelled at John, her hands on her face, head shaking. "The pigs are just dumb objects. They're pushed along by the flow. I can't make them stop and turn around. Look, they're in the pump stations now."

Dad raised a hand and pointed at the tablet Fedorov had set up. It had flopped over onto its screen during the fight. "Timer." Dad got nothing else out before losing consciousness. He still breathed, though.

Cassie put the tablet upright. The screen didn't show anything beyond the countdown to destruction in large white letters on a black background. It would have been ideal for the video guy to capture the last seconds, a distant shot of the explosions and then to pan to Dad and Cassie's faces. "We have twenty-three minutes to clear the pigs."

"Then it's over already," Becky said. "Like I told you, there's nothing we can do. We can't even get to Pump Station Two in under twenty minutes. Forget about the others."

Cassie looked at the pipeline map, desperation making her thoughts slow. She had done all she could. Without people down the line at the other pump stations to pull the pigs, stations 2, 3, and 4 were going to blow.

This is what it felt like to lose your hold on the edge of the cliff, to see the safety fall away to heaven as you spent the last moments falling to hell. "Is there someone who can disarm this briefcase?" she said. It was an absent question, like asking if anyone had mosquito repellent at a picnic— an annoyance to be dealt with.

John picked up a phone. He held it to his ear and asked a couple questions. Then, "We need Fox down here. The explosives are all triggered by a transmitter. It's a tablet. Power it down? If we're wrong, we—yes, I understand we're screwed either way, Doctor. That's why I want Fox. He's a computer guy—I see. Okay. Yes. Wait, um, Mr. Ingram is here. He had a heart attack. The woman who saved him has a gunshot wound. Several others do, too. Okay. Thank you."

John hung up. "The techie guy I know had to go into the field to pull a bomb from a well site. He's out. Dr. Sheldon is sending Dr. Limon here to treat the injured. We have to get this woman's bleeding under control. And she thinks we should just turn off the transmitter."

The black antenna sat on the desk, attached by cables to the tablet. A green light on a little black box at the base was the only indication the device did anything at all.

But the box worried Cassie. The little she knew about radio communication had come from using walkie-talkies with Kalov during her first round of training a year ago. The signal carried through the air like any old radio station. The reach of the signal was determined by the power of the transmitter. She didn't think such a small box could broadcast very far. So its signal couldn't reach the first pig, let alone the farthest one out.

She turned a slow circle, taking in the scene. What was she missing? Her eyes came to rest on the video camera. The whole thing had been staged as a video production, a way for Federov to serve a third goal. First had been ransom money. Second had been to destroy oil production here and drive up prices for Russian oil. Third had been a personal vendetta against her father, and the weird video had been central to that. But that told her the tablet and antenna were a bit of theater to make the video more tense and dramatic.

"The transmitter sends a signal to a higher-powered transmitter somewhere else, a repeater with enough oomph to reach the pigs down the line. And all the well-heads."

That felt right. But it also told her she couldn't power off the antenna or the tablet. The loss of signal from the tablet would likely trigger a sort of dead man's switch at the high-powered transmitter. Such switches were common on power tools and even exercise equipment like the tread-mills she used to run on in the summer. If the operator fell, a dead man switch turned the device off. But in this case, it would be like pressing a "detonate" button.

"We have to take out the relay transmitter," she said.

"Where would it be?" John had bunched up Dad's coat and was pressing it to Becky's wound. His hands were nearly black with blood and filth. His face hadn't fared any better. He was a mirror of her, she supposed.

Cassie knew exactly where the transmitter was. "As long as your truck's not out of fuel, I think we can make it."

They recruited a prisoner to look after Dad and Becky. Taking the briefcase and the transmitter with them, they fled the pig bay and raced toward the refinery.

The sniper was waiting for them.

Chapter Forty-One

5:40 pm

Fox Tils steered the snow machine to the well site, slowing to let the headlight show what dangers lay ahead. Based on the position of the camera, he knew that the bear and dead man were on the opposite side of the well shack.

He made a slow, wide turn. The headlight beam blazed from the animal's white fur. The animal looked back from its kill, eyes flashing.

Fox accelerated, revving the engine for maximum noise. The bear took that as a challenge and stood. Fox swore and swerved. The beast's snout and jaw were stained red with blood. The mangled body of the volunteer lay in the snow behind it.

Fox made a loop and stopped well away from the bear. He brought his AK-47 around and checked that the safety was off. He lined up the sight on the animal.

The beast had killed a man. That was an automatic death sentence for any wild animal anywhere in the world. Civilization couldn't tolerate such a specimen to live, for once it had tasted man-flesh it would forever see men as food.

But killing it went against Fox's nature. Especially since he'd started working on the recognition algos to help study the animals. He aimed his weapon high and fired a burst. The gun jerked awkwardly in his hand. The bear ducked and retreated.

Fox fired again, then yanked the throttle to make the snow machine lurch toward the animal. Another burst of bullets, this time at the ground near the bear's feet. Spouts of snow and permafrost kicked into the bear's face.

Finally it turned and loped off into the darkness. Fox didn't waste time watching it go. He zoomed right to the well shack door and jumped off. He was inside and shining a light around for the bomb in seconds.

"Where are you, you bastard?" he muttered. "Where the hell are you?"

But there was no bomb. He clicked on his radio. "Dr. Sheldon? Frennly? Can you check my well site logs and make sure there was ever any Russian motion here? I'm not seeing, like, any C4."

The response came seconds later. "We're watching your shack on the feed now." It was Dr. Sheldon's voice. "I can confirm Russian motion one hour thirteen minutes ago. Maybe they didn't leave a charge there for some reason."

Fox looked into every corner and nook of the machinery. Even at the ceiling. The support rafters and beams provided ideal spots, but there was nothing to find.

"Wait," Dr. Sheldon said. The radio hissed and crackled with static. "The video clearly shows that the Russian never left."

"What?"

"Fox. There's somebody in there with you."

"There can't be. His snow machine would still be outside."

"He never left, so he has to be there somewhere. Maybe he got injured. Maybe his snow machine broke down and he walked there. He would be half-frozen if that happened."

Fox kept his weapon up, flashlight braced to shine in the same direction as the barrel. He'd seen this done in a movie once. The posture might have felt badass if he wasn't so scared.

He glanced everywhere but didn't see any place a man could hide.

Until he spotted the hatch in the floor. A hinge on one side, a ring handle on the other. He had stepped over it three times, but hadn't noticed because it was made out of the same metal grating as the floor.

It was exactly where a cold man would go because of the warmth of the oil coming up from the earth. Fox propped the flashlight on a control panel and aimed it as best he could toward the hatch.

With one hand free he opened the hatch, pointing the AK-47 into the darkness.

Warm air welled out and washed over him. The flashlight shined into the gray eyes of a young man awkwardly trying to aim an AK back at Fox. Neither of them fired. Fox because of pure paralysis of mind. The Russian because his fingers were so frostbitten he could barely cup the weapon in his hands.

Fox lowered his gun and motioned for the Russian kid to do the same. And he *was* just a kid. Maybe nineteen. His lips were blue, and his entire body quivered.

"Do you speak English?" Fox asked.

"Yes. Are you going to shoot me?"

"No. Where is your bomb?"

The boy's eyes fell to a spot beneath the hatch. The C4 was stuck in place, armed and ready to blow. The kid had known he was going to die.

"Hand me your gun, yo," Fox said. "I'll help you."

The kid hesitated. He had no reason to trust Fox. The reverse was also true, Fox realized. But his instincts told him that this was one chance to avoid bloodshed. He wouldn't take the easy way out and just shoot the kid.

But first, the bomb. The Russian relented and lifted his arms as best he could. Fox took his AK and slung the strap over his shoulder. Then he pried the C4 brick from the wall and snipped the detonator wire. When the brick didn't blow up, he let out a huge sigh and laughed.

The Russian seemed relieved, too. Fox doubted the kid knew how the explosive worked. He'd likely seen the same movies Fox had, and probably thought cutting wires willy-nilly would make the thing go off.

Fox put the C4 in his parka pocket, the detonator in the other. Then he went down the rungs and started hoisting the kid out. Not easy. The boy's legs were almost as useless as his hands. But with some grunting and swearing, Fox got him out of the hatch.

He clicked the radio. "I've got the Russian. Bad frost-bite. Nearly hypothermic. Do I risk bringing him back to the control center?"

"Put him outside," Frennly said. "The bear's back."

Fox leaned against the shack door, arms holding the kid upright.

An idea came to him. A stupid, insane idea. But he decided to ask.

"Yo, is Denny White Eagle still around?"

"Why?"

"I'm thinking I know how to scare off that bear. Big time."

"I'll find him," Frennly said. "Meantime, shoot that Russian."

The kid heard the comment. He probably thought whoever was on the other end of the conversation was Fox's superior. He started to struggle. "No. Don't shoot me. I don't want to die."

Fox nudged the kid. "Shut up. If I was going to shoot you, I would have, like, done it by now." He dug in a pocket and found a half-eaten Snickers bar. He shoved it at the kid's mouth. "Eat this."

Denny White Eagle's voice came through, aged but clear. "Frennly told me about your predicament. I think I know what your question is. Here's what you do. I hope you have a knife. You need to cut off a slice about the width of your thumb. Then put the detonator in it. You'll have to sacrifice your flashlight."

Fox followed the instructions, and the wind continued to howl.

Chapter Forty-Two

5:40 pm

The sniper stood on the stairs leading to the refinery door. His rifle was aimed directly at John. Cassie put her arms up, aware that the Serdyukov 9mm in her hand and the shotgun in John's were not the best things to be waving around.

"Let me put this down," she said, slowly crouching.

The sniper allowed them to set their weapons down. "And the case," he said, motioning with the barrel of his gun for John to put the briefcase full of C4 on the floor.

"Listen, Fedorov is dead," Cassie said. "The others are dead. You're the last Russian here. There's no reason you can't leave us. We can't stop you, and you could get away before the Marines arrive."

He kept his cool gaze on her, unfazed by her words. Now that he was closer, Cassie noticed his age. He was at least sixty. This was not your average gunner. "Fedorov got the ransom money," she said. "If you have access to those accounts, you can have all of it. One hundred million dollars."

He didn't speak, and he didn't blink. But he stepped backward, one slow step at a time. And then he slipped through the door and was gone. Cassie looked at John and he looked back.

"He could've shot us," John said as he bent to retrieve his shotgun and the briefcase. "Why didn't he?"

Cassie couldn't know for sure, but she had an idea. "He reminds me of another Russian I know." Though there wasn't any physical resemblance to Kalov, there was a likeness in their postures. It spoke of similar training. Similar thinking. "Snipers are highly trained. Killing is a forward decision. The default choice is to not pull the trigger. He saw that I was right. He didn't need to kill us to get away with $100 million."

But that wasn't going to be true, she knew. If she survived, finding that man would be the object of her every waking hour. He may not have killed Val, but he was part of the group who had.

"I think we've given him enough time to get away," she said. "Let's go turn off that radio transmitter." Together they plunged into the acrid darkness of the refinery. The fire suppression had left the floor slick with a water and ash mixture that clung to their shoes.

The truck was still running. John got into the driver's seat and handed Cassie his shotgun. "Here. Take Old Betsy."

Cassie took it. "Old Betsy?"

He said, "There are more rounds in the glove box. I don't think there are any more Russians to shoot, though."

"Let's hope not." Cassie propped the tablet in her lap. The countdown had decreased to twenty minutes.

John whistled through his teeth. "Let's hope this truck's

fuel gauge isn't accurate. Because we're bottoming out on E."

"Nineteen minutes," Cassie said.

Since they didn't have time to conserve fuel by going slowly, John drove them down the ice-covered road at full speed.

Chapter Forty-Three

5:45 pm

The Russian kid's name was Ivan. He was eighteen and a half. He had perked up a little after eating the rest of Fox's Snickers bar. He was also intensely curious to watch Fox slice off a chunk of C4, press the detonator into it, and then wire it to the disassembled flashlight switch. "Bomb will explode when you switch on," Ivan said. "We will die."

Fox had said pretty much the same thing to Denny once the scope of the hacked-together explosive was explained to him. "I wasn't planning on making it easier for the bear to dine on my guts."

Denny explained that if Fox kept the door between him and the sliver of C4, the blast would project away from the shack and make a big boom. "You might blow out your eardrums," Denny had said, as if he was explaining that it might rain. "Just make sure you have enough wire between the switch and the explosive."

Fox now held the bomb in both hands. He stretched

the slack out of the wire. Five feet. "Won't this just do the Russians' job for them?"

"You don't have to set it off," Dr. Sheldon said over the radio. "But we're looking at the video feed, and that bear is pacing back and forth by the door. You could shoot it."

"*Da!* Shoot him," Ivan said, nodding vigorously.

Fox didn't want to shoot it. He sliced a bit off his C4 bomb to make the explosion smaller. All he wanted was a boom to scare the beast away. He cracked the door, tossed the C4 onto the snow, then closed the door, wire leading to the flashlight in his hands. He clicked his radio. "Tell me when the feed shows the bear isn't too close."

"I'll tell you," Frennly said.

"There's a lag between what's happening here and what you see on the video. About seven seconds."

"Got it."

"I'm ready."

"Now!"

Chapter Forty-Four

6:01 pm

The only radio station broadcasting from Deadhorse was KDHS. It didn't have a DJ. In fact, it didn't have any staff at all aside from the occasional maintenance guy who came up from Fairbanks once every three months to service the equipment.

KDHS amounted to a rather old computer server with a hard drive full of audio files. It broadcast country music 24/7, on an A.M. station. The broadcast antenna stood outside the Sag River Motel. A power station sat next to it, a gray box with a plain, utilitarian hinged door and two key holes.

"Two minutes," Cassie said.

John had taken Old Betsy from her. He put the barrel to the top keyhole and fired. The bear slug blasted a smoking hole in the metal. There was no sign of either lock mechanism remaining.

Cassie opened the door. Inside was a control panel and a big lever marked MAIN TRANSMITTER POWER. A safety button kept it secure, but she thumbed it aside and yanked the lever down.

There was no outward sign that it had worked. They went back to John's truck and tuned to the station. The only sound coming across was static.

The tablet read one minute. "This is it," Cassie said. "Now we have to pull this little antenna and disconnect it."

"Do it," John said.

"I hope everybody is out of the field," he said. "This little thing might have just enough power to reach the nearest wells." No point in delaying. It would either work or it wouldn't.

Cassie switched off the antenna's power and then unplugged the cable connecting it to the briefcase.

When nothing happened, she and John sighed with relief.

Her eyes opened slowly as a distant boom rattled the vents in the dashboard. And then another sounded. Another, and another. Finally the resonate thunder faded to stillness. John's face lit up with the faint glow of fire as a huge ball of flame rose to the sky in the distance.

"Oh no," Cassie said. Twisting, she looked toward the pump station. No explosion there. And that was no surprise. The briefcase meant to destroy it was on the floor next to Cassie's feet. It hadn't gone off.

"The field teams must not have gotten them all," John said, face grim. "We'd better get out to the monitoring center."

He backed up and started driving. He stopped at a fuel depot. "We have to be smart," he said. "There's so much to be done, it would be irresponsible to freeze to death on the side of the road because I was too stupid to get gas."

Cassie nodded, but she couldn't bring herself to care. What could be done anyway? They had failed. All she could think about was that Val had died in vain, her Dad had suffered a heart attack, and the poor artic foxes were now at risk because of Fedorov.

That sniper, whoever he was, had better run fast and he had better run far.

Chapter Forty-Five

<hr>

6:03 pm

The well shack trembled as the concussion wave passed over. The explosion had given Fox a second of total despair.

Finally, his brain figured out that he wasn't injured at all.

"So loud," he said, but barely heard his own voice. Danny White Eagle must have lost his mind if he thought that was just a little boom.

But then Fox looked at the flashlight in his hand. He hadn't even flipped the little slider switch on the side. He got to his knees and opened the door. Light washed in, blinding him. An enormous tower of flame stood high into the air, black curls of smoke billowing into the polar night sky.

"Damn." They must have missed removing a bomb.

"Bear? Dead?" Ivan asked.

The bear was gone. Fox didn't need any more entice-ment. He helped Ivan to his feet and half-carried him to the snow machine. "I hope you don't, like, freeze to death on the ride."

Ivan would have to sit behind him. He'd have to hold on to him. Fox looked into the kid's eyes. "Promise you won't try to throw me off this thing."

"I promise." The boy looked back at the now-fading column of fire. "What choice I have?"

"Good." They got on the snow machine and Fox headed back to the monitoring center. With the explosion here, he wondered how many more there had been. And had all the removal teams gotten clear before the wells had gone up?

Chapter Forty-Six

6:25 pm

"This is the central monitoring facility for the fields," John said as they approached the nondescript cluster of interconnected trailers. "This is where Dr. Sheldon and I ran into some trouble."

Cassie saw from John's face that the trouble had not yet ended for him. She touched his arm. "I'm sorry we didn't stop it in time. I really am."

"I know." He didn't say more. His face was hard, and Cassie knew what he was thinking. That if these wells weren't here in the first place, none of this would have happened. But he wasn't saying that, which meant he was trying not to blame her for what her father's business did.

They got out of the truck, ducking their heads against increasing wind. It came straight out of the west like a spike of ice. Snow blurred everything but the lights standing over the parking area.

The buzz of a snow machine came from the distance, growing louder. The headlight wavered as it cut through the growing blizzard. They waited to see who it was. When it was clear there were two men aboard, John went to greet them. "Peter?"

"What? No. This is Ivan. He's one of the bad guys."

"Fox?" John said.

"Yo, just help me get this kid into the building."

They each got under an arm and carried the man toward the facility. Cassie's jaw clenched as she studied the man's clothes. He was one of the Russians all right. "You should have left him out there."

"I couldn't," Fox said. He did a double-take. "Hey, aren't you what's-her-name?"

John made introductions while they got the man into a monitoring center. Cassie took in the array of computer monitors and the big screen with video feeds on it. "So do we know if any of the pump stations went up, too?"

A man by one computer stood and rubbed his head, face crumpled with confusion. "They're all online and flowing."

Dr. Sheldon was standing next to him. She came around to inspect the half-frozen Russian. But instead of shooting him with her .45, as Cassie half-wished to do, she checked his hands and nose. "He needs to be evacuated to Fairbanks. But that isn't going to happen with this storm coming on. We'd better get him to the clinic. I hope John returned my Ranger Rover with a full tank."

John winced. "Uh, about that . . . "

Cassie didn't care about the Russian kid's frostbite. "We can't leave here in the middle of a crisis. There are probably millions of gallons of oil pouring onto the surface right now."

"No, there isn't," Dr. Sheldon said, still looking suspiciously at John.

The other man, Frennly, was talking to Fox. The

bearded man raced to his computer and clicked his mouse like a madman. "Impossible."

"Actually, it isn't," Dr. Sheldon said. "Just improbable."

Fox looked at the big screen. "None of the wells blew up."

"We saw one go up," Cassie said. "And we heard a few more booms."

"I have telemetry and video feeds from all of them. They're all live and pumping."

"And they're flowing properly," Frennly said.

"What blew up?"

Dr. Sheldon was beyond the topic, now only concerned with her Russian patient. "John, please. Help me get him back to my truck. I can probably save his fingers."

"Your Ranger Rover is, uh, incapacitated," John said. "Some Russian snow machines sorta ran into it."

"Sorta? Either they did or they didn't."

"Oh, they definitely did. Thing is, one of them set your Ranger Rover on fire. And then it blew up."

Fox yelped. "Yo, Dr. Sheldon! My gait recognition algos are screaming. There's a match at Jack-Sixteen. It's your godson, Peter. He's waving at the camera." Fox waved at the screen and then caught himself.

Dr. Sheldon bowed her head, but only allowed herself a moment's relief. Cassie didn't know who Peter was, but clearly Dr. Sheldon had been worried about him.

"I still don't understand what blew up," Cassie said. "Aside from Dr. Sheldon's Range Rover."

John got Ivan to his feet and Frennly got on the other side. They started to carry-walk Ivan back outside.

The phone rang. Dr. Sheldon answered, listened, then hung up.

She smiled. No. She beamed. "Peter put seven of the bombs he removed into the track trucks the Russians used to get here. The fuel wagon is what sent up the big fire. I guess the other explosions were bombs our team pulled but didn't properly disarm. They left them on the tundra, so there will be some scorched holes, but no oil. We lucked out. Most of them did as told and put them in the gravel depot out past the airport. Nobody hurt, but Camp Deadhorse reported a rainfall of small stones just now. A few cracked windshields."

"So that's it?" Cassie said, feeling the exhaustion she'd been fighting hit her all at once. She struggled to remain standing. "We did it? We stopped it?"

Dr. Sheldon smiled, nodded, and followed John and Ivan into the cold. Cassie followed, too.

Yes, she thought, they'd stopped it. But it wasn't over. In fact, she was certain that it had just started.

Uncle Dev and Dad were waiting for her at the clinic. Dr. Limon had ferried everyone from the pump station on the Sno-Cat. The wounded had been treated, given infusions from volunteers desperate to help however they could. The frostbit Russian was put in a separate room and placed under the vaguely watchful eye of one of Harv's useless security men. The bristle-stache obstructionist was also waiting there. Upon seeing Cassie enter the small clinic, he came forward, opening the cuffs she left him wearing the last time she'd seen him. "I have a mind to arrest you and wait for the NSA folks to arrive. But it looks like only Marines are coming to secure the oil fields and Pump Station One. They told me to let you go. But you're to stay in Deadhorse until their commander can speak with you."

Cassie gave him her most charming smile and said, "Well, bless your heart."

He looked momentarily thrown, but then he returned the smile and flushed slightly. "I just hope you've learned your lesson to leave the policing to grown men next time."

Cassie didn't respond to this outrageous insult. She didn't have to. John, Dr. Sheldon, Fox, and several others shouted at the man and told him to shut up or get out.

Dad waved her to his gurney. "I have never been prouder of you than I am right now, honey. What you did today is beyond my comprehension."

"I'm my mother's daughter."

"Ain't that the truth. But you did some things that shouldn't have to be done." He shook his head, grimacing as he struggled with who his daughter had become. With what she'd become.

Some *things*. Already they were referring to the killing in abstractions. "I'll be okay, Dad."

He kissed her forehead, just as he had done when she was four. But she welcomed it. He knew she wasn't anyone's little girl anymore. She doubted he'd stop calling her that. And that was okay.

They rested there while Dr. Sheldon checked John and Cassie out. When she declared them healthy, they were free to go back to the Sag River Motel for a shower and some much-needed rest.

Chapter Forty-Seven

12:47 am

When Cassie's phone began jangling—seemingly only minutes after she'd fallen asleep—she shot from the bed, Fedorov's Serdyukov already in hand.

Heart slamming, she answered the phone.

"I know that Valentine is dead," Kalov said. His words were slurred. Cassie had never seen the man drink a beer, much less get drunk. "Killed by his own countrymen. For what? Money? Bah!"

Cassie hadn't forgotten about Val. But her numbed mind had not been capable of mourning him when she'd finally flopped onto her bed. She had simply fallen asleep.

But now, in the wakeful buzz of adrenaline, she pictured her dark-haired and beautiful Val. "He died trying to save me, Misha. You can be proud of him." Her voice caught. She gripped a fistful of bedsheets. She would not give in to the rise of tears. She refused. Not when Kalov was on the phone with her.

A grunt, or maybe a cough, came across the wire. It was a thin, low quality phone line full of clicks and buzzes. "Ah, Cassandra. Ah, Cassie." All that came through after that were sobs.

The heart-wrenching sounds of old Kalov's grief were too much to bear. Life without Val was too much to bear. Her resolve failed and she joined her Russian mentor in his grief.

Cassie never got back to sleep. Eventually the tears dried up and an exhausted numbness settled over her. And in that state an idea came to her. She got dressed, left the motel, borrowed John's still-running truck, and drove back to the clinic.

Harv's assigned security man was asleep on a chair outside the Russian kid's locked room. Cassie lifted the keys from the guard, unlocked the door, and slipped in. The room was lit only by the lights of some medical equipment. A heart rate monitor beeped out the slow, steady pace of the boy's pulse. He lay on the bed, his hands and feet bound in white bandages. More bandages crossed his face, covering his frostbitten nose.

The room smelled sterile. The way Cassie's heart felt.

She pressed her Serdyukov to his temple. "Wake up, sweetheart." She had to shake him a couple times to get him out of his sedated slumber. When his eyes finally cleared and he realized there was a gun to his head, he went still. "You are going to kill me, yes?"

"Not yet. At the pump station there was a sniper. An older man. You're going to tell me his name."

The boy's mouth moved like a landed fish, but nothing came out. And he became much more frightened by her question than he had been by the sight of a SRS to his head. "I don't know him."

Interesting. Whoever the sniper was, this kid was

willing to risk his life to protect him. That didn't make any sense. "You don't think I'll shoot you, do you?"

"I don't know. But look at me. I will lose fingers. Maybe nose. Perhaps it isn't good to live. Women will not like my face."

Cassie caught herself. As if seeing this scene from above, she noticed the trembling rage in her arm, and how tightly she clenched her teeth. She lowered the gun. "I won't shoot you, Ivan. I won't threaten you. I'm asking you, as someone who lost a person she loved, who was that sniper?"

"If I tell you, you will tell the CIA or NSA. He has people in those organizations. They will know I gave up name. He will kill me. Not bullet from long distance, not when I don't expect. He will have me taken where they put you in ground. Lock you in and you never get out. But they feed and give water and keep alive. Better you kill me now."

Cassie stuffed the weapon in the pocket of her parka and leaned over the bed. She put her face very close to Ivan's. So close she could see the flecks in his gray eyes. "I won't say who told me his name. I want to know for me, not to share with the incompetents in Washington."

His breath wheezed through the nostril holes Dr. Sheldon had cut in his bandage. Finally he whispered a name. Sergei Zherdev. Cassie didn't recognize it. She hadn't expected to. But now she had a place to start.

She kissed his forehead. "Go to sleep, Ivan. Rest easy. The prison you're going to sounds much nicer than the one Sergei Zherdev had in mind for you."

On the way out, she tossed the keys on the floor at the feet of the guard. "Wake up, buddy. There's a Russian bad guy in there."

She made it back to the Sag River Motel and back into

her bed. And then she did sleep. And her dreams were very violent indeed.

Chapter Forty-Eight

December 21, 10:16 pm

Kalov had the fire roaring and his beloved Rolling Stones playing quietly. On a turntable, of all things. He had made his signature dish for supper. Macaroni and cheese. "This is the last of the carbohydrates for you, Cassandra."

They ate the delicious comfort food in silence, but every once in a while she caught him looking at her. He had not asked her yet about Val's death. She would tell him everything she remembered many times over the next few days. She owed him that much.

When they were done, they retired to the little sitting area with the cable rug and the mismatched flea market furniture. Grom curled up on the floor atop Kalov's feet, twitching and whining occasionally as a doggy dream came over him. The fire made Cassie sleepy, too. Kalov closed his eyes and said nothing. He knew she had come to talk. He probably knew what she was going to say.

First things first. "I was in love with him, Misha. I never told him."

"He knew. I knew. I warned him. You surely know it was impossible. Totally out of the question."

"I know. But that doesn't mean I don't feel what I feel."

"That is why we have brains. To take the reins and keep us out of stupidity. Do not think I am insensitive, Cassie. But you will heal and move on. One day, Val will be a vague memory to you. You will not even remember him as he truly was, but as an idea you invented at an impressionable age."

Cassie absorbed the lecture. He had every right to say what he said, whether she wanted to hear it or not. But she wasn't done. She pulled her phone from her back pocket and brought up a photo. It was frame of a security video feed. Fox Tils had sent it to her once he'd gotten back to California. It showed part of the pump station and, very clearly, the face of the sniper. She held out the screen for Kalov to see. He studied the man's face but didn't betray even the slightest flicker of recognition. Good.

Cassie kept the phone out, screen toward Kalov. "His name is Sergei Zherdev."

Kalov pursed his lips and scratched his chin. "And you passed this information to the authorities?"

Cassie smiled and said, "Do you think I'm stupid?"

Kalov grinned, a full and genuine smile. And it was full of grim violence. "I do not. I most certainly do not. Well done. Very well done. I shall look into this Sergei Zherdev."

Chapter Forty-Nine

December 23, 7:45 pm

Father-daughter time in New York City turned out to be a bit slower-paced than Dad had wanted. Doctor's orders forced him to go slowly and not try to cover the entirety of Manhattan on foot. But Cassie enjoyed the lunch at Katz's Deli, and the shopping on Fifth Avenue was nice. It felt good to be back in really nice clothes, and she was in love with the new Louboutins Dad had bought her earlier that day.

The limo, the dinner at Club 21, the secrecy around what special show he was taking her to, all made her feel like a little kid again. And that was just fine.

When the limo pulled up to the theater, Cassie saw the marquee. "No way!"

She was thrilled. As much as she loved *The Lion King*, she'd seen it enough to be in it herself. This was something special. *Hamilton*.

"I bought tickets off a guy I know." That was Dad's way of saying he'd paid many times the face value online.

They had amazing seats and the theater was full of excited, nicely-dressed people, all eager to see the hottest show in years.

Dad made a last-minute bathroom run, so Cassie pulled out her phone. She'd gotten a message from a number she didn't recognize. She pulled it up.

The sender had included a picture. A white fox. The text read: *I saw this little guy and thought of you. This is John Goodnight BTW not some rando creeper.*

Cassie laughed and zoomed in on the fox's cute little face. She saved the picture as a new contact pic and added John Goodnight's name. She put the phone away and leaned back to enjoy the hubbub and the feeling of safety.

Her purse was on her lap. The clasp open. She could reach in and bring out her new personal carry, a Ruger LC9s Pro. The one Fedorov had taken from her bag was now in government custody. That suited her fine. She would never touch that particular weapon again. Besides, she had kept Fedorov's Serdyukov.

As the show started she settled in. She leaned over to her father and patted his hand. "Thank you, Dad."

He smiled. "You're welcome, sweetheart."

When the show was over, and she was cozily ensconced back in her suite at the Park Hyatt, another text came in. This one from Kalov. It read very simply: *I FOUND HIM.*

Cassie didn't bother packing. She had a small bug-out bag ready to go. She scribbled a note for her father and left it at the front desk. In an hour she was at the airport, private charter Learjet 60 standing by.

A bleary-eyed flight attendant handed her the requested cup of coffee. "The pilot says we'll arrive at Sawyer International in two hours. Can I ask why you're going to Michigan at this hour?"

"Death in the family."

The attendant made a surprised "oh" with her lips and retreated. As the plane lifted off, Cassie watched the lights of New York slip away beneath cloud cover. But above them, forever and ever, was a sky full of stars. That one to the north, just off the lip of the Big Dipper, was Polaris. It looked cold from here, but it was a star. An inferno.

Just like Cassie Smythe Ingram.

Before Polar Midnight there was "L.I.V.E."

Read the short story that started it all. First published in *Fiction River: Pulse Pounders Adrenaline*, "L.I.V.E" tells the thrilling story of exactly what happened to Cassie in the coffee shop in Houston.

Buy your copy today.

www.ingramcontent.com/pod-product-compliance
Lightning Source LLC
Chambersburg PA
CBHW050559190726
48283CB00007B/2199